THE GALAXY RAIDERS

By
WILLIAM P. McGIVERN

ARMCHAIR FICTION
PO Box 4369, Medford, Oregon 97504

*For more information about Armchair Books and products, visit our
website at…*

www.armchairfiction.com

Or email us at…

armchairfiction@yahoo.com

ALIEN INVASION FROM OUTSIDE THE SOLAR SYSTEM...

Were there aliens from another galaxy? There had been wild rumors of it for many years—tall tales that had perpetuated from one end of the Solar System to the other. However, there was no one in the hierarchy of the Earth Federation that had ever seriously believed in the mysterious legends of Galaxy X. Until now…

It was when a fleet of alien warships appeared on the edge of the Solar System that the Federation realized that they were faced with a horrible threat. And it was up to one man in one spaceship to try and somehow stop them—along with an edgy crew and a beautiful stowaway.

FOR A COMPLETE SECOND NOVEL, TURN TO PAGE 71

CAST OF CHARACTERS

STORM

This tough space commander was handed the job of saving the Earth from an alien invasion. The only thing standing in his way was a little humility.

MARGO

She stowed away on a spaceship headed for Jupiter. Little did she know it might well turn into a suicide mission.

MASTERSON

His arrogance put the lives of his fellow crewmen in mortal danger—especially when he trifled with the notion of mutiny.

MacDONALD

This aging engineer had to devise a way of stopping an entire alien space fleet—and he only had a few hours to do it!

KAREN

She was the lone survivor of an earlier expedition to Jupiter, but she now ruled her realm with a giant army of robots.

CARNEY

This big Irishman came down on the wrong side of a space mutiny, and it soon brought him far more than he bargained for.

CHAPTER ONE

"THE WIDE arched corridor and the imposing doors at its end were familiar to him, and he knew the feeling that came when the Four-man guard military guard snapped to attention at their approach.

His tight hand moved instinctively to return the salute, and then stopped short.

The rigid respect of the guards was not for him, John Storm knew. Hardly. It was the Vice Admiral at his side, who returned the salute casually and put a friendly hand on Storm's arm as the doors swung open.

"Go right in, John. They're expecting you, of course," he said. "It was damn nice of you to come after—well, bygones are bygones. I always say and a good thing too," he finished hastily.

"Oh, sure," John Storm said, and there only the barest sarcasm in his flat hard voice.

They walked together into a large bright room, unadorned except for floor-to-ceiling maps that covered the walls and the green and white standards of Earth Federation hanging above the conference table at the far end of the room.

Seated at the table were eight officers of the Federation, representing top authority in each world zone—men whose most casual word was considered important and whose commands could send millions of men and thousands of fighting units into action.

They stood as Storm approached and the Controller, a slender graying man who wore the yellow epaulets of a First Marshal, came forward and extended his hand with a smile.

"It's good to see you again, John," he said. "It's been eight—no—nine years, hasn't it?"

"Eleven," John Storm said, and a smile flickered on his strong dark face.

"Of course. Well, you know everyone, I think."

THE GALAXY RAIDERS

By WILLIAM P. McGIVERN

Storm glanced at the men behind the table and nodded. He knew them all. Stoddard, Logistics; Malcom, Communications; Baley, Supply; Millholland, Electronics; Crestweather, Space Arm—that was good. Space Arm!

They all sat down then and the Controller glanced at a paper before him, and then at Storm with a slight smile.

"You know why we asked you to come here, I suppose?"

"Yes." Storm said. He crossed his legs and settled back comfortably in his chair. There was a controlled and deliberate sense of power in every move he made. Too thick and massive through the shoulders to be considered well built, and too dark and bitter to be considered handsome, be was nevertheless a man to be looked at twice. His eyes were a quiet gray, and his hair was jet black and straight.

"Yes," he said again, "I know why you want me. The threat from space is more acute than it was eleven years ago—when I

Illustration by Edward Swiatek

was cashiered from the service for being a wide-eyed radical who wanted the Federation to build up its Space Arm."

The Controller spread his hands in a helpless gesture. "Mistakes were made then, John," he said. "We didn't see what was coming. Men like Commander Griffith and yourself—you were the casualties of our blindness."

The name of Commander Griffith brought a frown to Storm's face, and as the Controller talked soothingly and placatingly, a flood of bitter memories swept over him.

COMMANDER GRIFFITH had made the first long Space flight of history in the late Seventies—to Jupiter. Storm had been in his crew. It was not a military flight; there were no funds for that. Griffith, a dedicated, fearless and brilliant scientist paid for the trip from his own pocket. Accompanying him were his wife, Grace, and his daughter, Karen. They had stayed on Jupiter for three months and then had received a trans-space message from Earth ordering them to return. There had been a vicious public reaction to the trip from influential ignoramuses who said the mysteries of space were not for man to unravel, and now these fools had forced the Federation to order Griffith's ship the *Astro Star*, to return at once to Earth.

Griffith had refused and the Federation sent its entire fleet of four ships to Jupiter to enforce the order. They had arrested the crew, but Griffith, his wife and daughter, and a man named Thatcher had escaped into the wilds of mountainous volcanic ash that dotted the planet, and were deserted, left behind when the Federation crafts returned to Earth.

This was regarded as poetic justice by those who had fought the trip in the first place, but Storm had begun then to wage a campaign for the rescue of Commander Griffith and for an immediate development of the Federation's air arm, for even then Galaxy X was causing concern among the enlightened members of the command.

But John Storm was not tactful or diplomatic, or political. He raged at his superiors, conducted experiments of his own without official sanction, and he talked to newspapermen, radio reporters—to every agent of communication he could get to listen. The result was that he became a thorn in the sides of the top brass of the Federation, a stern logician, who went directly to the people instead of clearing things with his superiors and so he was arrested, court martialed, and thrown out of the service.

"...AND SO," the Controller said, "that's what we are hoping you'll do for us. Take a ship to Jupiter, not to look for Commander Griffith, since that I fear would be futile, but to establish an outer defense post there in case our worst fears of Galaxy X are realized."

"How many ships?" Storm asked.

The Controller looked embarrassed. "One," he said.

Storm stood up and dropped his cigarette on the floor, then ground it out with his heel. "You're still fools," he said bitterly. "You want me to establish an outpost to give you warning against any raiders from Galaxy X—and be in the first line of defense against them. Yet you talk of one ship!"

"Appropriations," the Controller said, with a helpless shrug. "We're not politicians, Storm. We have to trim our sails to their commands."

Storm looked over their heads to the bright green-and-white standards of the Federation and his thoughts went slowly back across the years of his bitter fight for a Space Arm and he knew that now, as then, he'd have to take any chance that was offered. But one ship! He rubbed his forehead and grinned bitterly. "All right," he said. "What rank do I take?"

"Commander. We couldn't do any better."

"Okay," Storm said impatiently. "Send me my orders as fast as you can."

He turned and without another word strode from the silent chamber...

THE SHIP was a shining tube of deadly beauty, four hundred yards long and towering a hundred yards in the air. From the tapering nose with its multiple banks of visi-screens, to the flaring fins and blast nacelles, the giant spacecraft was a tribute to the men whose dream had made it live.

Storm stood at the foot of the ramp leading to the amidships entrance and let his eyes travel over his ship. *His* ship! Far above him he saw the name gleaming in black on the soaring curve of the prow—*Astro Star II.*

He drew a deep breath and walked up the incline to the ship, returned the salute of the cadet on duty and went forward to his combination office and sleeping quarters.

Inside, Storm closed the door and sat down at his desk. He lit a cigar and began the laborious process of leading through the reports prepared for him on each man in his crew. He studied their firing records, their communication reports, their physical conditions and even glanced at their clothing allowance and inoculation charts.

Finishing, he pushed the neat stack of papers aside and slumped deeper into his chair. He smoked thoughtfully for several minutes, enjoying the heavy fragrance of tobacco and savoring the thought that the routine details of flight preparation were over and done with.

They were ready to go now. Six weeks had been spent in training. The men were as ready as they'd ever be. There were good men aboard, good officers too. But it would take the grueling job ahead to test them. How they'd stand up was anybody's guess.

He pushed a button at his elbow, then stood and poured himself a drink from the table at his reading chair. His apartment was sparely furnished. There was a cot, desk, reading chair, and of course his books and charts.

A knock sounded and he said, "Come in."

It was his chief engineer, MacDonald, a tall graying man with thoughtful eyes and a reserved manner.

"Yes, sir," he said. He stood at attention easily.

"That's all right, MacDonald." Storm said. "Will you have a drink?"

MacDonald hesitated almost imperceptibly; then said, "I think not, sir, if it's all the same to you."

"Very well."

Storm put his drink down. He had no flair for relaxing with his men, for being genial and off-handed. It didn't bother him particularly; he knew he was respected but not liked by most men. There was a wall of stubborn steel around him that rebuffed all but the most impersonal contact.

"We will blast-off sometime tomorrow morning, probably before eight, and not after nine. I want everything ready by six."

"Yes, sir. Will that be all?"

"That's all," Storm said curtly.

WHEN MACDONALD had gone Storm walked into the intercom panel and flicked open the switch. "Hear this," he said, in his hard flat voice, and in his imagination he could see men stopping their work in all parts of the craft, of men in bunks rising up one elbow, of sleeping men waking, as his voice, the supreme voice on the ship, was carried echoing throughout the corridors and compartments of the craft.

"Hear this," he repeated, "All leaves are cancelled as of now. No one will be allowed off the ship unless he has my written permission. All personnel except guards on duty will assemble in the forward gun chamber in fifteen minutes. That is all."

Storm flicked off the switch and went into his bedroom where he washed his face and hands and put on a clean shirt. He put on his tunic and fastened the command belt with its five-starred buckle about his flat waist.

Turning toward the door he saw himself in the mirror, and noticed the lines of exhaustion at the corners of his mouth, the hard look of his eyes. Readying the *Astro Star II* had meant twenty hours of work every day. It hadn't been fun; but there was nothing else he'd rather have done.

Smiling, he left his office and walked down the companionway to the forward gun chamber where he had scheduled the meeting of the ship's company.

THE DOORS leading to the gun chamber were ajar and Storm stopped as he heard a great shout of laughter from inside the room.

Someone called for silence and as the laughter faded another voice said, "Really, men, I'm not that funny. The credit should go to our indomitable skipper who supplies me with all the material."

Storm took an involuntary step forward, his great hands clenching. But he stopped as the carefree mocking voice beyond the doors continued speaking.

Storm knew the voice. It belonged to Captain Larry Masterson, a gunnery officer, whose recklessness and irresponsibility had worried him since the first day of training. He had thought of getting rid of him, but Storm didn't like admitting he couldn't handle the situation.

Larry Masterson now was telling the men in the gun chamber the circumstances of his first meeting with Commander Storm. The muffled laughter was a tribute to his ability as a mimic.

Storm pushed the doors open gently and watched with hands on hips, as Larry Masterson continued his story.

Masterson was facing a semi-circle of seventy or eighty crewmembers, and speaking in a broadly comic imitation of Storm's hard flat voice. "The hand salute," the young captain was saying, "is not intended to convey anything but respect. It is not a gesture by which one indicates high spirits or personality, Captain."

"Quite right," Storm said mildly, and walked into the room.

Larry Masterson stiffened suddenly and the circle of crewmembers after one horrified look at Storm raised their eyes in agonized innocence to a point high in the air.

Storm said to the captain, "You're carrying your childishness too far, young man. You're getting infantile."

Larry Masterson stared over Storm's shoulder, stiffly at attention, but there was a hint of secret laughter at the corners of his mouth.

"Captain," Storm said, "do you think you're amusing?"

Larry hesitated an instant before saying, "Yes, sir," in a meek voice.

Someone laughed; and Storm knew he was allowing the situation to become difficult.

"Report to my quarters in ten minutes," he said to the young captain, and then turned to face the semi-circle of crewmembers. They fell into immediate silence.

"I asked you to come here for one reason," Storm said, speaking in a tight clipped voice. "Leaves are cancelled, as you know, and you deserve to know why. Tomorrow morning we blast off for Jupiter. I—"

Someone let out a yell and then the entire crew was cheering. Storm watched them for a moment, then held up his hand for silence. He was not touched or impressed by the demonstration. It meant nothing. The time to cheer was when something had been accomplished.

"You know the job ahead of us," he said. "It may be difficult, tiresome and dangerous, but understand this, gentlemen, we will do that job. I will accept excuses, but not failure. Carry on."

STORM WAS lighting a cigar when a knock sounded on the door of his quarters. He opened the door and saw Captain Larry Masterson standing there at attention.

"Captain Masterson reporting as ordered, sir," he said.

"Come in," Storm said.

He puffed on his cigar until it was drawing to his satisfaction, then looked at the young officer and said, "Don't you like this assignment, Captain?"

Captain Masterson made the slightest of shrugs. "Is my attitude important, sir?"

"Not to me, but I thought it might be to you."

Storm studied the younger man thoughtfully. Larry Masterson was tall and slimly built, with curly blonde hair and merry blue eyes. Except for a certain untried look about his mouth he was an extremely handsome young man. Storm knew that he came from a wealthy, influential family, which had placed many of its members in top military and diplomatic posts. The boy's father was a retired secretary of Conservation, and several of his uncles had been in the World Parliament.

Storm said, "Are you worried about the uncertainties of inter-planetary travel, perhaps?"

The young captain flushed. "I asked for the assignment, sir. I've been a space flier since I graduated from the Cadet Center. I know what space is, sir."

"Oh, I'm sure you do," Storm said with heavy irony. "Then what is it that makes you undermine my authority aboard the ship?"

"Do I have to answer that question, sir?"

"I would prefer that you do," Storm said dryly.

"Very well, sir. I find it difficult to serve under an officer who has been dishonorably discharged from the service."

Storm stood motionless for an instant, and then he carefully knocked the ash from his cigar.

"That will be all, Captain."

"You asked for it," Masterson said with quiet contempt. "That's the way I feel and—"

Storm's voice cut harshly across his sentence. "I said, that will be all, Captain."

"Very well, sir."

When he had gone Storm stared at the closed door for several moments without moving. Then he pounded a fist into his palm and his eyes were hot and bitter.

CHAPTER TWO

THE BLAST-OFF was without incident. The mighty *Astro Star II* moved up through Earth's atmosphere under auxiliary power and then, at sixty thousand feet, the aft atomic rockets crackled into life.

The ship leaped upward trailing a mile-long stream of orange fire in its wake. It hissed through the thinning atmosphere and cleared the Heaviside layer in a matter of seconds. Void-bound, it wrenched itself clear from the pull of Earth and shot outward with flashing silent speed.

Storm left the bridge then and returned to his quarters where he snapped on the visi-screen. He watched the depths ahead for a few moments, noting asteroid clusters, and comets that appeared on their course. Everything was routine—so far. The powerful deflector rays of the *Astro Star II* spread thousands of miles beyond the ship and nothing smaller than a Class 1 comet could penetrate that buffer.

Nothing of incident occurred until the second day. Storm was at his desk checking reports from his sub-commanders on the operation of the ship, when his orderly knocked and entered with an anxious expression on his face.

"Sir, there's trouble in compartment B."

"What happened?" Storm said, rising from his chair.

"A cadet has gone berserk sir!"

"A little early for hysterics," Storm muttered, and went down the corridor toward compartment B at a half-trot. The door to the compartment was locked and there was no response to Storm's resounding knock.

He stared at the door for a second, then pulled his heat gun. Compartment B, he knew, was the sleeping and recreation quarters for the cadet members of the crew, most of them youngsters in their last year of training.

Storm adjusted his gun for a two-foot target and played a ray of white heat against the lock of the door. It dissolved instantly and he nudged the door open cautiously with his foot.

Through the aperture he saw that eight crewmen were standing against one wall with their hands raised in the air. They were all officers, and among them he noticed Captain Larry Masterson.

On the floor were lying two cadets in shorts and beside them were long handled brushes and buckets of soapy water. The two men were looking fearfully past a third cadet who stood above them with a heat gun in his hand. The gun was trained unwaveringly on the officers.

This cadet was a slightly built youth who wore the green tunic, black trousers and white cap of a first class cadet. Storm couldn't see his face.

"I don't intend to be treated as a child by you barbarians," he was saying in a light cool voice to the officers as Storm eased through the door and began to close in on him from behind.

"You may humiliate these other cadets if they allow it, but I'll put a hole through the first man who tries to give me a bath I don't need."

Storm moved with savage speed as he came up behind the cadet. His right hand chopped down in a blurring arc and the rock-hard edge of his palm cracked against the cadet's arm. The gun flew upward and Storm caught it in mid-air. The cadet cried out in pain and dropped to the ground, clutching his injured arm.

Storm glanced at the two cadets lying on the floor. "Get up," he said, and then he swung around to face the officers, who had lowered their arms and were facing him sheepishly.

"I think you men understand my orders about hazing," he said curtly. "Return to your rooms and consider yourselves under arrest. I will talk to you later."

Several officers had come in behind Storm with guns drawn. They put them away at a motion from him. He glanced down at the cadet who still lying on the floor clutching his arm, and said, "Report to me immediately in my quarters," and left the compartment.

"WHAT'S YOUR name?" Storm said to the cadet a little later in his office.

"Thomas, sir," the cadet said in a low voice.

Storm sat at his desk, a dark frown on his face. He studied the cadet carefully. The boy was slim, with fine features, fair skin and deep, vivid-blue eyes. His hair was black and cut short. He was older than Storm had first judged. There was a weary, tired bitterness in his face that contrasted oddly with the boyish fairness of his skin.

"What was the idea of that tantrum?" Storm asked quietly.

"I—I saw no reason to submit myself to the indignity of

being scrubbed with a stiff brush."

"You realize you could be shot for drawing a gun on a superior officer?"

"Yes, sir."

"How's your arm?"

"All right, sir." The cadet touched it with his other hand and winced painfully.

"Take off your jacket," Storm said, and turned to his desk. He wanted to get to the bottom of this situation, for any temperamental explosion like this might setoff a series of them, like a string of firecrackers. He found his resentment against Captain Masterson growing. Trust that young fool to precipitate such a situation.

He turned around and his anger suddenly sharpened as he saw the cadet still wearing his jacket.

"It's all right, sir," the cadet said hastily.

"By God, I don't give orders to hear the sound of my voice," Storm snapped. "Take off that jacket!"

The cadet made no move to obey and Storm's patience ran out. He stood and grabbed the young man by the arm and jerked him about. The cadet struggled in his grasp and kicked backward, at Storm's shins.

"You need a taste of discipline," Storm said grimly.

He twisted the cadet's uninjured arm sharply and brought him to the floor in a kneeling position. Then he gripped the collar of his jacket and ripped the garment down over his elbows. Buttons spattered the floor.

"Now stand up and finish the job," Storm said.

The cadet got slowly to his feet, and the jacket slipped from his arms and dropped to the floor.

"Turn around,'" Storm ordered.

The cadet obeyed slowly, smiling bitterly, and Storm suddenly felt the breath leave his lungs in a rush.

"Good God," he said.

The "cadet" was a girl.

SHE FACED him unashamedly, defiantly nude from the waist up, her shoulders thrown back and her head held high. Her breasts were small and firm and perfect and her waist could have been encircled with his two hands.

On her left forearm—the arm he had struck—was an ugly, swelling bruise.

"Put on that jacket," Storm said.

"A second ago you tried to jerk it off by main strength," the girl said, quietly.

Storm stooped and retrieved the jacket. He held it while the girl slipped into it awkwardly, favoring her injured arm.

Storm nodded to the chair beside his desk. "Sit down and we'll get to the bottom of this. You stowed away last night, I presume. Did you take Cadet Thomas' place?"

"That's right," the girl said.

"Where is Cadet Thomas now?"

"At my apartment. That is, he *was* there. I presume he has awakened by now. He probably has a horrible headache."

"You drugged him, took his uniform and papers, and came aboard. Why?"

The Girl said, "Did you ever know a man named Thatcher?"

"Thatcher?" Storm looked at the girl closely. "Yes. I knew a man by that name. He accompanied Commander Griffith to Jupiter eleven years ago. He remained there with Griffith to die."

The girl sprang to her feet. "No! That's a lie. He can't be dead."

"You knew him?" Storm said quietly.

The girl sat down again and her deep eyes grew bitter. "Yes. I knew him," she whispered. "I loved him. I was seventeen then and we were going to be married."

"You came on this trip hoping to find him alive?"

"There's a chance, isn't there?" the girl said. "Don't you see? I had to take it."

"No I don't," Storm said harshly. "You've ruined a young man's career, you've forced yourself on a trip where you'll cause trouble, just on the thin chance that your fiancé might still be alive," he rang impatiently for his chief medical officer. "What's your name?" he said.

"Margo."

Storm sat in silence, a heavy frown on his face, until the ship's medical officer appeared. He was a portly, gray-haired man with very red cheeks, which got even redder when Storm explained the situation to him.

"Well, well," he said, peering down at the girl as if she were some hitherto undiscovered fauna. "Well, well," he added.

"I understand what you mean," Storm said dryly. "Put her into a compartment away from the run of ship's business, and take a look at her arm. She will receive her meals there, and I'll have a guard posted to see that she stays put. Also, you'd better inform the crew of this development. Give them all the facts. I don't want a lot of stupid gossip and speculation started."

"Very well," the medical officer said. He nodded to the girl, who had gotten to her feet, and said, "Just come along with me, please," he started to offer her his arm, but seeing Storm's frown, cleared his throat and proceeded her from the room.

The girl paused. She looked at Storm and there was pity in her smile. "You've never loved anyone, have you?"

"You're excused," Storm said firmly, and turned to his desk.

CHAPTER THREE

THEY LANDED on Jupiter sixteen days later. Storm set to work immediately to convert a tiny section of the planet into an efficient space base. The men were restless after the enforced inactivity of the trip and needed a period of diversion, but Storm drove them with out let-up. He knew the danger, but he made no man his confidant.

They had landed in the shadow of an immense mountain. The weather was bitingly cold, the ground hard as flint.

The *Astro Star II* was unloaded and a headquarters building erected for Storm, and his records and graphs. Prefabricated dwellings were set up in a semi-circle about Storm's quarters, and towers were erected to hold the great lamps that bathed the area in warming light. Everything necessary for comfort and efficiency had been built on Earth and shipped in parts aboard the *Astro Star II*.

Storm ordered a separate hut built for the girl, Margo, and saw to it that she was lodged there with as much comfort as possible, although his bitterness toward her had not diminished.

When the encampment was made, Storm ordered the fighter space ships uncrated and assembled by a crew working days, while a night shift started the work of clearing a field, sinking blast-off tubes, and preparing a maintenance section.

The mood and keynote of the place was work. Storm drove the men, but drove himself twice as hard. He was everywhere at once, keeping an eye on all details, and occasionally throwing his big shoulder against a stanchion that refused to budge, or taking specifications into his office and working through the night to correct errors, or to adjust them to fit an emergency.

Tempers grew short. The men complained to their immediate superiors, but those officers were afraid to pass the complaints on to Storm. They knew what his reaction would be. He drove the work on by sheer will, and he kept himself going with black coffee liberally laced with whisky.

He had a telescope set up in his office, and this was focused on a visi-screen that he had taken from the *Astro Star II*. Storm spent part of each day studying the visi-screen. He made notes occasionally and consulted his charts. When he came away from the telescope everyone knew it was time to look busy. His temper was apt to be shortest then.

THIRTEEN days after the landing, the girl, Margo, came to his office. She had tried to see him everyday since they arrived but he had been too busy. This time she walked in the door and planted herself beside his desk.

"I must speak to you," she said.

Storm looked up from his work. He needed a shave and his eyes were tired. He saw that she had made herself a costume of sorts from camouflage material. She wore black leather boots, shorts made of yellow canvas, and a leather vest. Her legs were slim and shapely and her short black hair was brushed back above her ears in small flaring wings. Except for the bitter darkness of her eyes, and the sadness of the mouth, she was an exciting woman.

"What do you want?" he said, his voice blunt and unfriendly.

"I came here to find Thatcher," she said. "I—I want to look for him. Please let me go."

"No...once and for all, no!" Storm said, and slammed his fist down on his desktop. "You'd get lost and we'd have to take valuable men away from important work to look for you."

"Don't you have any heart at all?" she cried, and caught his arm as he got to his feet. "I must know if he's alive or dead. I've got to search for him."

Storm smiled mirthlessly. "You're on a planet roughly ten times the size of Earth. Where would you start to look for this man?"

"You were here with him and Commander Griffith," Margo said breathlessly. "You'd know where to look...are we in the same area now?"

"We are within a hundred square mile area of where we landed eleven years ago," Storm said. "But what good does that do? A hundred square miles is as vast a million square miles when you're on foot."

"You aren't going to send out a searching party?"

"No," Storm said flatly.

"What is so important about this work you're doing?" Margo cried. "You're killing your men, digging holes, and working all night to get spaceships ready. Is that more important than looking for human beings who still may be alive, who may need help?"

"My job comes first," Storm said angrily. "Now get back to your quarters."

Margo stood facing him, her breasts rising and falling under her quick breathing. Her eyes were flashing and Storm was suddenly acutely conscious of her as a woman. He saw the smooth swelling sweetness of her breasts, the long supple lines of her bare legs, the smooth column of her throat.

They were alone in a vacuum then into which nothing else could penetrate. Outside, the noises of work seemed distant and faint.

She came closer to him and suddenly her arms were around his neck and her mouth was pressed against his and her slender body strained against him. Storm felt a sharp desperate need that drove everything else from his mind.

And then he suddenly tore her arms from his neck and flung her away from him. She fell to the floor and began to sob.

Storm wiped his mouth with the back of his hand his face black and bitter. "You thought I had a price, didn't you? You thought to buy me, as you would buy a hungry man with a beefsteak. Get out!"

When he was alone he went into the bedroom and splashed cold water over his hands and face, and rubbed himself dry with a coarse towel. Then, he poured a canteen cup full of black coffee and dumped four ounces of whisky into it. He drank it down in three gulps and then adjusted the telescope and turned his eyes on the void.

He was still at the scope when MacDonald, his chief engineer, entered. They exchanged perfunctory salutes and MacDonald said, "The fighter ships are ready, sir. We had some trouble with the tubes on number three ship, but it's all cleared up."

"Good," Storm said. "Then we can blast-off any time now?"

"Well...yes, but I don't know that it would be the right thing."

"What do you mean?" Storm asked sharply.

"The men, sir. They're tired, worn out. If we start patrols now, it'll mean keeping extra crews at the field, plus the pilots and crewmembers for the flying—"

Storm lit a cigar and glanced almost involuntarily at the visi-screen. Then he turned back to MacDonald. "I'm not a martinet for the fun of it," he said. "But it is necessary that we use the men up to their last ounce of strength. That's all there is to it."

"Very well, sir," MacDonald said. "The ships are ready."

"Fine. You've done good work. Tell the flight captains to report to me here immediately."

THERE WERE four flight captains assigned to the *Astro Star II* to pilot the fighter ships she carried and these men were in Storm's office within five minutes. Boyd, a stocky light blond; Miller, a gangling, sleepy looking man with lightning reflexes; Carney, a grinning Irishman; and Larry Masterson, looking like a sullen angel, stood before Storm, who was seated at his desk.

The captains were tired now, their clothes dusty, their eyes bloodshot, and they needed shaves, baths and sleep.

Storm's first words caused an almost imperceptible sigh from all four men.

"Regular patrols will start tonight. Two ships will cruise this area continuously. During a change of relief, one ship will remain out, well away from the planet, and continue to reconnoiter, while the two ships of the next shift get away."

"What are we supposed to be looking for?" Larry Masterson said, sarcastically.

Storm ignored his tone. He turned, faced the visi-screen and pointed to a milky chain of star clusters in its upper left corner.

"You know something about Galaxy X, I presume?"

Three captains nodded, but Larry said, "The old bogey man, eh?"

Storm looked at him and said, "Men a damn sight smarter than you, Captain, think otherwise," he turned to the screen again. "Fifteen years ago we knew there was a life force in this galaxy. Commander Griffith proved to his own satisfaction that sections of this vast universe were at war with other sections of it. He theorized that one section might win a decisive victory and then turn its war-like attentions toward Earth.

"Commander Griffith was called a crackpot, of course, but time bas proven him right. There is one section of the galaxy in the ascendancy now. That section has been massing its life units along a chain of stars on the earth-side of the galaxy. Our mission is to patrol the area between Jupiter and the galaxy, to watch what happens to that star-chain on this side of the galaxy, and to relay our information to Earth."

"You say this starts tonight?" Larry said.

"Yes," Storm said, standing. "Why?"

LARRY LOOKED at the other three captains, and then squared his shoulders. His curly blond hair hung over his forehead and his face was smudged with dirt. "I'll speak for myself then," he said. "We're worn out with this damn work here. We need a day or two to get rested."

Storm laughed harshly. "You boasted to me once of loving to fly, of knowing what it was all about, of liking the Space Arm. Sure! You liked flying fat admirals and their wives on trips around the moon. You liked the idea of being a space flyer. You like the uniform. That's all the Space Arm has been for the last fifteen years, a repository of incompetents. Well…times change. We're going to work here and do our job. And the patrols will start tonight and continue twenty-four hours every day that were here. That's all, gentlemen."

Larry stared at Storm and his face and eyes were rebellious, hot. But he shrugged finally and strode from the office.

Storm sat at his desk for a few moments studying the visi-screen. He lifted his cup and drank a last mouthful of cold coffee and whisky, then ran a tired hand across his forehead. It was four in the afternoon. He went into his bedroom and threw himself down on the cot, an arm across his eyes. The fighter ships wouldn't blast-off for two or three hours yet, he estimated. Time for him to get some sleep. He closed his burning eyes.

But sleep wouldn't come. He thought of Margo, of the feel of her body against his, of the smoothness of her skin, the womanly sweep of her hips and breasts.

Storm clenched his big hands and tossed restlessly on the cot. She had said once to him that he had never loved! That was both right and wrong. He had loved and loved ardently, but the object of his passion was a cold abstraction. He had loved Earth. He had wanted it to be free and safe. But nothing had come from that love but a great amount of bitterness and shame.

At last without warning sleep came. His body triumphed. The swirling weary thoughts were conquered by the needs of bone and muscle. He slept deeply, dreamlessly, an arm across his eyes, one leg trailing on the floor.

CHAPTER FOUR

A SHOUT penetrated Storm's sleep. Another brought him to full wakefulness. He swung himself up and was striding into his office when the door flew open and a cadet dashed in, his face and eyes terrified.

"What is it?" Storm snapped.

"They're coming up the hill," the cadet gasped. "Major MacDonald sent me to get you. He—"

Storm shoved past the cadet and stepped outside. Directly ahead of him, about two hundred yards away, a slope began that led down into a broad valley. Storm had gone over the valley carefully the first day they arrived and found nothing but the usual purple-tinted, flint-like soil, and occasional tufts of vegetation tougher than steel wire.

Now Storm saw a knot of his men at the crest of the slope, and several men running back toward the compound.

He started to run.

Major MacDonald turned as he charged up and Storm was shocked at the ghastly pallor of the engineer's face. The man couldn't speak. He waved to Storm and pointed toward the valley.

Storm trotted up the sharp rise to the crest of the hill and looked out at the valley, and the sight that met his eyes brought an icy film of perspiration to his face.

Coming toward him with the inexorability of a glacier, were hordes of great metal monsters, rank after rank of them, stretching down into the valley as far as his eye reached. The clanking, grinding noise they made carried clearly on the dank cold air, and there was something in their progress, an inevitability in their approach, that raised the hackles on his neck.

They were moving faster than he had first judged. Within five minutes the vanguard of the weird creatures would reach the spot where the Earthmen were standing. Storm could see them clearly, now make out the details of their construction.

They stood six feet tall, with arms and legs attached in a semblance of the human form, and above the broad flat shoulders were bucket-like heads cut in square ugly angles, with slits for mouth and eyes.

Light from the artificial suns at the compound reflected off the rows of rivets on the machines, and as they moved forward toward Storm they winked and flashed as if charged with electricity.

Storm drew his heat gun and took careful aim on one of the foremost robots.

He fired a beam that hit the creature below its left knee joint. The metal dissolved and the robot fell ponderously to the ground where it lay like a broken toy.

But the remaining horde continued its inevitable, engulfing march.

"It won't do any good to shoot them," MacDonald said, desperately.

"No," Storm said. "Not with hand weapons, at any rate," he swung around to survey the situation. Men were coming out of their huts at the compound and staring toward the hill where Storm stood. To his right, a mile off, was the space ship field with the blast-off tubes pointing up to the sky, and beyond that was the mighty bulk of the *Astro Star II*. A tight grimace of satisfaction touched Storm's face as he saw the giant atomic cannons protruding from the hull of their ship.

"We'll retreat to the *Astro Star*," he snapped. "We can burn these robots down with one sweep of those starboard cannons."

"That's right," MacDonald said. "I didn't think of that!"

THEY BEGAN a careful but hasty retreat. Storm trotted ahead and rounded up all crewmembers at the compound and told them to head for the *Astro Star*. The girl, Margo, came out of her hut and he sent her along with the advance section from the crew.

Now the leading robots had topped the crest of the hill and were lumbering along toward the compound. But halfway there they changed direction and continued after Storm and his followers, who were bringing up the rear of the retreat.

"The damn things are after us!" MacDonald shouted. "They're passing up the compound entirely."

"Let's keep ahead of them, then," Storm said grimly. He didn't know whether the robots' intentions were lethal, but he didn't intend to investigate that possibility yet.

Suddenly a shout sounded at the head of the ragged column of Earthmen.

"Good God!" MacDonald cried.

Storm swung around and saw that another column of the massive robots had appeared on the slope below the space ship base. This contingent swarmed in seemingly endless numbers past the blast-off tubes and surged along to meet the first group.

Storm and his crew were caught in a pinchers movement.

They were cut off from the *Astro Star*.

Storm saw there was only one course left to take, which was to make a right angle turn and attempt to get around the first horde and back to the compound, where there were steel shelters and rifles.

Storm heard a scream then went through him like a cold knife. Wheeling, he saw that the girl, Margo, had fallen in the pathway of the advancing robots. She tried to rise, then fell back to the ground. One crewmember started back for her. The rest of the crewmembers were rushing to get out of the closing jaws of the robot attack.

Storm said to MacDonald, "Get to the compound, and into my office as fast as you can. You're in charge."

HE TURNED then and raced back toward Margo. The ground was uneven and treacherous beneath his feet, and he saw with horror that he and the leading robot were going to reach the girl at about the same time. The crewmember who had gone to her aid was a mechanic, a husky fearless man, but his face was ashen as he tugged at the girl's arm.

Storm whipped out his ray gun and burned the metal legs off the charging robot. The creature fell with a metallic crash, both great arms still reaching out for the two humans.

That gave them ten seconds.

Storm saw that Margo's face was white and drawn. She was pushing the crewmember away from her.

"Don't stay with me!" she gasped. "It's my knee. They'll get us both!"

Storm scooped her up in his arms and flipped his gun to the mechanic. "Cover us," he shouted to the man, and ran as fast as he could to get clear of the engulfing tide of robots.

There was a pathway now about fifty yards between the two waves of metal monsters, and through this rapidly narrowing channel Storm dashed with the girl. Beside him the mechanic was picking off robots, first on one side, then the other.

The robots, Storm saw, were slow in changing course. On a straightaway they could lumber ahead at surprising speed, but now some of them were starting to turn to follow him, and they performed this maneuver clumsily, haltingly.

It was this delay that gave him a chance to get away. He dodged through the last of the creatures as the two waves came together with a crack. Some of the robots were bowled over by the impact, and the others milled and churned around as they attempted to get clear and follow Storm.

By that time Storm was twenty-five yards up the side of the mountain, and from there he cut left and ran alongside the unorganized mass of robots. Some of the creatures on the fringe of the horde turned and began a clumsy ascent of the rocky hill, but Storm outdistanced them easily.

The compound loomed ahead. Every steel door was closed tight, and from every window squat deadly atomic rifles were thrust. Nothing stirred except the slowly moving muzzles that covered Storm, the girl, and the mechanic.

Storm trotted straight to his headquarters. His arms were aching and each breath seared his lungs painfully.

The door swung open and they were inside. The girl was lifted from Storm's arm and carried into his bedroom. Someone thrust a rifle into his hands.

Questions, babbled questions, beat at his ears. He held up a hand and called for silence in his harsh voice.

"I don't know what they are, how they operate, or who sent them," he said. "So don't worry about that now. By God, we're in for a fight! Don't waste a round. Shoot them in bunches if you can. Maybe we can build a wall of disabled robots that the rest can't climb,"

He told MacDonald to call him when the first robots appeared in the compound. Then he went into his bedroom.

The girl lay on his cot. She was pale and her mouth was twisted with pain.

"You said I'd cause trouble," she said weakly.

"Never mind that," he straightened her leg and then felt her knee gently. "Iothing broken," he said. "A bad wrench."

"It doesn't matter. What in the name of God are they?"

"I don't know. I'm going now. Are you afraid?"

"Yes," she said quietly. "But it's all right."

"Good girl," he said. He felt sorry for her. This was bad enough for a man. He put his hand awkwardly on her forehead in a gesture of comfort then got to his feet. He was turning to the door when MacDonald's voice, loud and fear-laden, shouted his name.

STORM hurried through the door into his office and pushed his way through the knots of men who were clustered there. MacDonald was at a window, staring out into the compound, his jaw slack with astonishment.

Storm edged him aside. In the compound, robots were drawn up in ranks on both sides of the encampment. Advancing through their center was the weirdest sight Storm had encountered in his life.

Leading a squad of robots was a tall, voluptuously proportioned girl, a magnificent Amazon with flaming red hair and ice-green eyes. She wore a brief, tight-fitting garment and a long purple cape that swirled back and away from her powerful shoulders. Her bare legs were slender and graceful, but the fine muscles that rippled in her calves as she advanced was an indication of steel-spun strength.

From a jeweled belt at her waist hung a gleaming tubular object from which poured a stream of light. In one gauntleted hand she carried a ray gun of ancient make, and the other was raised above her head in a defiant gesture as she stopped spread-legged before Storm's quarters.

"Come out, you crawling cowards!" she shouted in a brassy, full-lunged voice. "There is nothing here but a helpless girl and a few clumsy figures of steel."

Storm had hardly dared believe his eyes when he saw the girl. Now he jerked open the door and strode into the compound. He stopped a dozen feet from the girl, a hard smile on his face.

The girl watched him and the expression of belligerence on her face changed slowly to one of bewilderment.

"Yes," Storm said. "We know each other, Karen. You were eleven when I last saw you."

"You're Storm," the girl said slowly. "You came here with my father on that trip."

Storm nodded. He could hardly believe he wasn't living some strangely vivid dream. This was Karen Griffith, daughter of Commander Griffith, who had been left on Jupiter eleven years ago. Karen had not only survived, she had thrived.

"Your father?" Storm said, quietly.

"Dead," the girl said. "He and Ben Thatcher, and my mother have been gone a long while now. That pleases you, doesn't it?" she said, in a savage voice. "You and all the rest of Earth cowards. You deserted him, left him here to die."

"I did not desert your father," Storm said in an even voice. "I was dragged aboard the ship in irons and taken back to Earth by force."

"Lies, lies, lies!" the girl cried imperiously. She stepped back a pace, her hand dropping to the tube at her waist as members of Storm's crew crowded out behind him.

"Hold it!" Storm said sharply. He didn't know what she intended to do, but he surmised the tube controlled the robots in some manner. "We're not your enemies, Karen. We are here to continue your father's work. Earth is in danger Karen, grave danger. The danger your father foresaw and attempted to prepare Earth to face, is at hand—so close at hand that days may mean the difference of life and death to the entire planet."

"You expect me to care about the fate of Earth?" the girl cried in a scornful manner. "I would cheerfully hasten Earth's destruction with every means at my command."

"Your father didn't teach you that attitude," Storm said.

"My father was a poor, idealistic fool," Karen said, laughing. "He held no malice against Earth. He talked to me of tolerance of forgiveness. I listened and when he finished I spat at his feet. I saw what they had done to him. I saw the reward he received for his service, his dedication, his very life. There is no forgiveness, no charity in me, Storm—for you or your kind."

"We face each other as enemies then?" Storm said heavily.

KAREN LAUGHED, a ringing defiant laugh. "Yes, by Heaven, we do!" She turned a significant glance at the column of silent robots lined up on both sides of her, and stretching back for what seemed miles. Then she faced Storm again. "You've seen my pets at work. I warn you, Storm, I do not intend to make war. My life is my own, clean, alone, and unfettered. I will keep it that way with every weapon I control.

"I will not interfere with you. But…if you seek me out or attempt to disrupt my life, I will not rest until every man of yours is ground to powder beneath the feet of my army. Do you understand?"

Storm nodded. His face was dark, bitter, as he struggled against a mighty anger. He would have liked to get his hands on this imperious, defiant woman for ten seconds, but the thing that enraged him most was that she had every right in the world to her opinion and feeling. Why should she help Earth?

There was no reason. The girl had seen the gratitude of Earth, knew its pettiness. Who could blame her for the way she felt?

"Very well, Karen," he said. "We have our work to do, and you have a right to your own life. They won't come in conflict."

"They had better not," Karen said, with an ominous smile.

Still smiling she fingered the tube at her waist and the army of silent automatons began to rearrange themselves in formation. Karen backed away from the compound, her cool, ice-green eyes flicking contemptuously across the groups of silent men who watched her, and when she reached the crest of the slope, she wheeled and disappeared.

The last they saw was the flash of her purple cape, elusive and mysterious as smoke on the horizon.

CHAPTER FIVE

STORM TURNED and nodded to the crewmembers clustered at the entrance of his office. "Carry on with your regular work, men," he hesitated a moment, then added grimly. "You know as much about this thing as I do."

Entering his office, Storm found MacDonald standing by his desk. The engineer was grave.

"Two men were killed at the blast-off chute," he said. "They didn't get started fast enough."

"I see." Storm sat down at his desk and rubbed his forehead tiredly. He had been known in the service as a steel-hard, void-cold commander; but no one knew the effort it cost him to preserve that front of impersonality.

MacDonald filled a cup with coffee, poured whisky into it and brought it to Storm.

"You need this," he said. "You can't last much longer at this pace, you know. Why don't you rest tonight?"

Storm took the coffee and sipped it. He was touched by MacDonald's concern, and he didn't know quite what to say. "There's too much to do," he said finally. "But thanks just the same."

MacDonald nodded and left the office. Storm finished the coffee and stood up and walked into his bedroom. Margo still lay on the bed. She was staring at the ceiling. He saw that she had been crying.

"Knee hurt?" he said.

"No, it's stiff, that's all."

"Will you let me tape it for you?"

"Yes. Maybe I can walk then."

Storm got out a first-aid kit and pulled a chair beside the cot. He sat down and applied a tape cast to the injured knee.

"That may hurt a little," he said.

"No, it's all right."

He fought down a feeling of annoyance. "Well, something's hurting you. You're crying."

"She had a pretty loud voice. I heard about Thatcher."

"Oh," Storm said. He felt clumsy. "I'm sorry."

"Don't be sorry. It was the end of a dream. All dreams do end, don't they?"

"I don't know," Storm said, standing. "I think you can walk now."

She stood and tested the leg by walking haltingly to the door. "It's all right, I guess. Thanks, Storm." Turning, she limped across his office and he heard the door slam behind her.

Storm threw himself on the cot and pressed both hands against his aching eyes. There was faint, delicate fragrance in the room—a subtle essence as elusive as a smile.

He lay there, staring at the ceiling, stony-faced, wondering what had happened to him...

HALF AN hour later he pushed up on one elbow, frowning. Something was wrong. It took him a moment to decide what it was. There was no sound of activity from the compound. The normal, everyday bustle of work was lacking.

Storm walked out of his office and saw half a dozen men talking in a small group. Other groups were clustered in the compounds. No one was working.

The talk faded as he glanced from group to group, his jaw hardening grimly.

"I told you men to carry on your regular work," he said harshly. "Didn't you understand that?"

Larry Masterson, the young flight captain, moved out from a group and sauntered over to Storm. He stopped and lit a cigarette and blew smoke in the air. His blond hair hung over his forehead and there was a sardonic smile at his lips.

"We don't see much reason to get back to work, Commander Storm," he said mildly. "We're tired of being driven like dogs to satisfy your ego. We don't believe the fairy stories about Galaxy X, and we don't intend to invite more attacks from those murderous robots."

"You've said enough to hang yourself, Captain," Storm said grimly. He raked his eyes over the crewmembers clustered in the compound. "I'll give you exactly ten seconds to get on with your work."

He swung his arm up and watched the second hand on his watch move inexorably across the dial. Larry Masterson yawned elaborately.

Storm put his arm down and squared his big shoulders. "So it's mutiny, is it?" he said quietly.

"Oh, no, not at all," Larry Masterson said. "We think you're unfit to command this squadron, Commander. When we return to Earth it is you who will stand trial, not us. Now, we are relieving you of command."

"You don't know what you're doing!" Storm shouted.

"Yes, we do," Larry said, his voice hard. "We heard the pact you made with that murderous girl, and we intend to change it. We'll take her robots and put them to work for us, and we'll see that she causes no trouble."

Storm spun suddenly and dove for the door of his office, but half a dozen crewmembers sprang after him and caught him before he got inside. Struggling furiously he was borne to the ground.

The crew must have prepared for the attack. Storm realized, for steel hoops were produced, slipped about his arms and tightened until he was pinioned helplessly. Then he was jerked to his feet.

"You will be kept a prisoner until we return to Earth," Larry Masterson said. "Your treatment will depend on how you behave yourself."

"You'll die for this!" Storm raged.

"No. I'm merely trying to save all of our lives."

MacDonald, the tall, graying engineer, came forward slowly from the ranks and stood beside Storm. "I'm too old for mutiny," he said in a cold precise voice. "Commander Storm is my superior officer. I recognize no other."

"Very well," Larry said dryly. "You may accompany your commander into honorable imprisonment."

He was turning away when a clear but firm voice said, "If you move I will blast you straight to hell!"

Storm looked up and saw the girl, Margo, her face ashen, clenching a heavy gun in both hands and pointing it unwaveringly at Larry.

"Don't be a fool," he called to her. She stood at the edge of the compound, a slight, determined figure. "Release him," she said.

She didn't see the man slipping up behind her, nor did she see his hand until it came down suddenly and sharply, knocking the gun from her grasp. By then it was too late. She sank to the ground, weeping.

Larry shrugged. "Take these three down to the blast-off field and lock them up there. We've got work to do…"

CHAPTER SIX

THE PLACE they were taken to was a steel building used to house tools and supplies. It was a one-storied unit about twelve by fourteen feet, with glass windows that were strong as chrome steel.

Storm stood at one window staring across the mile-long sweep leading to the compound. He could see men moving about even at that distance, for the atmosphere was burned clear by the powerful sun lamps.

He stood there unmoving, his face black with rage, his eyes hot. He wanted nothing else in life but to get his hands on Larry's throat.

MacDonald joined him. "They may change their minds, you know," he said. "Some of those men have sense. When they start thinking this over they may snap out of it."

"I didn't ask for a recapitulation," Storm said harshly.

MacDonald cleared his throat. "Very well, sir," he said, and sat down with his back to the wall.

"Bite and snarl, that's all you know," Margo said hotly. "He stuck with you, didn't he, while the rest of your men mutinied?"

"Do you think he deserves some special credit for doing what he swore he would do when he was commissioned in the service?" Storm said.

"He wouldn't get it from you, at least," Margo said. "You think people should be made of steel, knowing nothing but duty, having no doubts, or problems, or anything but their dedicated service to Earth."

"Am I a monster because I want Earth to be safe?" Storm said.

"No," Margo said in a weary voice. "But you've never learned that two people can want the same thing in different ways. You treat disagreement with scorn instead of respect. Your men want what you want, Storm, but you drove them away."

"Shut up!" Storm said angrily.

"That's how you settle all issues. Very well. I'll shut up."

Storm watched the compound, his face stony. Soon he saw a figure leave there and head toward them, toward the blast-off field. When the man neared Storm recognized him as Boyd, the fighter pilot.

"Where are you going. Boyd?" he shouted.

Boyd grinned. "Just for a pleasure jaunt, my friend," he said and continued on. A little later Storm heard a ship take off under auxiliary power. He peered upward and saw the slim fighter streaking upward and then bank toward the mountains.

He frowned and rubbed his jaw trying to guess what the men were planning.

HALF AN hour later twelve men left the compound. They carried packs. The man in the lead walked like Larry, but at that distance Storm couldn't be sure.

For another hour he watched the compound, looking for more indications that might help him decide what was happening; but nothing of significance occurred. Men strolled across the compound to the hall, or moved in and out of their dwelling units, in normal, casual fashion.

He lit one of his stubby black cigars and glanced up at the thick, green sky. High and almost directly above the compound he saw a small black globe settling toward the ground. He watched it for a moment without expression and then his hands tightened instinctively.

"MacDonald," he said. "Come here."

Storm pointed to the descending globe. He didn't speak. MacDonald moved closer to the window and peered upward, a slight frown on his face.

They could see the object more clearly now. It was circular, saucer-shaped, and was spinning slowly as it descended. From ports on its narrow sides bright lights flashed.

"Well?" Storm said. He kept his voice quiet, even.

"I don't know," MacDonald said slowly. "Look at the compound."

The men at the compound had come out of their steel huts, were gazing upward at the settling globe. Some of them were waving.

"Fools!" Storm raged. He beat a fist into his palm. "The hopeless, damned fools! Don't they realize—"

The door behind them opened and a corporal came in, plainly worried. He looked at Storm awkwardly. "Sir," he said, "there's a— You've seen it, I guess."

Storm didn't answer. "Let me have your binoculars."

"Yes, sir," the corporal said, with relief in his voice. It was obvious he was willing, even anxious, for Storm to resume responsibility and command.

Storm studied the globe with the glasses. It was several hundred yards above the ground now, and moving slowly. He saw nothing revealing at close range. The ship was made of black metal, and the lights flashing from discs on its side were bright and dazzling.

As he watched, the discs revolved and beams of light struck down toward the compound.

MacDonald shouted involuntarily. "Watch out!"

Storm swung the glasses to the compound and saw that his men had been scattered to the ground like broken dolls.

The light from the still-settling ship played over them, flashed into the buildings, over the whole area, bathing it in a brilliant radiance.

The men under the light didn't move; they lay still in the undignified sprawl of death.

"Good lord!" Margo cried. "What happened to them, Storm?"

STORM FAILED to answer. He watched the ship as it stopped fifty yards above the ground, then, after a wait of several minutes, slowly dropped gently to rest in the compound.

A powerful tension grew in Storm. It wasn't fear. It was anticipation. He knew with calm strong certainty that he was about to meet the thing he had fought against all his life. He had never known the enemy; he had battled shadows. Now the curtain was lifted, the antagonists could face each other, measuringly, appraisingly, finally.

Apertures appeared in the sides of the ship and things moved out of it and onto the rocky ground of Jupiter.

Storm centered his glasses on the first of the creatures, and hot anger coursed through him as he made out details: fat, toad-like bodies, gray, scabrous skins, pendulous heads, and great round stumps of feet.

"It's incredible," MacDonald whispered. "They're—they're old, older than hell."

"The last crawling filth of a dead universe," Storm said. "They want the plains and flowers of Earth now. They need its sun and air and young vigor."

They counted five of the creatures. They watched in fascinated silence as the invaders moved sluggishly about the compound, in and out of the buildings. Then, after this examination the creatures came together for several minutes near their ship. Finally four of them left the compound and traveled in the direction of the slope where the robots had first appeared—and where the twelve crewmen had gone.

Once started they moved with greater speed, and in a matter of seconds they had disappeared over the crest of the hill.

For several minutes no one spoke. Storm glanced at Margo and saw that her cheeks were wet but her eyes were flashing defiance.

"Good…that's good," he said gently. "Maybe if you thought about them all of your life you might turn into the kind of person I am. It's not a nice thing to turn into, of course. Nobody likes you very much," he turned to the corporal, who snapped to painful attention. "Let me have your rifle," he said.

Holding the rifle in readiness. Storm stepped carefully through the door and dropped to his stomach. He wriggled ahead for perhaps a hundred yards until he reached a slight rise from where he could clearly see the creature that had remained behind in the compound.

He settled himself on his stomach and put the stock of the rifle into his shoulder, enjoying the feel of cool metal against his cheek. He sighted on the toad-like creature and began to squeeze the trigger gently.

The creature moved back and forth restlessly, as if sensing that something was wrong. From its waist hung a small disc that glowed brightly. The beam from the disc flashed about in a wide questing circle as the creature moved in an aimless circle.

Suddenly the ray of light flashed to a greater length and leaped across the plain toward the blast-off field, toward Storm.

Storm fired a blast of heat at the creature, as light from the disc struck him full force. For an instant a terrible, unendurable pain swept over him. Then it was gone. He clambered to his feet, shaking his head like an injured animal.

The creature was lying on the ground, and attempting to move, to crawl. Storm fired two more blasts and the movement stopped.

MacDonald came hurrying up and caught Storm's arm. That light—what was it?" he gasped.

"I don't know. But another tenth of a second and I'd have been gone. My first shot got him just in time. Let's get going."

THE COMPOUND was a nightmarish scene of death. Men lay sprawled on the ground, slumped at workbenches, or collapsed in their cots. No one was alive.

Storm made directly for his headquarters. Inside he snapped on the visi-screen above his desk. MacDonald was at his heels.

They stood looking at the void, at the mightly jeweled star-chin on the Earth side of Galaxy X. Beneath it, several inches on the screen, but billions of miles in the void, was a shadowy cluster of black dots, thousands of them, poised in space.

Storm spoke matter-of-factly, bitterly. "You are looking at the space fleet of Galaxy X. They're ready. Are we, MacDonald?"

He turned without cutting off the machine and went outside. There were no clear thoughts in his mind. He didn't know what they could do.

He heard a ship overhead and instinctively he ducked; but the whine of the auxiliaries was familiar, and when it flashed into sight he recognized it as one of their own fighters, the one Boyd had left in an hour or so before.

Storm watched the ship circle for a mooring at the blast-off field, and then he trotted in that direction, the heat rifle still in his hands.

CHAPTER SEVEN

WHEN STORM, MacDonald, and the girl had first been led away. Larry had outlined his plans quickly to Boyd, the squarely built light blond, and Carney, the Irishman. They were in Storm's office.

"For better or worse we're in charge," he said crisply. "Our necks depend on what we do with our authority. If we do a sensible job, it will prove we were right. If not, we'll hang as mutineers."

"Hell, everybody is back of us," Carney said, his voice shaking.

"Okay, fine. First we have to find the girl...the one Storm called Karen. We've got to find out how she controls those robots and make sure she doesn't use them against us. Here's my idea: Those robots must return to some central area and they're probably still on the way there. Boyd, you take a fighter ship and cruise around this area until you pick up the trail. Meanwhile Carney and I will take a party in the same general direction the robots took. When you establish contact, radio us the directions and we'll close in on the girl. Okay?"

There were a few questions, a few details to iron out, then Boyd left on the double for the blast-off tubes. Larry told Carney to select a party of twelve men and pack enough supplies to last them a week.

When both men had gone, Larry lit a cigarette and sat down in Storm's chair. He frowned at the tip of his cigarette for a few minutes. He had been trained in the best ideals of the service. Mutineer in his eyes was a mad dog. Yet he had taken that step, confident he was right. The babbling about Galaxy X had never impressed him. It was an old scare story of those who wanted Earth to build bigger armies, bigger space ships. It was one of those semi-sacrosanct fables that everyone discussed gravely, but no one believed. At least none of the cadets in his class had believed it, and they were a well-informed, sophisticated group.

Suddenly he realized it was Commander Storm's desk he was sitting at and he got up hastily, with the uncomfortable certainty that he didn't belong there.

But that was foolish. Storm would have killed them all with his fanatic's ideas; and if Storm hadn't, then the girl with the robots might well have.

Larry lit another cigarette and pushed the hair from his eyes. He had had but one quick glimpse of this girl, but something about her, some quality of defiance and arrogance in her attitude, made him eager to see her again, eager to test that steel...

IT WAS AN hour later that he received the first radio message from Boyd. His party was halted near the narrow mouth of a valley. They were about ten Earth miles from the compound, and the air was stingingly cold, while the flakes of flint like dust hurled by the wind made their progress slow and difficult.

Larry raised a jubilant hand as Boyd's deep sure voice came over the portable unit:

"It's the valley ahead of you, Captain. Bear right, into an opening in the mountain. That's where, every robot has disappeared."

"Check," Larry snapped with satisfaction.

The men with him had heard the message and they pressed forward with renewed enthusiasm as Larry led the slender column through the narrow opening of the valley. His eyes swept along the right side of the vast, purple mountain that soared above their heads to the green-colored sky.

He found the opening Boyd had spotted about a quarter

of a mile from the valley entrance, and its appearance immediately suggested Herculean labor combined with intelligence. The aperture was fifty yards square and led to a shaft that seemingly stretched into the heart of the mountain, a tunnel with silk-smooth walls and gracefully arched ceiling high above the stone flooring.

They followed the shaft for nearly half a mile before it turned to the right. As they followed this new route they heard a swelling, murmuring sound that seemed to emanate from the heart of the mountain.

An iridescent glow from the sheer, glass-smooth walls provided illumination as they proceeded cautiously down the gleaming corridor. The sound was becoming more intense now; it was a gigantic humming that echoed from the walls and set up a throbbing in their ears.

Larry glanced at Carney uneasily, then shrugged. There was nothing to do but keep going.

A quarter of a mile ahead they saw that the corridor fanned out on both sides before ending abruptly—leading to nothing but bright and empty space.

They hurried along this last stretch and the swelling sound now filled their heads with an almost intolerable clamor.

Reaching the widening section of the shaft, Larry moved forward more cautiously to the very lip of the floor, until he could look down into the pit where the roaring sounds seemed to originate.

Carney crowded alongside him with the other members of the party as Larry heard somebody say, "Good lord" in a hushed voice.

HALF A mile below them, and extending as far as they could see, was a mighty vault cut into the granite heart of the mountain. Working deep in that immense pit were thousands and thousands of the ponderous, carefully moving robots.

The sight of that incredible metal army spreading for miles in all directions was enough to catch at their throats with a nameless horror.

Carney touched Larry's arm and said in an awed voice: "Do you see what they're doing? They're making more robots. Look! There on your left! They're coming off that line, getting up, and walking ahead under their own power!"

Larry rubbed a hand over his forehead. He saw squads of the creatures carrying loads of metal, others working with ringing sledges, and that other groups were working at long tables supporting fabulously intricate machines.

"Let's keep going," Larry said to Carney. "We've got to find that girl. You can imagine what would happen if she ever turned *this* loose on us."

They stood indecisively for a moment at the cross-corridor, above the great pit. Larry finally sent half the party to the left while he, Carney, and four others, proceeded to the right.

At the next cross-corridor Larry selected two men and told them to follow it for half an hour, then return to the main corridor. Again, a quarter of a mile on, he sent two more men down a cross-corridor, while he and Carney continued on alone. For a mile they went ahead, then they came to a third cross-corridor and Larry looked helplessly at Carney.

Carney shouted an answer to the unspoken question on Larry's face. "We might as well follow it. If we find nothing we might as well collect the men and get out of here."

The new corridor did not run straight. Instead it curved back and forth, and was considerably narrower than the one they had just left. As they followed its undulations the noise from the robot factory faded away to a gentle, distant murmur.

Then, as they rounded a corner, Larry caught Carney's

arm. Ahead was a wide arched door on the right side of the corridor.

They approached it cautiously. There was no knob or handle but it swung inward slowly, silently, as Larry put his shoulder against it.

Beyond the door was a short, narrow hall that turned to the right and led them to a pair of closed doors.

Larry stopped before them, his heart beating almost audibly.

HE PUT HIS hand against the panel of one and pushed. Through the aperture formed by the opening door he saw a large, high-ceilinged room with gleaming walls and a metal floor that shone like aluminum.

He eased the door open another few inches, and his breath caught as he saw the red-haired girl.

She was lying on a low oval bed in the center of the room and her full, sharply pointed breasts rose and fell with her even breathing. Her eyes were closed, and she was apparently asleep.

Larry glanced at Carney, put a cautioning finger to his lips, and then stepped through the arched doorway into the room. Carney moved quietly at his heels.

The girl who had called herself Karen turned restlessly as they moved toward her. She wore a light silken garment open at the throat and extending halfway to her bare knees. The pale silver light from the walls glinted on her fiery red hair and glazed the milky smoothness of her slender, exquisite legs.

On a table beside the bed Larry saw the belt she had worn the first time he had seen her, and the tube with which she had seemed to control the robots. Also, close to her hand, was the ancient ray gun.

Carney moved up beside Larry and as he did so his foot

slipped on the silk-smooth floor. He lost his balance and fell to one knee with a thud.

The girl sat upright with the instinctive, light-swift reaction of an animal in danger, her icy green eyes flicking across the faces of the two men.

For a second they stared at one another in a tense, breathless silence, and Larry saw the muscles in the girl's arms and legs beginning to coil.

"Calm down, beautiful," he said softly. "We're not going to hurt you."

"I told you not to follow me," the girl said, a slow ominous anger in her voice. "I want nothing from you but to be let alone."

"Cut it out," Larry said curtly. "You're an Earth girl, and you can't live here like this."

"You fool!" the girl cried, and with a flashing movement that caught them both by surprise, she flung herself from the bed and lunged for the ray gun.

Larry dove after her, catching her about the waist as she wheeled, gun in hand, to face them. A bolt of dazzling silent heat shot past his shoulder, as his attack deflected her arm.

Carney closed in on the girl as she struggled with Larry.

"I've got her!" he yelled, lunging for her arm.

But the girl swung Larry about with savage, incredible strength, and Carney's hands closed on empty air. As he stumbled forward she slugged him across the side of the head with the gun barrel. He went down in an inert heap.

LARRY suddenly stepped back from the girl and chopped his hand down on her forearm. The gun clattered to the floor and she lunged at him with a cry of anger and pain.

"Stop it, you hellcat!" Larry panted.

"Never!"

"Okay, you asked for it," Larry said. He caught her arm

and pulled her close, then snapped a short hard right to the point of her jaw. She slumped against him, her eyes glazing, and he caught her before she could fall to the floor.

Lifting her in his arms he carried her to the bed, then stripped off his belt, and Carney's, and bound the girl's elbows and ankles.

Breathing hard, he bent over Carney and looked at the ugly lump on his head. The fallen man was breathing, but showed no signs of regaining consciousness.

Larry sat down beside the girl on the bed and waited until her eyes flickered open. For an instant she stared at him without comprehension; then she attempted to move, only to become aware of the bonds at her arms and ankles. A spasm of defiant fury contorted her face and she began to writhe and twist on the bed.

"You'll die for this!" she panted.

Larry held her by both shoulders to keep her from rolling onto the floor. He said, "You're a spoiled and unpleasant brat, Karen. The thing you need is a thorough spanking and a short lecture on the fact that you're not the most important and wonderful person in the universe. Possibly then you might start behaving like a human being."

"I hope I never behave like the humans I've known," the girl cried. "The humans who left my father to die, humans like you and that clod on the floor who know no rule but strength, no rules but the ones you make. I'd die before I molded myself after you."

Larry felt almost helpless before the blazing fury and conviction in the girl's eyes. In a way, he could see that she had reason behind her attitude.

"Now listen to me just a minute, please," he said, in a calmer voice. "We probably seem like savages to you in one sense. But try to understand our attitude. We're a small group of Earthmen who have been driven to the point of collapse by a neurotic commander. We—"

"You mean Storm?" the girl said. She had ceased struggling, and interest showed in her face.

"That's right. The man is a maniac. So we put him in irons—and took a hell of a chance in doing it! Now we want to get safely back to Earth and present our story to the Earth Federation. Frankly those robots of yours scared us and we intend to make sure they don't attack us again. That's why you find yourself in the spot you're in."

LARRY'S last words were colored with faint sarcasm, but the girl appeared not to notice.

"What is it Storm feared?" she said. "Why did he come here?"

Larry shrugged. "The old familiar bedtime story about Galaxy X. You know, the one they use to frighten children with on Earth. Storm, being slightly cracked, eats it up. He'd kill himself and everyone of us to fight this non-existent menace."

"My father often talked of Galaxy X," the girl said. "When—" A troubled frown appeared on her face. "I'm not sure of time anymore. But once he told me he built the robots to fight for Earth against the galaxy."

Larry saw that her mood had changed, that her attention was arrested by his story. He decided to take advantage of that to get information.

"We saw the robot pit on the way here," he said. "Do those creatures actually make themselves, or was I drunk?"

"They make themselves, of course. Father worked for years to make them self-perpetuating. They've gone on since he died, reproducing themselves to the last rivet and coil."

"How are they controlled?"

That question broke the girl's oddly submissive mood. She stared at him as if she had suddenly awakened. Suddenly she strained against her bonds, and cried, "I'll tell you nothing more. Release me at once."

Larry smiled at her and folded his arms. "You have to learn humility, Karen. I'm not going to release until you tell me what I want to know, and give me your promise you'll behave. Think that over, young lady, while I take a look at my friend."

He bent over Carney, his back to the girl and the tall doorway, and began shaking the man's shoulder gently. Carney stirred and his lids fluttered.

"That a boy," Larry said.

A sound from the girl caused him to turn quickly. She was staring past him, toward the doorway, and the expression on her face sent a cold tremor of alarm down his spine.

Her face was ashen, her breath laboring in gasps. Her teeth were closed on her lower lip, and a thin trickle of blood stained her chin. But it was her eyes that sent horror into Larry's soul. They were wide, staring, agonized.

Her lips moved, and she whimpered, "No!" in complete terror.

LARRY wheeled, still on his knees, and the sight that met his eyes contracted his throat with nauseating horror.

Standing silently in the doorway were four creatures that could have been spawned only in the nightmares of a diseased and ravaged mind.

Leprous gray in color, squat and thick as great toads, they stood on clumsy round feet, while their heads, huge and pendulous, swung slowly back and forth.

They were old, hideously old and evil, and the folds of flesh that hung in putrefying folds and loops over their bodies, looked as if it had been created from slime and filth.

About their waists were belts that supported pale, gleaming discs. The discs glowed with gelid light, their beams playing downward on the floor at their feet.

Larry swallowed dry terror and rose instinctively to his feet. He took a step backward—and then a beam of light flashed upward and caught him in its glare.

Instantly pain—numbing, incredible, maddening pain—flamed through every muscle, tendon and nerve of his body. He was transfixed, held motionless in its grip. He tried to fight, tried to throw himself to the floor, to scream. But the light was binding as a mold of steel. He stood rooted and paralyzed in the dreadful beam until his limbs were on the point of cracking and his skull felt as if it were ready to split like a rotten melon.

From the corner of his straining eyes he saw Carney move suddenly, lunging toward the ray gun on the floor, but as he did a beam of light from another of the creatures flashed out and Carney screamed—a scream torn from the depths of his soul. Blood streamed from his nose and mouth and he dropped to the floor like an animal crushed by some monstrous weight.

The light receded from the limp, huddled body, and Larry knew he was dead, the life driven from him forever by one touch of the creature's light.

The creatures hadn't yet moved except for the swinging, swaying motion of their great heads, but now they advanced slowly into the room and fixed their sunken eyes on the girl.

The light that held Larry in a grip of agony left him suddenly, and he fell to the floor, drained and helpless. From where he lay he could see the girl, see the creatures advancing slowly toward her, their eyes moving over her body as restlessly as ants.

"They're asking me about the robots," she cried brokenly. "Their minds are in mine-like fingers, probing and twisting."

"Good God!" Larry gasped.

"No!" the girl screamed suddenly, drawing back. "No!

No! No! I'll tell you nothing, you rotting fiends!"

The intruders were motionless for a moment, but Larry sensed they were communicating with one another.

Then a whimpering cry broke from his lips as one of the creatures moved closer to the bed, and light from the disc at his waist flashed over the girl's slim figure.

CHAPTER EIGHT

THE TWO bodies lay sprawled at a cross-corridor beside the vast robot pit in the heart of the mountain. Storm dropped to his knees beside them, saw instantly that both men were dead. He said to MacDonald, "We're on the right track."

They stood there—Boyd, MacDonald, and Storm—all staring ahead along the gleaming corridor. Boyd had told Storm of Larry's plans, and they had set out after the twelve-man party leaving Margo and the corporal behind at the compound.

"These were two of the men Larry took with him. I'm sure," Boyd said.

"Okay, let's keep going. And keep your guns ready," Storm said. "If we find those damn things we'll only get one chance."

They went on, heat guns drawn and held in readiness, until they reached a corridor that ran off in a long curve. In that respect it was different from the other halls they had passed, and for that reason Storm decided to follow it. He knew they were looking for a needle in a haystack, and their chances of success were slim. But they had to keep on.

As they followed the new course, they became aware that the sounds from the pit were fading behind them. Half a mile on they came to a door in the right side of the wall.

Storm glanced at MacDonald, a look that told him to be

ready for anything, and pushed the door open, slowly. They stepped through the door into another corridor and followed that to a pair of high doors that were standing slightly ajar.

Storm looked into the room, then grabbed Boyd by the arm and jerked him against the wall. MacDonald had seen also, and he had ducked down on the opposite side of the corridor.

Ahead, through the door, they saw the four gray monsters from the galaxy standing near a long bed on which the red-haired girl lay helplessly bound.

Light from the discs at the waists of the creatures played across her slender straining figure, transforming her hair into a halo of foaming gold and coating the alabaster whiteness of her flesh with shimmering radiance.

Her body was bent in a straining tortured arc. Her bare feet pressed flat against the hard matting of the bed, her head was thrown back in agony.

She was held in the vise-strong grip of the light, helpless as a victim on a rack, and every muscle and tendon of her body quivered and trembled against the incredible agony she was undergoing.

Storm whispered, "Boyd, take the one on the right. MacDonald, the left. Now!"

HE SNAPPED up his gun and sent a searing blast of destructive heat through the head of one creature. Every nerve in his body knew a macabre satisfaction as the leprous, putrefying flesh disintegrated into streams of obscene slime.

MacDonald and Boyd fired with the same deadly accuracy, and Boyd leaped into the room and dashed toward the remaining creature.

"Get down!" Storm shouted.

Boyd's impetuous charge brought him in the line of fire. MacDonald cursed and tried to find an opening to blast at the slowly turning creature. But he was too late.

And so was Boyd. He had waited too long to fire, and a lashing, vengeful beam of light from the creature's disc cut him down in a crumpled heap.

Storm fired twice—deliberately, coldly—and the fourth and last of the galaxy raiders crashed to the floor in a mass of putrescent ooze.

MacDonald hurried to the side of the girl, removed the bonds and helped her to a sitting position. She was conscious, but her face was ashen and drawn and she was trembling violently. MacDonald put an arm about her shoulder and held her close.

Storm's face tightened as he saw Larry Masterson getting to his feet. The young captain's face was strained and gray. He looked unseeingly at Storm, then turned to the girl and stumbled to her.

"I know what it was," he said, in a choked voice. "They—did it to me. I know what you stood—for us."

"Captain Masterson," Storm said in a cold precise voice. "You will consider yourself under arrest."

Larry turned to him slowly, a hand moving uncertainly to his face. He sighed and there was a bare trace, a ghost of a weary smile on his lips.

"You were right, of course," he said. "Hanging's too good for me."

Storm turned to MacDonald and suddenly the helplessness of their position was plain to him. Out in the void a great fleet of ships from Galaxy X was poised to strike at Earth. And here they were, three men and a girl—a helpless, futile unit.

MacDonald's thin, whipcord body looked tired, and a strand of graying hair hung over his forehead, but his hard soldierly face was still firm, knife-sharp.

"Your orders, sir?" he said.

Storm hesitated, then shrugged. He said dryly, "There's nothing to say, is there?"

"Perhaps not," MacDonald agreed. "But we still have our brains and a source of power that has probably never been equaled in the history of the universe. I mean the robots, of course."

"You're right," Storm said, and suddenly new excitement, new hope kindled in him. He turned and strode over to the girl. He looked directly into her ice-green eyes. "Will you help us?" he said. "Will you tell us how the robots are controlled?"

"Of course," the girl said. Her eyes were listless, her face dispirited; but slowly as Storm held her gaze, her expression began to change. Her eyes came alive, color touched her cheeks. "I'll do anything to drive creatures like these into the pit of hell where they belong." She shook her head suddenly, and moved her shoulders. "Whatever they did to me doesn't seem to have a permanent effect. I'm all right—but I'll remember...one second under that light gives you a sensation to take to your grave."

She swung her legs off the bed and got to her feet. "Come with me," she said.

SHE LED them out of her quarters and along the edge of the vast robot pit to a stairway cut in the solid, granite-hard walls of the vault. Ascending this stairway for a nearly a quarter of a mile, they entered a great dome-shaped chamber fitted out as a laboratory. In the center of the room a great machine rested, a machine fully fifty yards tall and a hundred yards in diameter at the base, with sides of curving metal that gleamed like silver.

"This was my father's workshop," Karen said.

MacDonald stared about, his eyes finally stopping on the machine. From its depths they could hear a gentle murmur.

"This is what motivates the robots I suppose," he said, in a musing voice. Data is fed in here and transmitted into electrical impulses that affect radio cells in the robot's heads or bodies. Is that it?"

"Yes," Karen said. "The blueprint of what you want has to be made with care, and takes time. After the blueprint is made it is fed into the machine, which does everything then, even to correcting small errors."

"Where are your father's records?" MacDonald said, his voice sharp. "We can't waste a minute."

Karen indicated a long desk at one side of the chamber and soon MacDonald was surrounded by charts, graphs and records. He studied them for several minutes, then shrugged helplessly.

Storm said, "Fabulously complicated, eh? It's as I feared."

"I can help," the girl said.

"Thank you," MacDonald said. He tapped a pencil thoughtfully on the desk. "It's complicated, of course, but not fabulously so. The principle, the basic idea is simple enough, and is used by every office on Earth today. It's a question of extension. But to extend it as far as this machine indicates your father did is rather staggering. The machine has a million choices at a million separate points in even the simplest diagram. To attempt to make something complicated—that is, to make the robots make something—well, that gets one into mathematics of an extraordinary nature."

"And we need something complicated," Storm said grimly.

"Exactly...battering rams, projectiles, something of that sort," he rubbed his forehead and then squared his shoulders stubbornly. "We'll give it a try—Karen and I. Won't we Karen?"

"Why, certainly," the girl said, actually breaking a slight smile. "And we'll do it, too."

She looked at Larry as the smile on her face grew, but he

avoided her eyes. "What's the matter?" she asked.

"Nothing," he muttered.

She put her hand on his arm. "I'm not angry with you. I think you used your best judgment. Don't brood about it now."

"That's not possible," he said.

Storm cleared his throat, "The captain and I will return to the compound, MacDonald. Carry on here, and we'll keep in touch."

"Right, sir."

Storm and Larry left the great vaulted room together, and the girl stood silent by MacDonald, staring after them, a curious expression on her face.

STORM watched the visi-screen in his office every hour of the day. Margo and the corporal made his meals, and twice in the next forty-eight hours Karen came down to report on their progress. She said that MacDonald was becoming more optimistic.

"Fine," Storm growled, and returned to the visi-screen.

The spreading space fleet of Galaxy X was still in position. He had noticed some motion among ships on the outer edge of the formation, and for several hours he was sure the attack on Earth was commencing.

During that time he paced to and fro before the huge visi-screen, his mood black. Margo brought him coffee and stayed with him. He was learning he could talk to her.

"You see," he said, jerking a thumb at the screen, "they're restless. That could be because the ship they sent here hasn't returned, and they're getting ready to come after it. Or maybe they're getting ready to make for Earth."

"Well, it won't help to growl around like a tiger. Sit down and have some coffee."

"I suppose you're right," he sat on the edge of his chair

and hammered a fist into his palm. "If MacDonald can just get a model ready in time. Karen said he seems optimistic."

"She's pretty cheerful herself," Margo said.

Storm shot a look at her. "What do you mean?"

"Naturally you wouldn't notice," Margo said dryly. "But she seems a bit taken with Larry."

"That's fine." Storm said. "She can have the satisfaction of loving a traitor who will die on our return to Earth."

"Storm...maybe you should reconsider that."

"That's all I want to hear about it," Storm said coldly. "You can leave now. I've got work to do."

LATER THAT day Storm snapped on the telescreen they had connected with MacDonald. The connection was made at the opposite end and the engineer's lean face appeared. He was smiling.

"Glad you got in touch with us, sir," he said. "We've got the model," he held up a slim metal tube—the size of a cigar—for Storm to see. In the background Karen, too, was smiling.

"It's very much like the V-2 rockets used after World War II, except of course it's made for space, and is about a hundred times as fast. I'm making a blueprint of this now to feed into the machine. Work should get under way here by tonight."

"Great, great," Storm said. He was grinning, he knew; but he couldn't help it. To have a weapon once more, to be able to strike! "I'll be in touch with you again a few hours from now."

"Right, sir."

Storm snapped the switch and MacDonald's face disappeared. He walked back and forth for several minutes, making plans, seeing already in his mind's eye the fight that would develop between their robot-built missiles, and the fleet from Galaxy X. The tactics, strategy, and deployments, of such an attack crowded everything else from his consideration.

For half an hour he was oblivious to everything else. Then, having done as much as he could to explore all contingencies, he put the matter from his mind and turned back to the visi-screen.

He saw instantly that all his plans were pointless—the fleet from Galaxy X was moving, slowly but inevitably, away from Jupiter.

They were reassembling, forming in a wedge-shaped cluster that had its spear-end aimed toward the Earth.

Storm stared at the screen for a full thirty seconds, then wheeled and—with a mighty oath—snapped on the contact with MacDonald.

"The attack is starting," he said, harshly, when MacDonald appeared. "They're forming to blast-off for Earth. What chance have we got?"

"I need hours yet," MacDonald said, his voice strained. "The blast-off pits are being made now, thousands of them. Gawd, it's immense, it's staggering, what we can do—*could* do in just a few more hours."

"How about the projectiles?"

"The blueprint is in the machine. Within a few hours the first will be ready. The directional apparatus—everything will be set."

Storm glanced at the visi-screen. The movement of the great Galaxy X fleet was proceeding at a smoother, faster rate.

"Do what you can, MacDonald. We won't quit, but we need a miracle now. They'll be out of range in half an hour."

"There's no chance then," MacDonald said, his voice dull and empty.

"Keep at it!" Storm said harshly. "By God I'll take

excuses, but not failure."

He walked to the visi-screen and stood glaring at the shadowy clusters of ships—ships he knew to be moving at incredible speed beyond his reach. He felt almost like smashing his fist into the screen to destroy a sight he hated to watch.

A knock on the door sounded, and he said, "Come in."

IT WAS Larry Masterson. The young captain stood at attention, his eyes level.

"Well?" Storm snapped.

Larry glanced at the visi-screen. He said, "They're leaving, aren't they, sir? They're leaving for Earth."

"What of it?" Storm said coldly.

Larry flushed. "I know what you think of me, sir. You have good reason to, of course. But Earth is my home, my country. You can't believe I love it, I know. But I do. I want to help now," he pointed suddenly to the visi-screen. "I want to stop them, sir."

"Yes?" Storm said. "A laudable ambition. How would you go about it?"

"Let me take the *Astro Star* after them," Larry said eagerly. "She's faster and bigger by far than their units. All they have is numbers. I could disrupt their formations, burn hundreds of them from the void before they—well, before it was over. Don't you see, sir, it's our only hope. Earth's only hope. I can delay them an hour, maybe two, and by then MacDonald may have the self-propelled missiles ready to shoot after them."

Storm stood stock-still a moment, then wheeled and snapped on telescreen. When MacDonald appeared Storm said, "You may get those extra hours you need, after all. Listen, I'm going after that fleet in the *Astro Star*. You're in command here. If you get your missiles up in time, and all goes well, you can return to Earth in one of the fighters."

"You're committing suicide, sir," MacDonald said.

"Possibly, but that's beside the point. You understand your orders? Get that fleet from Galaxy X, then return to Earth in one of the fighters. And, MacDonald—for God's sake—make them believe you when you get there. Stay at their throats until they build a Space Arm. That's all."

"Very well, sir," MacDonald said.

He suddenly straightened and raised his arm in a crisp salute.

"Goodbye, sir."

Storm returned the salute, then snapped off the switch.

When he turned he saw that Margo had entered and was standing by the door. Larry was staring at him with hot flushed eyes.

"You can't leave me out of it," he cried. "It was my idea. You can't deprive me of a chance to clear myself."

"You'll have your chance for that on Earth, after due process of court-martial," Storm said. "I wouldn't trust you to take the *Astro Star*. You'd probably bypass the alien fleet and scuttle for home."

"Take me with you. I'm a gunnery officer. A good one. I can help."

"No!" Storm cried, and the word fell like a bar of iron in the room. "I go alone."

MARGO clapped her hands together in applause, but her expression mocked him.

"Now you finally have what you want," she said. "You can die alone for Earth. You can prove conclusively that no one else really cared for Earth, that everyone else was stupid, cowardly and indifferent. They'll put up statues of you!"

Storm said, "I want none of those things. Why do you deliberately misunderstand me?"

"Because you're such a bitter, twisted, wonderful person," Margo cried out. She walked up and pounded a fist against his chest. "There was never a man like you, Storm. You're strong and fine and good in some ways, but a brooding freak in others. You see no viewpoint but your own. Here on this compound more than one hundred and fifty men died for Earth; here a man named Thatcher died for Earth; here Boyd and Carney died for Earth, and Karen and Larry suffered for Earth.

"Some of those people thought you a madman; but they gave you the credit for loving Earth, for wanting to do the right thing, even though it was opposed to what they wanted. But you can't do that in return. For you, there's only one way…Storm's way. Other ways are wrong, criminal, even traitorous. I said once you never loved anyone. I think I was wrong. You appear to love yourself with an all-consuming passion. There's no room for anyone else."

Storm turned from her and sat down slowly, heavily at his desk. He put a hand to his face, over his eyes.

"You are wrong," he whispered. "I believe I do love someone," he looked up at Margo then, and his eyes devoured the fine lines of her face, the flaring wings of black hair that swept back above her ears, the slim, vital, quick-moving strength of her body.

She met his gaze for a long, tense moment, and then a touch of color came to her cheeks and she turned away, tears coming to her eyes. "Then take us with you," she said, brokenly. "Let us love something and die for it, too. Don't be selfish, Storm. Give us that much."

For a moment the silence was thick and oppressive in the small room. Dust motes danced in the still air, and tiny shadowy ships moved on the visi-screen.

Storm put his head down and rubbed his eyes, then he got slowly to his feet. He spoke and his voice was strong and sure, but there was a reserved quality in it that hadn't been there before.

"All right," he said, "let's go."

CHAPTER NINE

AHEAD OF them the fleet from Galaxy X loomed and spread across the forward visi-screen of the *Astro Star II*.

Storm was at the controls, Margo beside him. Larry was in the waist of the ship, at the batteries of atomic cannons.

"It's incredible," Margo whispered. "There must be hundreds of thousands of them."

"They've seen us too," Storm said. He pointed. "See that formation at the rear. They're dropping back."

"How long now?"

"Minutes."

Margo's hand tightened on his arm. "I don't care. I know what you feel toward me. I was afraid I'd never know for sure."

Storm touched her hand. "It's not much, really," he said. "I mean, it's so damn little to have, actually. We've had time for nothing. We just know how we feel…that's all. You don't mind that too much?"

"No, not too much," Margo said.

Storm smiled a little and said, "That's all the talking we have time for. I'm throwing on the boosters now."

"Okay," she smiled. "You're a good pilot fighter?"

"Very good," he said. He was glad in a small way that he was, and that she was going to see him working. "Yes…in fact I'm damn good," he said, and flipped the booster switches and flung the ship in a mighty arching dive across the top of the rear echelon of the fleet from Galaxy X.

The *Astro Star* flashed through the void—a streaking, silver flash of speed, and from their waist a solid wall of flame suddenly lashed out and struck against the alien ships.

Storm made two more looping passes that brought Larry's batteries into position, and then they were streaking on toward the main body of the fleet. The rear echelons had joined the black nothingness of the void.

"Larry, much as I hate to give him credit, is damn good," Storm said to Margo. "But now the fun is over."

Ahead, the main section of the fleet had changed course swiftly and was deploying its units across the path of the *Astro Star II.*

Storm hurled his ship into combat with a cluster of ships in the dead center of the formation. Lights flashed out from the enemy ships and he felt the *Astro Star* lurch and shudder under their impact. He knew a fin was gone by the sudden slipping list he went into, but be corrected that by stepping up the blast from the rockets on that side.

From the sides of the *Astro Star* the atomic cannons flashed solid walls of light, and the ships from Galaxy X were burned out of existence—by the hundreds.

But their numbers were inexhaustible, and they flung themselves at the *Astro Star* in increasingly confident waves, as the mighty ship began to slow down and lose its maneuverability.

Like a crippled shark attacked by thousands of tiny parasites, the *Astro Star* was gradually weakened, crippled.

Storm swore as it failed to answer his hand. He flung it out in a screaming dive that should have brought him clear of danger, but only made his position worse.

THE FIGHT ranged across thousands of miles of space and in spite of the destruction brought by the powerful cannons of the *Astro Star*, the inevitable end came closer with each blazing, flame-filled moment.

Soon the *Astro Star* would lose its speed, its ability to

maneuver; and then the attacking ships could draw back and blast away until its mighty hull weakened, its sections collapsed, and it died in the void.

Storm caught Margo's hand.

The ship was sluggish now, almost as if it were bound by thick heavy atmosphere. It was becoming nothing more than a huge target.

Margo's fingers tightened convulsively on his hand.

"Look, Storm!" she cried.

Storm swung his eyes to the visa-screen, and a grin split his weary face, light danced in his eyes.

"Thank God!" he shouted.

Streaming across the screen toward the Galaxy X fleet were eight flashing columns of projectiles, slim, deadly, inevitable.

Tiny flames glowed from exhaust blasts at their rear as they arced through the void to close with their targets—to close inevitably, implacably, irresistibly.

Storm gave the *Astro Star* every last ounce of power, throwing on all the rockets and the auxiliary, and like a spirited horse answering the demand of its master, the ship lurched ahead and cleared the galaxy fleet in a mighty soaring arc. They were not a second too soon, for the area they left was transformed in a matter of seconds to a scene of violent destruction.

The slim missiles flashed into the heart of the Galaxy X fleet. Hundreds of them were burned down, but thousands more poured into the cataclysmic fight. Storm, watching, saw thousands more breaking away from the pull of Jupiter and flashing up to fulfil their mission.

Storm cut his auxiliary power and headed for their base.

Margo was laughing and crying and Storm knew how she felt as he put his arms about her and held her close.

CHAPTER TEN

STORM stood up as the door of his office opened and Larry came in. It was four hours later, and they knew by then that the threat to Earth was gone. The fleet from Galaxy X was debris.

"There's nothing much to say," Storm said. "Maybe we've both learned something out here, Captain. I know I have."

"You called me 'Captain'?" Larry asked.

"No, it wasn't a slip of the tongue, if that's what you mean," Storm said, a trace of a smile on his lips. "You're a captain of the Earth Federation...and a good one."

Larry grinned and put out his hand. "All I want, now or ever, is to stay in your command, sir."

"I appreciate the sentiment," Storm said dryly, "although I realize you don't mean it." He glanced through the window, saw Karen passing, and released Larry's hand. "There, for instance," he said, "is something you want, too."

Larry smiled, saluted, and left.

Storm stood in the doorway of his office, smoking a cigar, and studying the atmosphere of the planet. It was clear and clean. Soon they would leave here, cleaving through that atmosphere to the silent void that lay between the planets of his universe. A void that was now free.

He saw Margo coming from her hut at the end of the compound. She saw him and waved.

Smiling, he waited for her.

THE END

If you've enjoyed this book, you will not want to miss these terrific titles...

ARMCHAIR SCI-FI & HORROR DOUBLE NOVELS, $12.95 each

D-1 **THE GALAXY RAIDERS** by William P. McGivern
SPACE STATION #1 by Frank Belknap Long

D-2 **THE PROGRAMMED PEOPLE** by Jack Sharkey
SLAVES OF THE CRYSTAL BRAIN by William Carter Sawtelle

D-3 **YOU'RE ALL ALONE** by Fritz Leiber
THE LIQUID MAN by Bernard C. Gilford

D-4 **CITADEL OF THE STAR LORDS** by Edmond Hamilton
VOYAGE TO ETERNITY by Milton Lesser

D-5 **IRON MEN OF VENUS** by Don Wilcox
THE MAN WITH ABSOLUTE MOTION by Noel Loomis

D-6 **WHO SOWS THE WIND...** by Rog Phillips
THE PUZZLE PLANET by Robert A. W. Lowndes

D-7 **PLANET OF DREAD** by Murray Leinster
TWICE UPON A TIME by Charles L. Fontenay

D-8 **THE TERROR OUT OF SPACE** by Dwight V. Swain
QUEST OF THE GOLDEN APE by Ivar Jorgensen and Adam Chase

D-9 **SECRET OF MARRACOTT DEEP** by Henry Slesar
PAWN OF THE BLACK FLEET by Mark Clifton.

D-10 **BEYOND THE RINGS OF SATURN** by Robert Moore Williams
A MAN OBSESSED by Alan E. Nourse

ARMCHAIR SCIENCE FICTION CLASSICS, $12.95 each

C-1 **THE GREEN MAN**
by Harold M. Sherman

C-2 **A TRACE OF MEMORY**
By Keith Laumer

C-3 **INTO PLUTONIAN DEPTHS**
by Stanton A. Coblentz

ARMCHAIR MASTERS OF SCIENCE FICTION SERIES, $16.95 each

M-1 **MASTERS OF SCIENCE FICTION, Vol. One**
Bryce Walton—"Dark of the Moon" and other tales

M-2 **MASTERS OF SCIENCE FICTION, Vol. Two**
Jerome Bixby—"One Way Street" and other tales

INTRIGUE IN EARTH'S OUTER ORBIT

Tremendous and glittering, the Space Station floated up out of the Big Dark, truly a sight to behold. Lieutenant Corriston was one of many who had come to see its marvels, but he soon found himself entrapped in its unsuspected terror.

For the grim reality was that some deadly outer space power had usurped control of the great artificial moon. A lovely woman had disappeared; passengers were being fleeced and enslaved; and, using fantastic disguises, imposters were using the Station for their own mysterious purposes.

Pursued by an unearthly monster and hunted with super-scientific cunning, Corriston struggled to unmask the mystery. For upon his success depended his life, the woman he loved, and possibly the future of Earth itself.

CAST OF CHARACTERS

CORRISTON
He saw all the amazing sights of the Space Station…in fact, he saw too much!

HELEN RAMSEY
A beautiful woman, Corriston longed for her; but her notorious father made her a virtual prisoner.

HENLEY
One thing was dreadfully certain, with him for a friend one would never have need of an enemy.

HAYES
His decision could well mean the beginning of the end for an entire planet.

CLAKEY
He was a bodyguard by trade, but Clakey needed special protection himself.

CLEMENT
There was something unusual about him, as though—at times— he seemed to be leading a double life.

SPACE STATION #1

By
FRANK BELKNAP LONG

ARMCHAIR FICTION
PO Box 4369 Medford, Oregon 97501-0168

*For more information about Armchair Books and products, visit our
website at…*

www.armchairfiction.com

Or email us at…

armchairfiction@yahoo.com

CHAPTER ONE

IT WAS A LIFE-AND-DEATH struggle—cruel, remorseless, one-sided. Corriston was breathing heavily. He was in total darkness, dodging the blows of a killer. His adversary was as lithe as a cat, muscular and dangerous. He had a knife and he was using it, slashing at Corriston when Corriston came close, then leaping back and lashing out with a hard-knuckled fist.

Corriston could hear the swish of the man's heels as he pivoted, could judge almost with split-second timing when the next blow would come. He was bleeding from a cut on his right shoulder, and there was a tumultuous throbbing at his temples, an ache in his groin.

The fact that he had no weapon put him at a terrifying disadvantage. He had been close to death before, but never in so confined a space or in such close proximity to a man who had certainly killed once and would not hesitate to kill again.

His determination to survive was pitted against what appeared to be sheer brute strength fortified by cunning and a far-above-average agility. He began slowly to retreat, backing away until a massive steel girder stopped him. He was battling dizziness now and his heart had begun a furious pounding.

He found himself slipping sideways along the girder, running his hands over its smooth, cold surface. To his sweating palms the surface seemed as chill as the lid of a coffin, but he refused to believe that it could trap him irretrievably. The girder had to end somewhere.

The killer was coming close again, his shoes making a scraping sound in the darkness, his breathing just barely audible. Corriston edged still further along the girder. Inch by inch he moved parallel to it, fighting off his dizziness, making a desperate effort to keep from falling. The wetness on his shoulder was unnerving, the absence of pain incredible. How seriously could a man be stabbed without feeling any pain at all? He didn't know. But at least his shoulder wasn't paralyzed. He could move his arm freely, flex the muscles of his back.

How unbelievably cruel it was that a ship could move through space with the stability of a completely stationary object. How unbelievably cruel at this moment, when the slightest lurch might have saved him.

The girder was stationary and immense, and in his tormented inward vision he saw it as a strand in a gigantic steel cobweb, symbolizing the grandeur of what man could accomplish by routine compulsion alone.

In frozen helplessness Corriston tried to bring his thoughts into closer accord with reality, to view his peril in a saner light. But what was happening to him was as hard to relate to immediate reality as a line half remembered from a play. *See how the blood of Caesar followed it, as if rushing out of doors to be resolved if Brutus so unkindly knocked or no...*

But the killer wasn't Brutus. He was unknown and invisible and if there had been any Brutus-like nobility in him, it hardly seemed likely that he would have chosen for his first victim a wealthy girl's too talkative bodyguard and for his second Corriston himself.

The killer was within arm's reach again when the barrier that had trapped Corriston fell away abruptly. He reeled back, swayed dizzily, and experienced such wild elation that he cried out in unreasoning triumph. Swiftly he retreated backwards, not fully realizing that no real respite had been granted him. He was free only to recoil a few steps, to crouch and weave about. Almost instantly the killer was closing in again, and this time there was no escape. Another metal girder stopped Corriston in mid-retreat, cutting across his shoulders like a sharp-angled priming rod, jolting and sobering him.

For an eternity now he could do nothing but wait. An eternity as brief as a dropped heartbeat and as long as the cycle of renewal and rebirth of worlds in the flaming vastness of space. Everything became impersonal suddenly: the darkness of the ships between-deck storage compartment; the Space Station toward which the ship was traveling; the Martian deserts he had dreamed about as a boy.

The killer spoke then, for the first time. His voice rang out in the darkness, harsh with contempt and rage. It was in some respects a surprising voice, the voice of an educated man. But it was also a voice that had in it an accent that Corriston had heard before in verbal documentaries and hundreds of newsreels; in clinical case histories, microfilm recorded, in penal institutions, on governing bodies, and wherever men were in a position to destroy others—or perhaps themselves. It was the voice of an unloved, unwanted man.

The voice said: "You're done for, my friend. I don't know what the Ramsey girl told you, but you came looking for me, and it's too late now for any kind of compromise."

"I wasn't looking for a deal," Corriston said. "If it's any satisfaction to you, Miss Ramsey told me nothing. But I saw a man killed; and I couldn't find her afterwards. I think you know what happened to her. Knife me, if you can. I'll go down fighting."

"That's easy to say. Maybe you didn't come looking for me. But you know too much now to go on living. Unless you—wait a minute! You mentioned a deal. If you're lying about the Ramsey girl and will tell me where she is, I might not kill you."

"I wasn't lying," Corriston said.

"Hell…you're really asking for it."

"I'm afraid I am."

"It won't be a pleasant way to die."

"Any way is unpleasant. But I'm not dead yet. Killing me may not be as easy as you think."

"It will be easy enough. This time you won't get past me."

Corriston knew that the conversation was about to end unless something unexpected happened. And he didn't think there was much chance of that. Had he been clasping a metal tool, he would have swung hard enough to kill with it. But he wasn't clasping anything. He was crouching low, and suddenly he leapt straight forward into the darkness.

His head collided with a bony knee and his hands went swiftly out and around invisible ankles. He tightened his grip, half expecting the knife to descend and bury itself in his back. But it didn't. The other had been taken so completely by surprise that he simply went backwards, suddenly, and with a strangled oath.

Instantly Corriston was on top of him. He shifted his grip,

releasing both of the struggling man's ankles and remorselessly seizing his wrists. He raised his right knee and brought it savagely downward, again and again and again. A cry of pain echoed through the darkness. The killer, crying out in torment, tried to twist free.

For an instant the outcome remained uncertain, a seesaw contest of strength. Then Corriston had the knife and the struggle was over.

Corriston made a mistake then of relaxing a little. Instantly, the killer rolled sideways, broke Corriston's grip, and was on his feet. He did not attempt to retaliate in any way. He simply disappeared into the darkness, breathing so loudly that Corriston could tell when the distance between them had dwindled to the vanishing point.

Corriston sat very still in the darkness, holding on tightly to the knife. His triumph had been unexpected and complete. It had been close to miraculous. Strange that he should be aware of that and yet feel only a dark horror growing in his mind. Strange that he should remember so quickly again the horror of a man gasping out his life with a thorned barb protruding from his side.

It had begun a half-hour earlier in the general passenger cabin. It had begun with a wonder and a rejoicing.

Tremendous and glittering, the Space Station had come floating up out of the Big Dark like a golden bubble on an onrushing tidal wave. It had hovered for an instant in the precise center of the viewscreen, its steep, climbing trail shedding radiance in all directions. Then it had descended vertically until it almost filled the lower half of the screen, and finally was lost to view in a wilderness of space.

When it appeared for the second time, it was larger still and its shadow was a swiftly widening crescent blotting out the nearer stars.

"There it is!" someone whispered.

It had been unreasonably quiet in the general passenger cabin, and for a moment no other sound was audible. Then the whisper was caught up and amplified by a dozen awestruck voices. It became a murmur of amazement and of wonder, and as it increased in volume, the screen seemed to glow with an almost unbelievable brightness.

Everyone was aware of the brightness. But how much of it was subjective no one knew or cared. To a man in the larger darkness of space, a dead sea bottom on Mars, or a moon-landing ship wrapped in eternal darkness on a lonely peak in the Lunar Apennines may glow with a noonday splendor.

"They said a space station that size could never be built," David Corriston said, leaning abruptly forward in his chair. "They quoted reams of statistics: height above the center of the Earth in kilometers, orbital velocity, relation of mass to maneuverability. The experts had a field day. They went far out on a limb to convince anyone who would listen that a station weighing thousands of tons would never get past the blueprint stage. But the men who built it had enough pride and confidence in human skill to achieve the impossible."

The girl at Corriston's side looked startled for an instant, as though the ironclad assurance of so young a man was as much of a surprise as his unexpected nearness, and somehow even more disquieting older.

She was certainly somewhat older than he was—about three or four years. She was an exceptionally pretty girl, her fair hair fluffed out from under a blue beret, her ship's lounge jacket a youth—accentuating miracle of casual tailoring that would have looked well on a woman of any age. She had the kind of eyes Corriston liked best of all in a woman: longlashed, observant, and bright with glints of humor.

She had the kind of mouth he liked too—a mouth which suggested that she could be, by turns, capricious, levelheaded, and audaciously friendly with strangers without in any way inviting familiarity. There was a certain paradoxical timidity in her gaze too. It was manifesting itself now in an obvious reluctance to be startled too abruptly by space engineering talk from a young man who had taken her companionability for granted and who was obviously given to snap judgments.

She brushed back the hair on her right temple, her brown eyes upraised to study Corriston more closely.

He hoped that she would realize upon reflection that she was behaving foolishly. He had taken a certain liberty in talking to her as he would have talked to an old acquaintance in a long-awaited meeting of minds. On the big screen a space station that couldn't be built was sweeping in toward the ship with eighty-five years of unparalleled scientific progress behind it.

First had come the Earth satellites, eight of them in their neat little orbits. They had used low-energy fuels, had kept close to the Earth, and no one had seriously expected them to do more than record weather information and relay radio signals. For fifteen years they could be seen with small telescopes and even with the unaided eye on bright, cloudless nights in both hemispheres.

First had come these small, relatively unimportant artificial moons and then, on a night in October 1972, the first space platform had been launched. Soon the sky above the Earth was swarming with radar warning platforms, a dozen men to operate them, and carrier-based jets equipped with formidable atomic warheads.

Nevertheless, how could anyone have known that in another twenty years interplanetary space flight would become a war-averting reality? How could anyone have known that by the year 2007 there would be human settlements on Mars and by the year 2022 the actual transportation to Mars of city-building materials?

CHAPTER TWO

CORRISTON WAS beginning to feel uncomfortable. He wished that the girl would say something instead of just continuing to stare at him. She seemed to be interested in his uniform. She appeared to be gazing at him interrogatively, as if she wanted to know more about him before promising anything.

He wondered what her unconscious purpose was. Did she see in him the quiet, determined type who was all set to accomplish something important. Or was she regretting he wasn't the hard-living, cynical type who had been everywhere and done everything?

Well, one way to find out was to be himself: a man average in every way, but with a hard core of idealism in his nature, a creative mind and enough independence and self-assurance to give a good account of himself in any struggle which brought his central beliefs under fire or placed them in long-range jeopardy.

And so Corriston suddenly found himself talking about the Station again.

"Not many people have grasped the importance of it yet," he said. "One station will service our needs, instead of fifty-seven, one tremendous central terminal and refueling depot for all of the ships. Do you realize what that could mean?"

Abruptly there was a startling warmth in the girl's eyes, an unmistakable look of interest and encouragement.

"Just what could it mean?" she asked.

"Any kind of steady growth across the years leads to centralization, to bigness. And that bigness becomes time-hallowed and magnified out of all proportion to its original significance. The Space Station is no exception. It started with the primitive Earth satellites and branched out into fifty-seven larger stations. Now it's tremendous, a single central station that can impose its influence in ship clearance matters with an almost unanswerable finality."

A shadow had come into the girl's eyes. "But not completely

81

without checks and balances. The Earth Federation can challenge its supremacy at any point."

"Yes, and I'm glad that the challenge remains a factor to be reckoned with. As matters stand now the Station's prestige can't be implemented with what might well become the iron hand of an intolerable tyranny. As matters stand, the Station is actually a big step forward. People once talked of centralization as it were some kind of indecent human bogey. It isn't at all. It's simply a fluid means to an end, a necessary commitment if a society is to achieve greatness. If the authority behind the Station respects scientific truth and human dignity—if it remains empirically minded—I shall serve it to the best of my ability. No one knows for sure whether what is good outbalances what is bad in any human institution, or any human being. A man can only give the best of himself to what he believes in."

"Sorry to interrupt," an amused voice said, "but the captain wants you to join him in a last-minute celebration: a toast, a press photograph—that sort of nonsense. A six-hour trip, and he hasn't even been introduced to you. But if you don't appear at his table in ten minutes he'll throw the book at me."

Corriston looked up in surprise at the big man confronting them. He had approached so unobtrusively that for an instant Corriston was angry; but only for an instant. When he took careful stock of the fellow his resentment evaporated. There was a cordiality about him that could not have been counterfeited. It reached from the breadth of his smile to his gray eyes puckered in amusement. He was really big physically, in a wholly genial and relaxed way, and his voice was that of a man who could walk up to a bar, pay a bill and leave an everlasting impression of hearty good nature behind him.

"Well, young lady?" he asked.

"I'm not particularly keen about the idea, Jim, but if the captain has actually iced the champagne, it would be a shame to disappoint him."

Corriston was aware that his companion was getting to her feet. The interruption had been unexpected, but much to his surprise he found himself accepting it without rancor. If he lost her for a few moments he could quickly enough find her again; and somehow he felt convinced that the big man was not a torch-carrying admirer.

"I'll have to stop off in the ladies' lounge first," she said.

She had opened her vanity case and was making a swift inventory of its contents. "Two shades of lipstick, but no powder! Oh, well."

She smiled at the big man and then at Corriston, gesturing slightly as she did so.

"We've just been discussing the Station," she said. "This gentleman hasn't told me his name—"

"Lieutenant David Corriston," Corriston said quickly. "My interest in the Station is tied in with my job. I've just been assigned to it in the very modest capacity of ship's inspection officer, recruit status."

The big man stared at Corriston more intently, his eyes kindling with a sudden increase of interest. "Say, I wonder if you could spare me a few minutes. When my friends ask me I'd like to be able to talk intelligently about the terrific headaches the research people must have experienced right from the start. The expenditure of fuel alone…"

"See you in the Captain's cabin, Jim," the girl said.

She moved out from her chair, her expression slightly constrained. Was it just imagination, or had the big man's immoderate expansiveness grated on her and brought a look of displeasure to her young face? Corriston couldn't be sure, and his brow remained furrowed as he watched her cross the passenger cabin and disappear into the ladies' lounge.

"I'm Jim Clakey," the big man said.

Corriston reseated himself, a troubled indecision still apparent in his stare. Then gradually he found himself relaxing. He nodded up at the big man. "Sit down, Mr. Clakey," he said. "Ask me anything you want. Security imposes some pretty rigid restrictions, but I'll let you know when you start treading on classified ground."

Clakey sat down and crossed his long legs. He was silent for a moment. Then he said: "You know who she is, of course."

Corriston shook his head. "I'm afraid I haven't the slightest idea."

"She isn't traveling under her real name only because her father is a very sensible and cautious man. You'd be cautious too, perhaps, if you were Stephen Ramsey."

Clakey's gaze had traveled to the ladies' lounge, and for an instant he seemed unaware of Corriston's incredulous stare.

"You mean I've actually been sitting here talking to Stephen Ramsey's daughter?"

"That's right," Clakey said, turning to grin amiably at Corriston. "And now you're talking to her personal bodyguard. I'm not surprised you didn't recognize her, though; very few people do. She doesn't like to have her picture taken. Her dad wouldn't object to that kind of publicity particularly, but she's even more cautious than he is."

The door of the ladies' lounge opened and two young women came out. They were laughing and talking with great animation and were quickly lost to view as other passengers changed their position in front of the viewscreen.

The door remained visible, however—a rectangle of shining whiteness only slightly encroached upon by dark blue drapes. Corriston found himself staring at it as his mind dwelt on the startling implications of Clakey's almost unbelievable statement.

"Biggest man on Mars," Clakey was saying. "Cornered uranium; froze out the original settlers. They're threatening violence, but their hands are tied. Everything was done legally. Ramsey lives in a garrisoned fortress and they can't get within twenty miles of him. He's a damned scoundrel with tremendous vision and foresight."

Corriston suddenly realized that he had made a serious psychological blunder in sizing up Clakey. The man was a blabbermouth. True, Corriston's uniform was a character recommendation that might have justified candor to a moderate extent. But Clakey was talking outrageously out of turn. He was becoming confidential about matters he had no right to discuss with anyone on such short acquaintance. Corriston suddenly realized that Clakey was slightly drunk.

"Look here," Corriston said. "You're talking like a fool. Do you know what you're saying?"

"Sure I know. Miss Ramsey is a golden girl. And I'm her bodyguard...important trust...sop to a man's egoism."

An astonishing thing happened then. Clakey fell silent and

remained uncommunicative for five full minutes. Corriston had no desire to start him talking again. He was appalled and incredulous. He was debating the advisability of getting up with a frozen stare and a firm determination to take himself elsewhere when the crazy, loose-tongued fool leapt unexpectedly to his feet.

"She's taking too long!" he exclaimed. "It just isn't like her. She'd never keep the captain waiting."

As he spoke, another woman came out of the ladies' lounge. She was small, dark, very pretty, and she seemed a little embarrassed when she saw how intently Clakey was staring at her. Then a middle-aged woman came out, with a finely-modeled face, and a second, younger woman with haggard eyes and a sallow complexion who was in all respects the opposite of attractive.

"She's been in there for fifteen minutes," Clakey said, starting toward the lounge.

"It takes a good many women twice that long to apply makeup properly," Corriston pointed out. "I just don't see—"

"You don't know her," Clakey said, impatiently. "I may have to ask one of those women to go in after her."

"But why? You can't seriously believe she's in any danger. We both saw her go into the lounge. She made the decision on the spur of the moment and no one could have known about it in advance. No one followed her in. You were sitting right here watching the door."

But Clakey was already advancing across the cabin. He was reeling a little, and a dull flush had mounted to his cheekbones. He seemed genuinely alarmed. Corriston was about to follow him when something bright flashed through the air with a faint swishing sound.

A startled cry burst from Clakey's lips. He clutched at his side, staggered, and half-swung about, a look of incredulous horror in his eyes.

Corriston's mouth went dry. He stood very still, watching Clakey lose all control over his legs. The change in the stricken man's expression was ghastly. His cheeks had gone dead white, and now, as Corriston stared, a spasm convulsed his features, twisting them into a horrible, unnatural caricature of a human face—a rigidly contorted mask with a blanched, wide-angled mouth and bulging eyes.

A passenger saw him and screamed. His knees had given way and his huge frame seemed to be coming apart at the joints. He straightened out on the deck, jerking his head spasmodically, propelling himself backwards by his elbows. Almost as if with conscious intent, his body arched itself, sank level with the floor, then arched itself again.

It was as though all of his muscles and nerves were protesting the violence that had been done to him, and were seeking by muscular contractions alone to dislodge the stiff, thorned horror protruding from his flesh.

He went limp and the barbed shaft ceased to quiver. Corriston had a nerve-shattering glimpse of a swiftly spreading redness just above Clakey's right hipbone. The entire barb turned red, as if its feathery spines had acquired a sudden, unnatural affinity for human blood.

Corriston started forward, then changed his mind. Several passengers had moved quickly to Clakey's side and were bending above him. Someone called out: "Get a doctor!"

Corriston turned abruptly and strode toward the ladies' lounge. Brushing aside such scruples as he ordinarily would have entertained, he threw open the door and went inside.

He called out: "Miss Ramsey?" When he received no answer he searched the lounge thoroughly. There was no one there. He was thinking fast now, desperately fast. He hadn't seen her come out and neither had Clakey. He'd seen four women come out: three young women and an elderly one. None of them faintly resembled the girl he'd been talking to.

The first young woman had emerged almost immediately. He remembered how intently Clakey had been watching the door. Clakey had sat down to discuss the Station with him, and in less than two minutes the first young lady had emerged. Then neither of them had taken their eyes from the door for five or six minutes. The second young lady had apparently known someone in the crowd. She had seemed annoyed by Clakey's persistent stare and had disappeared quickly. The elderly woman had looked her age. Her walk, her carriage, the lines of her face had borne the unmistakable stamp of genteel aging, and the dignity inseparable from it. The last woman had been the drab creature.

Corriston had a poor memory for faces and he knew that he couldn't count on recognizing any of them—except perhaps the elderly woman—if he saw them again.

It was good that he could smile, even at his own inanities. It relieved tension. Almost instantly the smile vanished. His aspect became that of a man in deadly danger on the brink of a hundred-foot precipice, a man completely in the dark and yet grimly determined not to go over the edge or take a single step in the wrong direction.

Where, he asked himself, do women ordinarily go when they vanish into thin air? Wasn't it pretty well established that ghosts were likely to follow the path of least resistance and fulfill obligations entered into in the flesh?

The captain's cabin! The captain would be disappointed if she failed to appear at least briefly at his table; and she had promised to do so. It was a wild, premeditated assault on the rational, but putting the irrational aspect of it aside, it was also realistic and reasonable. If by some incredible miracle she had eluded Clakey's vigilance and actually slipped from the lounge, she would almost certainly have gone straight to the captain's cabin.

CHAPTER THREE

CORRISTON LEFT the ladies' lounge faster than he had entered it. He shut the door firmly and stood for an instant staring at the passengers who had gathered in an even tighter knot around Clakey and were making it difficult for an alarmed young ship's doctor to get to him. He was quite sure in his own mind that Clakey would not need the assistance of a doctor.

Then he turned and headed for the captain's cabin. Anyone could have gotten in. The door was ajar and there was no one guarding it. He threw the door wide and everything was just as he'd expected to find it: It was completely empty.

No guests at all to welcome Corriston to the big, empty cabin. Then he saw that there was another door opposite.

Corriston was getting scared, really scared. There was an odd, detached, whimsical feeling at the surface of his mind, but it cloaked something distinctly sinister. He had more than half-expected the captain to be absent from his cabin. But something about the silence and the emptiness chilled him to the core of his being.

With an effort he shook the feeling off. He didn't know where the inner door led. He hesitated for an instant, realizing that the mere existence of a second door could complicate his search to the point of futility. If it led to a second cabin—well and good. But if it didn't...

He strained his ears to catch the sound of voices. There were no voices. He could have simply crossed to the door and looked beyond it. But the state of his nerves, and an odd habit he had of being precise and cautious under tension, made him explore the other possibilities first.

The door might conceivably be a trap. A trap does not have to be contrived in advance with some clearly defined purpose in mind. Circumstances can take a door or a window and turn it into a trap. A glove or a weapon left lying about can be picked up by an innocent man and snare him most damnably by seeming to point up his guilt.

What purpose did the inner door serve? Did it open on a corridor leading back to the general passenger cabin? If it did, it wouldn't be a trap; it would simply have "blind alley" stamped all over it.

Corriston suddenly realized that he was succumbing to a crazy kind of inaction. The door could lead almost anywhere, and if he had any sense at all he'd go through it fast.

Go through it he did, in six long strides. He'd been right about one thing—the blind alley part. He found himself, in not quite total darkness, in what was unquestionably an intership passageway. There was just light enough for him to make out the shadowy walls on both sides of him. Rather they were like metal bulkheads that gave off just enough reflected light for him to see by.

He wouldn't have considered ten or twelve seconds spent with a pocket flash a waste of time. But he had no pocket flash. The best he could do was stretch out both of his arms to determine just how far apart the bulkheads were. They were less than six feet apart.

Well, no sense in measuring the walls. A girl he'd talked to and liked instantly had vanished in a dark world, and he knew now that there was more than mere liking in the way he felt about her. He didn't dare ask himself how much more, not in so confined a space and with his chances of finding her again dwindling with every second that passed.

The passageway ended in a blank wall, less than forty feet from its beginning. Corriston saw the wall and was advancing toward it when he suddenly realized that the deck itself wasn't continuous. In his path, and almost directly underfoot, a companionway entrance yawned, so unexpectedly close that another short step would have sent him plunging into it. He saw the faint light reflected on its circumference and halted just in time to avoid a possibly fatal fall.

He knelt and stared down into a spiraling web of darkness. He could see a faint glimmer of light on metal and knew that he was bending above either a circular staircase or a companionway ladder. It turned out to be a staircase. Down it he went, moving cautiously, holding on to the supporting guide rail as he descended deeper and deeper into the darkness.

The darkness became almost absolute when the stairs ended. For a moment, at least, what appeared to be utter blackness engulfed him. Then gradually his vision became more effective. He could make out the faint outlines of stationary objects, of depths beyond depths, of crisscrossing lines and angles.

In utter darkness the glint of metal often seemed to draw the eyes like a magnet, to make itself known even without illumination. But there seemed to be a faint glow far off somewhere. He couldn't be sure, but light there should have been if—as he more than half-suspected—he was in one of the ship's below-deck ballast or storage compartments.

The deck beneath his feet was straight and level and cluttered with no impediments. He moved forward warily, testing every step until a wall of metal stopped him. He halted abruptly, felt along the barrier and became aware that it was studded with small bolts and was just a little corrugated. Exhibit A: one supporting metal beam, rough and slightly uneven in texture. Abruptly he reached the end of it and found himself underway again, still moving cautiously to avoid unseen pitfalls. He had not progressed more than a dozen feet when he heard the scrape of footsteps other than his own, and someone moved up close to him and blocked his way in the darkness.

For an instant the wild thought went through his mind that the someone was the captain. But he had seen and talked with the Captain and that self-contained, blunt-spoken man wasn't nearly as big physically as the path-blocker seemed to be.

The someone did not speak. But Corriston could sense the enmity flowing from him, the utter refusal to budge an inch, the determination to make his nearness a deadly threat in itself. Then the someone moved back a step. The far-off light could hardly have been an illusion, because for the barest instant Corriston could dimly make out the huge bulk of the man and the glint of the knife in his hand.

Two big men in the space of half an hour! The first had ceased to draw breath and the second was his killer. Corriston was suddenly sure of it. He knew it instinctively.

Then began the struggle that had almost robbed Corriston of his life, the cruel, one-sided, impossible-to-win struggle in total darkness.

And Corriston had won it.

Now almost in disbelief, Corriston looked down at the knife he had taken from the loser, telling himself that it was impossible that so much could have happened in so short a time and that he could still be alive at the end of it.

The wound in his shoulder was no longer painless, but it had ceased to bleed profusely, and his exploring fingers convinced him that the knife had severed no more than a superficial ligament. He strained his ears in the sudden quiet, listening for a possible return of his adversary. He did not think that the defeated man would attempt a second attack. But there was no telling what he might or might not do. Probably he'd ascended the companionway by now and was mingling with the other passengers.

The final link in Corriston's search had snapped. Even while battling for his life, he had felt close to the vanished girl. The man who had killed Clakey had been at least a link, a link that, short of Corriston's total defeat, might have been seized upon with physical violence and made to yield up its secret.

Now Corriston found himself wondering if the defeated man had been telling the truth. Had the link been nonexistent from the first? Was the killer as completely in the dark as he was as to the whereabouts of Ramsey's daughter?

It was difficult to believe that the man had been lying. Despite his hatred and denials he had offered Corriston a deal: "Tell me where the girl is and I may not kill you." The deal part had been a lie, of course. He would have gone on and attempted to kill Corriston anyway. But his plea for information, that tentative, cunning feeler in the dark had seemed genuine.

What had been the man's purpose in killing Clakey? Why had Clakey been murdered in the general passenger cabin, in plain view of the other passengers? Because the killer had seen the girl go into the lounge and thought she was still there? And because he wanted free and instant access to her, with Clakey out of the way? It was the only answer that made sense.

The killer must have known that Clakey was in Ramsey's employ and had been guarding Ramsey's daughter. Why then had he been unable to take advantage of his crime in any way? Apparently neither he nor a possible confederate had succeeded in what almost certainly had been a pattern of violence directed at Ramsey through his daughter—a plan obviously worked out in advance, ready to be put into operation the instant a promising opportunity presented itself.

Into Corriston's mind flashed an ugly picture of the girl pinioned by strong arms and with a handkerchief pressed to her face. She had ceased to struggle and was being spirited quickly away. The picture became even more intolerable when he saw her held captive in a cabin difficult to locate, at the mercy of men without compassion.

But for some reason he'd never cease to be thankful for, it hadn't happened that way. Something had gone wrong with the plan, and the killer didn't even know when and why and how she had vanished. Sharing Corriston's frustration, he had been struggling simply to save himself, to keep Corriston from identifying and exposing him. The fury he'd displayed was not difficult to understand.

Corriston found himself becoming more confident again, less dominated by despair. The change in his mood surprised him but he seized upon it gratefully and started building on it. There was only one logical next move. He must find the captain quickly and enlist his help. He must take the master of the ship fully into his confidence. With every gift of persuasion at his command, he must make the captain see how the danger of Ramsey's daughter was mounting and would continue to mount with every minute that she remained unfound.

He still felt dizzy, and his head was aching a little, but he moved quickly through the darkness, his faculties heightened by an intensity of purpose which enabled him to find the companionway without colliding with obstacles or taking a wrong turn. Up the stairway he climbed, still clutching the knife, prepared for a possible second encounter with its original owner.

An attempt to regain the knife by trickery and stealth would not have surprised him. In fact, it was not at all difficult for him to picture a silent form flattened against the stair-rail, waiting for just the right moment to come hurtling toward him out of the darkness. For a moment, as he ascended, the strain became almost unendurable. Then the darkness dissolved above him, and he was advancing toward the captain's cabin through the narrow passageway that he had spanned with his arms spread wide.

He did not stop to span it this time. He emerged into the cabin and stood for an instant blinking in the sudden light. The cabin was still deserted. It was anybody's guess where the captain had gone or when he would be returning, and Corriston decided not to wait. He walked to the door, opened it and stepped out into the general passenger cabin.

No one saw him immediately. There were several passengers fairly close to him, but they were being attentive for the moment to the words and gestures of a tall, dignified looking man with observant brown eyes, a ruddy complexion, and gold braid on his shoulders. The tall man was Captain John Sanders.

"I'd be a hypocrite and a liar if I said there was no justification for alarm," Sanders was saying, in a voice loud enough to carry to where Corriston was standing. "Strict regulations prescribe that sort of thing. But it's no way for a captain to keep the respect of his passengers."

Corriston felt himself stepping forward before he even thought about it. But he halted abruptly when the captain said: "There's a murderer on the loose aboard this ship. You may as well accept that fact right now. Each of you has to be on his guard. It's only right and proper that you should keep your eyes and ears open, and stay worried. If you do, our chances of catching up with him before the ship berths should be reasonably good."

The captain paused, then went on quickly: "We'll get him eventually. You can be sure of that. He'll never get past the inspection each of you will have to undergo when we reach the Station. But if we catch him before we reach the Station, you'll be spared an investigative ordeal distinctly on the rugged side."

Corriston was suddenly aware that he was being stared at. Everyone was staring at him.

"My God!" the Captain cried out, staring the hardest of all. "Where did you get that wound? Who attacked you? And what were you doing in my cabin?"

Corriston walked up to the Captain and said in a voice that trembled a little. "May I talk to you privately, sir? What I have to say won't take long."

"Why not?" Sanders demanded. "That uniform you're wearing makes it mandatory. All right, come back into my cabin."

They went back into the cabin. The captain shut the door and turned to face Corriston with a shocked concern in his stare.

"You've had it rough, Lieutenant. I can see that."

"Plenty rough," Corriston conceded. "But it's not myself I'm worried about."

"Did you know that a man has just been murdered?"

"I know," Corriston said.

"With a poisoned barb. A Martian barb. It's a plant found only on Mars. We have him stretched out on a table in the sick bay now. But he isn't sick; he's a corpse. Tell me something, Lieutenant, did you just tangle with the man who did it?"

"I think so," Corriston said. "In fact, I'd stake my commission on it."

"I see. Well, you'd better tell me about it. Tell me everything."

Corriston told him.

The captain was silent for a long moment. Then he said, "But we've no Miss Ramsey on the passenger list. And I certainly didn't invite her to drink a toast with me in my cabin. Are you sure of your facts, Lieutenant?"

Corriston's jaw fell open. He stared at the captain in stunned disbelief "Of course I'm sure. Why should I lie to you?"

"How should I know? It's unfair to ask me that. If Ramsey's daughter was on this ship, you can rest assured I'd have known about it. After all, Lieutenant—"

"But she was on board and you didn't know. Isn't that obvious? Look, she was traveling incognito. The trip to the Station takes only five hours. Perhaps in so short a trip—"

"No 'perhaps' about it. I'd have known."

"But she is on board, I tell you. I talked to her. I talked to Clakey. Don't make me go over the whole thing again. We've got to find her. Ramsey's enemies would stop at nothing. I'm afraid to think of what they might do to his daughter!"

"Nothing will happen to his daughter. She's on Earth right this minute in her father's house, as safe as any girl that wealthy can ever be. Lieutenant, listen to me. I've got a great deal of respect for that uniform you're wearing. Don't make me lose it. When you come to me with a story like that—"

"All right. You don't believe me. Will you check the passenger list, just to be sure?"

"I'll do more than that, Lieutenant. I'll assemble all of the passengers and check them off personally. I'll give you an opportunity to look them over while I'm doing it. Later you can ask them as many questions as you wish. There'll be a murderer among them, but that shouldn't disturb you too much. You've already met. Perhaps you can identify him for us. Ask each of the men who made a non-existent Miss Ramsey disappear and the one who turns pale will be our man."

Suddenly the captain reddened. "I'm sorry, Lieutenant, I didn't mean to be sarcastic. But a murder on my ship naturally upsets me. I'll be completely frank with you. There's a very remote possibility that Miss Ramsey actually is on board without my knowledge. She hasn't had much publicity. I believe I've only seen one photograph of her, one taken several years ago. But you've got to remember that a captain is usually the first to get wind of such things. It comes to him by a kind of grapevine. She's a golden girl—actually the goldenest golden girl on Earth."

CHAPTER FOUR

NOW CORRISTON was in a steel-walled cell and the captain's voice seemed only a far-off echo sympathizing with him.

And it was an echo, for the captain was gone and he would probably never see him again. It was all very simple—that part of it—all very clear. The captain had faithfully kept his word. The captain hadn't let him down. But any man can end up a prisoner when everyone disbelieves him and he has no way of proving that he is telling the truth.

It was hard to believe that a day and a night had passed, and that the Captain *had* kept his word and gone ahead with the roll call. It was even harder to believe that he, Corriston, was no longer on the ship, but in a sanity cell on the Space Station, and that the ship was traveling back toward Earth.

He shut his eyes, and the events of the past thirty hours unrolled before him with a nightmare clarity, and yet with all of the monstrous distortions which a nightmare must of necessity evoke.

Darkness and time and space. And closer at hand the frowns of forthright, honest men appalled by mental abnormality in a new recruit, an officer with a steel-lock determination to keep the truth securely guarded and safe from all distortion.

There had come the tap on his shoulder and a stern voice saying: "You'd better come with us, Lieutenant." He had just told the captain the whole horrible story. He had not been believed.

"Tell me about it," said the recruit in the bunk opposite Corriston. "It will help you to talk. Remember, we're not prisoners. We mustn't think of ourselves as prisoners. We can go out and exercise. We can walk around the Station for a half-hour or so. We've only got to promise we'll come back and lock ourselves in. They trust us. It could happen to anyone.

"Space shock. Not a fancy word at all. I'm getting over it; you've a certain distance to go. Or so they say. But we're still in very much the same boat and talking always helps. Talk to me,

Lieutenant, the way you did last night."

Corriston looked at the pale youth opposite him. He had close-cropped hair and friendly blue eyes, and he seemed a likeable enough kid. He was Corriston's junior by several years. But there was an aura of neuroticism about him that made Corriston uneasy. But hell, why shouldn't he get it off his chest. Talking just might help.

"It's true," Corriston said. "Every word of it."

"I believe you, Lieutenant. But quite obviously *they* didn't. Why not strike a compromise? Say I'm one-tenth wrong in believing you and they're nine-tenths right in not believing you. That means there may be some little quirk in what happened to you that doesn't quite fit into the normal pattern. Put that down to space shock—a mild case of it. I'm not saying you have it, but you could have it."

The kid was grinning now, and Corriston had to like him. "Okay," he said. "You can believe this or not. The captain lined all of the passengers up and checked them off by their cabin numbers. I didn't see her. Do you understand? She just wasn't there! I thought I recognized two of the women who had come out of the ladies' lounge, but I couldn't even be sure of that. One of the two denied ever having stepped inside the lounge, and the other was vague about it."

"I see."

"The captain really sailed into me for a moment, lost his temper completely. A fine officer you are, Lieutenant. It's painful to be on the same ship with the kind of officers the training schools turn out when the Station finds itself short of personnel. Is the Station planning to trust ships' clearance to hallucinated personnel?

"All right, you talked to a girl—some girl. She didn't even tell you she was Ramsey's daughter; Clakey told you. And he's dead. Not only is he dead, he wasn't listed on the passenger list as Clakey at all. His name was Henry Ewers. I don't know what you believed, Lieutenant. I don't care what you think you saw. You tangled with someone and he stabbed you. He was real enough . . . obviously the man who killed Ewers. But you let him get away, so even that isn't too much to your credit."

"If I had been you," the kid said, "I've had knocked him down."

"No." For the first time Corriston smiled. "To tell you the truth, the captain is a good guy. He's one of those blunt, moody, terribly human individuals you encounter occasionally, men who speak their minds on all occasions and are instantly sorry they did. You have to like them even when they seem to insult you."

"He made up for it then?"

"I'll say he did. He knew that when we landed the officials would be breathing right down my neck. He wanted to give me every chance. So he kept the officials away from me until I'd convinced myself Ramsey's daughter just couldn't be on board.

"He let me look at every piece of luggage that was taken off the ship. He had some cargo to unload and he let me inspect that too, every crate. Most of the crates were too small to conceal a drugged and unconscious girl—or any girl for that matter. The ones that weren't, he opened for me and let me look inside.

"He let me watch every passenger leave the ship. Then, when all of the passengers had left, he stationed officers in the three main passageways and I went through the ship from bow to stern. I went into every stateroom and into every intership compartment. No one could have kept just a little ahead of me or behind me, dodging back into a compartment the instant I'd vacated it. They would have been instantly spotted by one of the officers.

"The Captain wasn't to blame at all for what happened later . . . when I tried to convince the commanding officers here that I was completely sane."

"I see. He must have' really liked you."

"I guess he did. And I liked him."

The kid nodded. "And the murderer's still at large. That makes it rough for the sixty odd passengers they're holding in quarantine. How long do you think they'll hold them in the Big Cage?"

"As long as they can. They'll keep them under close guard and increase their vigilance every time there's a suspicious move in the cage. They'll be screened perhaps a dozen times. But most of them are influential people. Most of them have booked passage on the Mars run liner that's due here next week. They can't hold them forever. They'd start pulling wires on Earth by short wave and there'd be a legislative uproar.

"Suppose they refuse, to let them send messages?"

"They won't refuse. I'm sure of that."

The kid was thoughtful for a moment. Then he said: "Tell me more about Ramsey. Just what do you think is happening on Mars?"

"No one knows exactly what is happening," Corriston said. "But to the best of my knowledge the overall picture is pretty ugly. The original settlers have their backs to the wall with a vengeance. Now there are armed guards at their throats. Ramsey has taken over. He has resorted to legal trickery to freeze them out.

"There are perhaps fifty important uranium claims on Mars and Ramsey has consolidated all of the holdings into single major enterprise. To say that he's cornered the market in uranium would be understating the case. He has taken possession by right of seizure, and the colonists can't get to him. They're living a hand-to-mouth existence while he lives in a heavily guarded stronghold behind three miles of electrified defenses."

The kid nodded again. "Yes, that's the picture when you unscramble it, I guess. But most of it is kept hidden from the general run of tourists."

"Naturally. Ramsey has the power to keep it under wraps."

"Do you think the colonists had anything to do with Clakey's murder and Miss Ramsey's disappearance? Or I guess I should say Henry Ewers' murder."

"Clakey, Ewers—his name doesn't matter. I'm convinced that he was Miss Ramsey's bodyguard."

"But you haven't answered my question."

"I can't answer it with any certainty. Did the colonists hire a killer and book passage for him on the ship? It's difficult to believe that the kind of men who colonized Mars would resort to murder."

"But there are a few scoundrels in every large group of men. And what if they became so desperate they felt they had to fight fire with fire?"

"Yes, I'd thought of that. It may be the answer."

CHAPTER FIVE

A HALF-HOUR later the kid was taken away and Corriston found himself completely alone. There are few events in human life more unnerving than the totally unexpected removal of a sympathetic listener when dark thoughts have taken possession of a man.

The kid wasn't forcibly removed from the cell. He left without protesting and no rough hands were laid on him, no physical violence employed. But he was not at all eager to leave, and if the guards who came for him had eyed him less severely, his attitude might have been the opposite of complacent.

"Sorry, kid," one of them said. "Your discharge has been postponed. Somebody on the psycho-staff wants to give you another test. I guess you didn't interpret the ink blots right."

He looked at Corriston and shook his head sympathetically. "It's tough, I know. Once you're here, waiting to be released can wear you down. I shouldn't be saying this, but it stands to reason it might even slow up your recovery a bit. It's easy to blame the docs, but you've got to try to understand their side of it. They have to make sure."

When the door clanged shut behind the kid, Corriston crossed to his cot, sat down, and cradled his head in his arms. The fact that he was still free to go outside and walk around the Station was no comfort at all. That kind of freedom could be worse than total confinement. He could never hope to escape from observation. The guards were under orders to watch him, and wherever he turned there'd be eyes boring into the back of his neck.

On Earth, a man under surveillance could duck quickly into a side street, run and weave about, and emerge on a broad avenue in the midst of a crowd. He could walk calmly then for a block or two, and turn in at a bar. He could drown his troubles in drink.

There were bars on the Station, of course. But Corriston knew that if he tried to mingle with officers of his own rank on the upper levels, he'd quickly enough find himself drinking alone. He could picture the off-duty personnel edging quickly and resentfully away from him, as though he'd suddenly appeared in their midst with a big, yawning hole in his skull.

Suddenly utter weariness overcame Corriston. He loosened his belt, elevated his legs, and relaxed on the cot.

He was asleep almost before he could close his eyes. How long he slept he had no way of knowing. He only knew that he was awakened by a sound—the strangest sound a man could hear in space. It was as if a gnat or a mosquito had developed a sudden, avaricious liking for his blood type and was determined to gorge itself to bursting at his expense.

The buzzing seemed to go on interminably as he hovered between sleeping and waking. On and on and on, with absolutely no letup. Then, abruptly, it ceased. There was a faint swishing sound and something solid thudded into the hardwood directly above him.

With a startled cry Corriston leapt from the cot, caught the iron edge of the bed-guard to keep from falling, and stared up in horror at the shining expanse of wall space overhead.

The cell was in almost total darkness. But from the barred window opposite, a faint glimmer of light penetrated in a diffuse arc, just enough light to enable him to make out the quivering stem of the barb.

It was a barb. This was so beyond any possibility of doubt. It had lodged in the hardwood scarcely a foot above his cot and it was still quivering.

Cold sweat broke out on Corriston's palms as he realized how close death had come, and how almost miraculous had been his escape. Had he raised himself to slap at the "mosquito" the barb could just as easily have buried itself in his skull.

Corriston hesitated for an instant, his eyes on the barred window and the faint glow beyond. Then his gaze passed to the wall switch. He decided against switching on the light immediately. He stooped low and moved quickly to the window, taking care to keep his head well below the sill.

For a moment he listened, his every nerve alert. There was no stir of movement in the darkness beyond the sill, nothing at all to indicate that someone was crouching there.

Finally, with an almost foolhardy recklessness, he raised his head and stared out between the bars. He could see right across to the wall opposite. The wall was less than eight feet away, and the space between the wall and his cell appeared to be unoccupied. This did not surprise him.

It was utterly silly to think that a man intent on willful murder would have lingered for any great length of time in so narrow a space. After having shot his bolt, his immediate concern would have been to get away as quickly as possible.

No, definitely, the man was gone, and if he had more barbs to release he would choose another time and place. Even then Corriston did not switch on the light. He had no particular desire to examine the wood-embedded barb in a bright light. He could see it clearly enough from where he stood. It was exactly like the barb that had sealed the lips of that blabbermouth Clakey.

Corriston went back to his cot and sat down. He told himself it would be highly dangerous to leave the cell and give the killer another chance. He had saved himself by refusing to slap a non-existent mosquito. But in the shadows of the Station there would be no mosquitoes—non-existent or otherwise. The killer would simply crouch in shadows, await his chance, and take careful aim.

What he had to do was find Miss Ramsey, and prove his sanity. If he stayed in the cell, the shadows would continue to deepen about him, would become intolerable, and perhaps even drive him to the verge of actual madness.

He had to convince the killer that he couldn't be silenced easily and perhaps not at all.

Corriston stood up. He ran his hands down his body, taking pride in its muscular solidity, its remarkable integrity under strain. He still felt lithe and confident; his physical vitality was unimpaired.

He had really known all along that he would be leaving the cell. On Earth you could dodge into a narrow alley between tall buildings or lean on a stroller platform and be carried underground so fast that your pursuers would be left blank-faced. If he stayed alert he could do the same thing on the Station, even though there were no moving pavements to leap upon. Quite possibly he could even slip out unnoticed. They might not even be watching the cell door because he had behaved himself so well up to now. Psycho-cases were permitted to roam, but if they stayed in their cells precautions would naturally be relaxed in their favor.

Corriston now was about to develop a sudden, unanticipated impulse to roam. The fact that he was completely sane gave him an edge over the space-shocked recruits. There is nothing quite so terrifying to a man who doubts his own sanity than the thought that unseen eyes are keeping tabs on him. He feels guilty and acts guilty and almost invariably his caution deserts him.

Corriston was quite sure that he could carry it off, even if he felt eyes boring into his back the instant he left the cell. He'd simply bide his time and seize the first opportunity which presented itself.

Actually, it was easier than he'd imagined it could be.

He simply opened the cell door, walked out; and there was no one in sight to observe him. So far, so good. The corridor outside was completely deserted, and when he reached the end of it there was still no one. He turned left into a large, square reception room and crossed it without hurrying, his shoulders held straight. Photoelectric eyes? Yes, possibly, but he had no intention of letting the thought worry him. If he were being watched mechanically, there was nothing he could do about it and somehow he didn't think that he had crossed any photoelectric beams. Certainly no doors had swung open or closed behind him, and photoelectric alarm system without visible manifestations could be dismissed as a not too likely possibility.

When Corriston emerged in the glass-encased, wide-view observation promenade on the Station's Second Level, he was no longer alone. On all sides, men and women jostled him, walking singly and in pairs, in uniform and in civilian clothes, or hurrying off in dun-gray, space-mechanic anonymity.

The promenade was crowded almost to capacity, and yet the men and women seemed mere walking dots scattered at random beneath the immense structures of steel and glass that walled them in. A feeling of unreality came upon Corriston as he stared upward. He deliberately moderated his stride, as if fearful that a too rapid movement in anyone direction might send him spinning out into space with a glass-shattering impetus which he would be powerless to control.

It was an illogical fear and yet he could not entirely throw it off, and he did not seriously try. It was not nearly as important as the possibility that he might be being followed. There was no one behind him who looked in the least suspicious, and no one in front of him either. But how could he be completely sure?

The answer was that he couldn't. He had to trust his instincts, and so far they had given him every assurance that he was moving in a free, independent orbit of his own, completely unobserved.

And then, quite suddenly, he ceased to move at all.

Something quite startling was taking place throughout the length and breadth of the observation promenade. The men in uniform were exchanging alarmed glances and departing in haste. The civilians were crowding closer to the panes. They were collecting in awestruck groups of blinding light crisscrossed high above their heads.

They were all looking in one direction, but a few of them had been taken so completely by surprise that they stood motionless in the middle of the promenade. Corriston was one of the motionless ones, but his eyes were quick to seek out the nearest viewpane.

At first he thought that a gigantic meteor had appeared suddenly out of the stellar dark and was rushing straight toward the Station with a velocity so great as to be almost unimaginable.

Then he realized that it wasn't a meteor. It was a spaceship. And it wasn't rushing straight toward the Station. It had either bypassed or encircled the Station and passed beyond it, for it was now heading out into space again. He could see the long, bright trail left by its rocket jets, the diffuse incandescence in its wake.

CHAPTER SIX

AN OFFICER with two stripes on his shoulder was standing almost at Corriston's elbow. He hadn't turned to depart, and for some reason he seemed reluctant to do so. The spaceship's erratic course seemed to absorb him to the exclusion of all else.

He started swearing under his breath. Then he saw Corriston and a strange look came into his face. He looked at Corriston steadily for a moment, then looked quickly away.

Corriston edged slowly away from him and joined the nearest group of civilians. They were all talking at once and it was hard to understand precisely what they were saying. But after a moment a few enlightening fragments of information greatly lessened his bewilderment.

"That freighter was preparing to land at the Station, but for some reason it couldn't make contact. It never even began to decelerate."

"How do you know?"

"I asked one of the officers—that gray-haired man over there. He was plenty worried. I guess that's why he talked so freely. He'd had some kind of dispute with the captain, apparently. He told me that trouble developed aboard that freighter when it was eight or ten thousand miles away. An emergency message came through, but for some reason the captain kept it pretty much to himself."

Watching the freighter's hull blaze with friction as it went into a narrow orbit about Earth, Corriston tried hard to make himself believe that the particular manner of a spaceman's departure was simply one, tragic aspect of a calculated risk, that men who lived dangerously could hardly expect to die peacefully in their beds. But it was a rationalization without substance. In an immediate and very real sense he was inside the freighter, enduring an eternity of torment, sharing the agonizing fate that was about to overtake the crew.

Nearer and nearer to Earth the freighter swept, completely encircling the planet like a runaway moon with an orbital velocity so great the eye could hardly follow it.

"It will blast out a meteor pit as wide as the Grand Canyon if it explodes on land," someone at Corriston's elbow said. "I wouldn't care to be within a hundred miles of it."

"Neither would I. It could wipe out a city, all right—any city within a radius of thirty miles. This is really something to watch!"

The freighter had encircled Earth twice and was now so close to its blue-green oceans and the dun-colored immensity of its continental land masses that it had almost disappeared from view. It had dwindled to a tiny, glowing pinpoint of radiance crossing the face of the planet, an erratically weaving firefly that had abandoned all hope of guiding itself by a light that was about to flare up with explosive violence and put an end to its life.

The freighter was invisible when the end came. It was invisible when it struck and rebounded and channeled a deep pit in a green valley on Earth. But the explosion, which followed, was seen by every man and woman on the Station's wide-view promenade.

There were three tremendous flares, each opening and spreading outward like the sides of a funnel, each a livid burst of incandescence spiraling outward into space.

As seen from the Station the flares were not, of course, so tragically spectacular. They resembled more successive flashes of almost instantaneous brightness, flashes such as had many times been produced by the tilting of a heliograph on the rust-red plains of Mars under conditions of maximum visibility.

It takes an experienced eye to interpret such phenomena correctly, and among the spectators on the promenade there were a few, no doubt, who were not even quite sure that the freighter had exploded.

But Corriston had no doubts at all on that score. The full extent of the tragedy would be revealed later by radio communication from Earth.

There was a long silence before anyone spoke. The group around Corriston seemed paralyzed by shock, unable to express in words how blindly hopeful they had dared to be, or how fatalistic from the first. There were a few moist eyes among the women, an awkward, almost reverent shuffling of feet.

Then the young man at Corriston's elbow cleared his throat and said in a barely audible whisper: "It didn't come down in the sea."

"I know," Corriston said. "It came down in North America, close to the Canadian border."

"In the United States?"

"Yes, I think so. We can't be sure. It's too much to hope there was no destruction of human life after an explosion of that magnitude."

Corriston suddenly realized that he was behaving like a man who had taken complete leave of his wits. He was drawing more and more attention to himself when he should have been bending all of his efforts toward making himself as inconspicuous as possible.

Fortunately the agitation of everyone on the promenade was helping to remedy his blunder. His wisest course now was simply to recede as an individual, to move silently to the perimeter of the group and just as silently vanish.

He was confident that he could accomplish it. He began elbowing his way backwards until there were a dozen men and women in front of him. He let himself be observed briefly as a grim-lipped spectator who had taken such an emotional pounding that he could endure no more. Suddenly he saw his chance and took it. There was another small group of civilians close to the group he had joined, and he ducked quickly behind them, using their turned-away backs as a shield. He edged toward a paneled door on his right, his only concern for the moment being a comparatively simple one. He must get away from the crowded promenade as swiftly as possible.

He reached the door, swung the panel wide, and stepped into the long, brightly-lighted compartment beyond without a backward glance. Almost immediately he perceived that he had committed an act of folly. The compartment was a promenade cafeteria and it was crowded with an overflow of agitated men and women discussing the tragedy in heated terms.

Keep cool now. None of these people are interested in you. Keep cool and keep on walking. There's another door and you can be through it in less than a minute, Corriston told himself.

There was a pretty waitress behind the long counter, and as he came abreast of her she smiled at him. For an instant he hesitated, eyed the stool opposite her, and fought off an incongruous but almost irresistible impulse to sit down. Quick warmth and sudden sympathy. Yes, he could do with a bit of both, Corriston thought.

It was sheer insanity, but he did sit down. He eased himself into the stool and ordered a cup of coffee.

"Something with it?" the waitress asked. "A sandwich, or—"

"No, no, I don't think so," Corriston said quickly. "Just the coffee."

The waitress seemed in no hurry to depart. "It was pretty terrible what happened. Wasn't it?"

"Did you see it?" Corriston asked.

"I saw most of it. I saw the ship go past the Station and start to explode. I saw that black wing, or whatever it was, drop off. Then someone started shouting in here and I came back. They say it crashed on Earth."

"That's right," Corriston said, telling himself that he was a damned fool for wanting to look at her hair and hear her friendly woman's voice when every passing second was adding to his danger.

"You saw it crash?"

Corriston nodded. "I just came from the promenade."

"That was a crazy thing to ask you. How excited can you get? I saw you come through that door. You looked kind of pale."

"I still feel that way," Corriston said.

The waitress then said a surprising thing: "I wonder what it is about some men. You just have to look at them once and you know they're the sort you'd like to be with when something terrible happens. You know what I mean?"

"Sure," Corriston said. "Any port in a storm."

The waitress smiled again. "I don't mean that, exactly. Please don't think I'm handing you a line. There's just something…comfortable about you. You go all pale when something bad happens to other people. That's good; I like that. It means you can feel for other people. You're a gentle sort of guy, but I bet you can take care of yourself and anyone you care about. I just bet you can."

The waitress flushed a little, as if afraid that she had said too much. She turned and walked slowly toward the coffee percolator at the far end of the counter.

He was glad now that he had ordered the coffee. The coffee would help too. He suddenly felt that he was under observation, that hostile eyes were watching him. But it was no more than just a feeling; and coffee and sympathy might drive it away.

How blindly, stupidly foolish could a guy be? Corriston thought. *If he had any sense at all he wouldn't wait for the coffee. He'd get up quickly and head for the door at the other end of the cafeteria. He'd either do that, or swing about abruptly and attempt to catch the silent watcher by surprise.*

Corriston decided to wait for the coffee.

The waitress looked at him strangely when she returned. She set the coffee down before him and started to turn away, her eyes troubled. Then, suddenly, she seemed to change her mind. She leaned close to him and whispered: "You'd better leave by the promenade door. That man over there has been watching you. I know him very well. He's a Security Guard."

Corriston nodded and stared at her gratefully for a moment. He was more relieved than alarmed. It was far better to have a Security Guard watching him than a killer with a poisoned barb. He wasn't exactly happy about it, but he was confident he could elude the agent.

The waitress' eyes were suddenly warm and friendly again. "Space shock?" she asked.

"So they claim," Corriston said. "I happen to think they're mistaken."

He started sipping the coffee. It was hot but not steaming hot. He could have tossed it off like a jigger of rye but he had some quick thinking to do.

"Tell me," he said. "Just where is that guard sitting?"

"At the other end of the counter," the waitress replied, the anxiety coming back into her eyes. "He's close to the door. You'd have to go past him. Maybe I'm wrong, but I think you want to get away from him. So you'd better go the way you came—by the promenade door."

"That's not too good an idea, I'm afraid," Corriston said. "He'd follow me and get assistance on the promenade. What's beyond the other door? Where does it lead to?"

"It opens on a corridor," the waitress said quickly. "If you can get past him you might have a better chance that way. There's nothing but a corridor with two side doors. One opens on an emergency stairway that goes down to the Master Sequence Selector compartments."

She seemed to take pride in her knowledge. Due to a space-shocked guy's difficulties, the Master Sequence Selector had become an important secret shared between them. Corriston wondered if she knew that the Selector functioned on thirty-two separate kinds of automatic controls. If he ever got the chance, he'd come back and tell her exactly how grateful he was. Right at the moment one consideration alone dominated his thinking. If he could get past the guard he could hide out in an intricate maze of machinery. Even if they sent a dozen guards down to look for him it would take them some time to locate him. He could hide-out and gain a breathing spell.

The waitress had a very small hand. Abruptly Corriston clasped it and held it for an instant, his fingers exerting a firm, steady pressure. "Thanks," he said.

Corriston swung about without glancing toward the end of the counter. He'd pass the guard quickly enough; there was no sense in alerting the man in advance. As for recognizing him, that would be no problem at all. You couldn't mistake a Security Guard no matter what kind of clothes he wore.

Corriston took his time. He walked slowly, refusing to hurry. A man under surveillance should never hurry. He should be casual, completely at his ease, for there is no better way of keeping an observer guessing.

He kept parallel with the long counter, his shoulders swaying a little with the assurance of a man who knows exactly where he is going. Presently the entire length of the counter was behind him, and he was less than a yard from the door.

He hadn't glanced once at the counter. He didn't intend to now. One quick leap would carry him through the door and beyond it, and to hell with recognizing the guard. When it was touch and go and odd man out, you altered your plan as you went along.

He'd seen a girl disappear when everyone said it didn't happen. Confined to a psycho-ward, he had simply walked out, eluded a killer, and watched a ship explode on the green hills of Earth. He'd survived all that, so how could one lone Security Guard stop him now?

He was preparing to leap, when something got in his way—a shadow—a shadow for an instant between himself and the door, and then a dark bulk stepping right into the shoes of the shadow and filling it out.

The Security Guard was not at all the kind of person he'd expected him to be. He was not a big ape, not even a muscular-looking man. He had simply seemed big for the instant he took to fill the place of his shadow. He was a man of average height, average build. He blocked the doorway without bluster, looking very calm and relaxed. Only his eyes were cold and accusing and dangerously narrowed as he surveyed Corriston from head to foot.

"I'm afraid you'll have to go back to the ward now," he said. "You picked a bad time to take a turn about the Station. Ordinarily you'd be privileged to do so. That's part of the therapy. But you picked a very bad time."

"I'm beginning to realize that," Corriston said. "I couldn't help it, though. I had no way of knowing that freighter was out of control. I'm afraid you've made a mistake, too, though. I'm not going back to the cell."

Corriston had been watching the man's right arm. Suddenly it went back and his fist started rising, started coming up fast at an angle that could have sent it crashing against Corriston's jaw.

Corriston had no intention of letting that happen. He sidestepped quickly and delivered a smashing blow to the pit of the guard's stomach. The blow was so solid that it doubled the guard up. His knees buckled and he started to fold.

Corriston didn't take the folding for granted. A second blow caught the man squarely on the jaw and a third thudded into his rib section. For an instant he looked so dazed that Corriston felt sorry for him.

He was still half-doubled up when he sank to the floor and straightened out. He straightened out on his side first, and then rolled over on his back and stopped moving. His lips hung slackly, his eyes were wide and staring.

The look on his face gave Corriston a jolt. It was a very strange look. The fact that his features had become slack was not startling in itself, but there was something unnatural, unbelievable, about the way that muscular relaxation had overspread his entire countenance. His features were putty-gray and they seemed to have no clearly defined boundaries.

His nose, eyes, and forehead looked as if the ligaments which held them together had snapped from overstrain or had been severed by a surgeon's scalpel...severed and allowed to go their separate ways without interference.

In fact, there was no real expression on the man's face at all— no recognizably human expression—not even the stuporous look of a man knocked suddenly unconscious.

There was agitation now in the cafeteria, a hum of angry voices, a rising murmur that was coming dangerously close. Corriston shut his mind to it. He knelt at the guard's side and swiftly unbuttoned the unconscious man's heavy service jacket. He felt around under the jacket until he was satisfied that he could move on through the doorway with a clear conscience. The guard's heart was beating firmly and steadily. There was a reassuring warmth under the jacket as well, a complete absence of clamminess.

Suddenly the guard groaned and started to roll over on his side again. Corriston didn't wait for him to complete the movement. He arose quickly and was through the door in four long strides.

He preferred not to run. He was not so much fleeing as seeking a security he was entitled to, a reasonably safe port in a storm that was threatening to take away his freedom by blanketing him in a dark cloud of unjust suspicion and utter tyranny.

The corridor was as deserted as he'd hoped it would be. With no one to get in his way or sound an alarm, he had no difficulty at all in locating the emergency passageway that descended in a rail-guarded spiral to the Master Sequence Selector. He kept his right hand on the safety rail as he moved downward into the darkness. For the first time he felt extremely tired.

CHAPTER SEVEN

THE DRONE of machinery in a high-vaulted, metal-walled compartment awakened Corriston. It was for the most part a steady, low, continuous sound. But occasionally it ceased to be a drone, in a strict sense, and became high-pitched. It became a shrill, almost intolerable whine, impinging unpleasantly on his eardrums and preventing him from going to sleep again.

For interminable minutes he lay stretched out at full length in the lidded, coffin-like rag bin into which he had crawled, a lethargic weariness enveloping him like a shroud. Above his head steel-blue surfaces crisscrossed, vibrating planes of metal and wire intricately folded back upon themselves.

After a moment, when the steady drone was well in the ascendancy again, he sat up and stared about him. He had a throbbing headache and there was a dryness in his throat that made swallowing difficult.

He was certainly not an exceptional man in regard to such matters. During moments of crises he could remain fairly calm and self-possessed but the aftermath could be killing.

He felt now as if all of his nerves had been squeezed together in a vise. He looked at his wristwatch and was amazed to discover that he had slept for eight hours. If a search had been made for him, he had no reason to complain about his luck. He hadn't even closed the lid of the bin. But perhaps the oil-stained waste he had drawn over himself had given them the idea that he was just more waste underneath. Perhaps the guards didn't give a damn whether they found him or not. It was quite possible. On a low official level a cynical desire for self-comfort could dominate the thinking of a man.

It was quite possible that the guards who had been sent down to search for him—or one of the guards, at least—had been angry at his superiors. Just a quick look and to hell with it—that must have been his attitude.

It made sense in another way. They wouldn't suspect the bin because the bin was so conspicuous and obvious a hiding place. The Purloined Letter sort of thing. Crawl into an empty coffin at a funeral and no one will give you a second glance. All dead men look alike.

The Master Sequence Selector compartment was a coffin, too— a big, all-metal coffin arching above him and hemming him in. If he hoped to get out of it alive, he'd have to do more than just beat on the lid with his fists.

Almost instantly he was ashamed of his thoughts. He had been extremely lucky so far. The funeral was over, the sod firmly in place. They would not be likely to dig him up on suspicion, and he could stay buried until he starved to death.

The worst would be over when they found him. The thirst torment would be the worst, but if it became unbearable he would still have the choice of surrendering himself.

Quite possibly he would die of thirst. Quite possibly he could shout his lungs out and still remain trapped. If a search had been made and they had failed to find him, sullen anger might have tempted them to do an unthinkable thing. They might have locked the door of the compartment so that the corpse would have no opportunity of escaping prematurely and making them look like fools.

Corriston was just starting to climb out of the bin to investigate the truth or falseness of that utterly demoralizing possibility when he heard the sound. It was a very peculiar sound, three or four times repeated, and he heard it clearly above the low drone of the Selector's automatic controls.

He stood up in the bin, straining his ears. It came again, louder this time. It was only a short distance away and it was a voice sound, unmistakably a voice sound.

He climbed out of the bin, grasped a metal rod that projected from one of the crossbeams, and descended cautiously to the base of the Selector. The droning increased for an instant, rising to a whine so high-pitched that he could no longer hear the voice.

He started moving around the edge of the Selector, keeping well within its shadow, watching shafts of dull light move backwards and forwards across the floor. He hardly expected anyone to leap out at him. The voice had not seemed quite that near; in fact, he was by no means sure that it had come from the compartment at all. But if not from the compartment, where?

He found out quickly enough. There was a square, window-like grate a few feet from the Selector's automatic control panel, set high up on the wall. A faint, steady glow came from it.

Corriston paused for an instant directly below the glow, measuring the distance from the floor to the aperture with his eyes. He strained his ears again, waiting for the whine to subside. It continued shrill, but suddenly he heard the voice again, heard it above the whine.

There was stark terror in the voice. It was despairing and desperate in its pleading, and it seemed to Corriston that he would remember it until he died. He thought he recognized the voice, but he couldn't be sure.

It was perhaps merciful that he couldn't, for the grate was at least ten feet above the floor and had he known beyond the faintest shadow of doubt that it was Helen Ramsey's voice, his inability to reach her would have been fiendish torment.

He hoped only one thing—that he had to reach that voice in time.

First of all he had to stay calm. Even a calm man could not hope to scale a ten-foot wall with his bare hands, but an agitated man would have no chance at all. Something to stand on! A box—anything!

A box would help, a ladder would be better. But what were his chances of finding a ladder in the Selector compartment? Not good at all. Still, he could search for a ladder. Quickly now. No time to waste, but don't lose your head. Take thirty seconds, a good long thirty seconds to look around for a metal ladder. There just might be one standing somewhere against the wall.

There was! Not one ladder, but two, leaning against the wall directly opposite the glimmering front section of the Selector.

It was amazing how desperation could change a man. In the great moments of danger and desperation small, neurotic concerns ceased to matter.

He was sure now. He had recognized the voice beyond any possibility of doubt. The ladder scraped against the wall and swayed a little, and for an instant he feared it might slide out from under him. He paused to make sure, and then went swiftly on up until his head was level with the grate.

He grasped the heavy grillwork with both hands and raised himself higher. He could see clearly through the grill into the compartment beyond now. The entire compartment was visible from where he stood. It was small and square and dimly lighted by an overhead lamp, and there was a paneled door leading into it.

Close to the door a man was standing. Corriston couldn't see his face. He was half turned away from the wall opposite him, and the girl who was struggling to escape from him was more than two-thirds concealed by his massive shoulders.

He was holding her in a tight, merciless grip. He had locked one hand on her wrist and was preventing her from moving either backwards or forwards. It was costing him no effort. He simply stood very straight and still while she struggled vainly to free herself.

Immense strength seemed to emanate from him, complete assurance and a coldly calculating kind of brutality that appeared to be slowly undermining her will to resist. Her struggles became less frantic second by slow second, and that she was about to stop struggling altogether was evident from the way her right arm had begun to dangle and her body to sag.

The man was holding her by the left wrist in a left-handed grip. He was cruelly twisting her wrist and suddenly she cried out again in pain and despairing helplessness.

The blood started mounting to Corriston's temples. He began tugging at the grate with both hands, exerting all his strength in a desperate effort to dislodge it. It began to move a little, to become less firmly attached to the wall. He could feel it moving under his hands, rasping and creaking as it loosened inch by inch.

He was covered with sweat. Already in his mind he had killed the man, and Helen Ramsey was tight in his arms, happy and alive.

The man did not seem to hear the rasp of the grate coming loose. He neither turned nor raised his head. His free hand had gone out and across the girl's face. But if he had struck her on the face, she gave no sign. She did not recoil as if from a blow and there was something strange about the movement. It was as if the man had reached out to tear something from the girl's face—a veil or a mask.

His hand whipped back empty but his fingers were oddly twisted, as if he had clawed at something that had failed to come free.

Corriston pulled back his shoulders and his posture on the ladder grew more erect. He knew that his exertions might send the ladder toppling but it was a risk he had to take.

The grate was freely movable now. He could move it backwards and forwards, six or eight inches each way; but he still could not rip it completely free.

He kept on tugging, his neck cords bulging, the ladder swaying dangerously. The grate could be moved upward now, just a little. No, it was finally coming completely loose. He could move it in all directions and even push it outward at right angles to its base.

Twice he heard Helen Ramsey cry out again, and her screams became a goad that turned his wrists to steel. With a sudden, convulsive wrench he twisted the grate sideways. It came loose in his hands. It was so surprisingly light that an incongruous rage surged up in him. It was cruelly perverse, intolerable, that he should have been so long delayed by a thin sheet of metal that hardly seemed to have any weight at all.

He swung about on the ladder and let the grate drop. It struck the floor a few feet from the Selector and rebounded with a clang loud enough to wake the dead. The ladder swayed again, and he had to grab the edge of the aperture quickly and with both hands to keep himself from toppling.

He pulled himself forward through the aperture on his stomach, taking care not to dislodge the ladder. His temples were pounding and his palms sticky with sweat. He did not look down until he was completely through, dreading what he might see.

He passed a hand over his eyes. It was unbelievable, but he had to believe it. The man was gone and the girl was now alone in the compartment.

Had the man fled in sudden fear, knowing that Corriston would be consumed with a killing rage that would make him a more than dangerous adversary? Corriston didn't think so. The man had looked quite capable of putting up a furious struggle. More likely he had disappeared to keep himself from being recognized, or because he had accomplished his purpose.

Blind, embittered anger again boiled up in Corriston. Had the man waited, he would have rejoiced and been less angry. He would have taken a calm, deep breath and slowly set about the almost pleasant task of killing him.

He felt cheated, outraged. Then his concern for Helen Ramsey made him forget his rage. Had she been felled with a blow, or had she simply fainted? He started down, then hesitated.

The ladder first. Before he descended it was necessary to make sure that the ladder would be in the same compartment with him, set firmly against the wall, directly under the aperture. If he were prevented from leaving the compartment by the corridor door, he might find himself needing the ladder. Without it he might be descending into a trap that could close with a clang and abruptly imprison him.

Getting down into the compartment was the worst part, just putting the ladder into place and not knowing how badly hurt she was.

What if she's dead? he thought. *What if he killed her with a single blow? He looked strong enough. He could have killed her. God, don't let me think of that. I mustn't think it.*

His feet touched the floor. He let out his breath slowly, turned and crossed the floor to where she was lying. He went down on his knees and lifted her into his arms. She lay relaxed in his arms, face up, quiet, her lips slightly parted.

He looked down into her face, and for a moment his mind went numb, became still, so that there was no longer a whirling inside his head—only a chilling horror.

She seemed to have two faces. One was shrunken and almost torn away, a shredded fragment of a face. But enough of it remained for him to see the shriveled flesh of the cheeks, the puckered mouth, the white hair clinging to the temples. It was the face of an old woman but so fragmentary that it could not even have been called a half-face. And even though it had been almost ripped away, it seemed still to adhere firmly to the face to which it had been attached, and to blend with it, so that the features of both faces intermingled in a quite unnatural way.

Not quite, though; Helen Ramsey's face was sharper, more distinct—all of the features stood out more clearly. And when Corriston's stunned mind began to function normally again, he realized that the old woman's face was—had to be—a plastic mask.

It took him only an instant to remove the ghastly thing from features that he could not bear to see defaced.

He had to pry it loose, but he did so very gently, exactly as a sculptor might have pried loose a life mask from the face of a recumbent model.

He held it in his hand and looked at it, and a little of the horror crept back into his mind.

It was the merest fragment, as he had thought. Thin, flexible, a tissue-structure of incomplete, aged features, and with an inner surface that was very rough and uneven, as if something had been torn from it.

He could have crumpled it up in his hand, but he did not do so. With a lack of foresight which he was later to regret—a lack which was to prove tragic—he simply flung it from him, as though its ugliness had unnerved him so that he could no longer endure the sight of it.

Helen Ramsey was a dead weight in his arms, and for a moment he feared that she had stopped breathing. So great was his fear, so paralyzing, that his hand on her pulse became rigid, and for a moment he could neither move nor think.

Then he felt the slow beat of her pulse and a great thankfulness came upon him.

He knew then that he must get help as quickly as possible. He eased her gently to the floor, walked to the door and locked it securely. Then he returned to her and took her into his arms again. He spent several minutes trying to revive her. But when she did not open her eyes, did not even stir in his arms, he knew that he could not wait any longer.

CHAPTER EIGHT

AN INEXORABLE kind of determination enabled Corriston to get to the Station's central control compartment, and confront the commander, when the latter, absorbed by matters of the utmost urgency, had triple-guarded his privacy by stationing executive officers outside the door.

Commander Clement was a small man physically, with a strangely bland, almost cherubic face. But his face was dark with anger now—or possibly it was shock that he was experiencing—and the heightened color seemed to add to his dignity, making him look not merely forcibly determined, but almost formidable. His white uniform and the seven gold bars on each epaulet helped a good deal too. It was impossible to determine at a glance just how great was his inner strength, but Corriston knew that he could not have gotten where he was had he not possessed unalloyed resoluteness.

He was standing by a visual reference mechanism that looked almost exactly like a black stovepipe spiraling up from the deck. There was a speaking tube in his hand, and he was talking into it. He seemed completely unaware that he was no longer alone.

Had Corriston been less agitated he would have felt a little sorry for the officer who had admitted him. The officer had been so impressed by Corriston's gravity and the earnestness with which he had pleaded his case that he had stepped forward and opened the door without question, assuming, no doubt, that Clement would look up instantly and see Corriston standing just inside the doorway.

Now the door had closed again, Clement hadn't looked up, and the officer was going to be in trouble. But Corriston had no time and very little inclination to worry about that. What Commander Clement was saying into the speaking tube had a far stronger claim on his attention.

"It's the worst thing that could have happened," Clement was saying. "We can't just brazen it out. It's going to mean trouble, serious trouble. What's that? How should I know what happened? When you're carrying a certain kind of cargo a thousand things can go wrong. The ship went out of control, that's all. The first radio message didn't tell me anything. The captain was trying to cover up to save himself. He didn't even want me to know.

"You bet it can happen again. We've got to be prepared for that, too. But right now—"

Commander Clement saw Corriston then. His expression didn't change, but it seemed to Corriston that he paled slightly.

"That's all for now," he said, and returned the speaking tube to its cradle.

He looked steadily at Corriston for a moment. A glint of anger appeared in his eyes, and suddenly they were blazing.

"What do you mean by coming in here unannounced, Lieutenant?" he demanded. "I gave strict orders that no one was to be admitted. If I didn't know you were suffering from severe space shock . . ."

"I'm sorry, sir," Corriston said quickly. "It's very urgent. I think I can convince you that I am not suffering from space shock. I've found Miss Ramsey. She's been badly hurt and needs immediate medical attention."

The Commander looked as if a man he had thought sane was standing before him with a gun in his hand. Not Corriston, but some other, more violent man. For a moment longer he remained rigid and then his hand went out and tightened on Corriston's arm.

"By heaven, if you're lying to me!"

"I would have no reason to lie, sir. It proves I'm not a space-shock case. But that's unimportant now. She's safe for the moment. No one can get to her. I bolted the door on the inside. Unless—"

Corriston went pale. "No, there's no danger. I drew the ladder up and returned it to the Selector compartment. Then I threw the lock on the emergency door."

"Start at the beginning," Clement said. "If she's in danger we'll get to her. Take it easy now, and tell me exactly what happened."

Corriston went over it fast. He said nothing about the mask. Let Clement find that out for himself.

Commander Clement walked to the door, threw it open and spoke to the executive officer who was stationed outside. The officer came into the control room.

"Stay with Lieutenant Corriston until I get back," Clement said. "He's not to leave. He understands that."

He turned back to Corriston. "I'm afraid you'll have to consider yourself still under guard, Lieutenant. I have only your word that you found Miss Ramsey. I believe you, but there are some regulations even I can't waive."

"It's all right," Corriston said. "I won't attempt to leave. But please hurry, sir."

Commander Clement hesitated, then said with a smile: "I knew about the guard you knocked out, Lieutenant. You're a very hotheaded young man. That's really a court martial offense, but perhaps we can smooth it over if you're telling the truth now. You were in the position of a man imprisoned for a crime he didn't commit. If he can prove his innocence, the law is very lenient. He can escape and still get a full pardon, even a pardon with apologies. It's a different matter, of course if he kills a guard to escape. You didn't."

Corriston was tempted to say, "I think perhaps I tried to, sir," but thought better of it. He'd ask Clement later why the guards who had been sent down into the Selector compartment had failed to find him. It wasn't important enough now to waste a second thought on, but just out of curiosity he would ask.

He didn't have to. After Clement had departed the executive officer told him. "They made a pretty thorough search for you," he said. "Or so they claimed. But they had been drinking heavily—everyone of them. Maintaining discipline can be a terrible headache at times. There's a lot of objectivity about the commander and he doesn't try to crack down too hard. He knows what it means to be out here for months with nothing to break the monotony. Hell, if we could send for our wives more often it wouldn't be so bad."

Corriston's palms were cold. He stood very still, wondering how long it would take the commander to return with the news he wanted to hear.

"The question is whether life is really worth living without a woman to talk to," the executive officer went on. "Just to lie relaxed and watch a pretty girl move slowly around a room. It does something for you."

Corriston wished the man would keep quiet. Under ordinary circumstances he could have sympathized heartily. He couldn't now. There was only one girl he wanted to see walk around a room, and she might just as well have been at the opposite end of space.

She wasn't walking around a room now. She was lying helplessly sprawled out, waiting for rescue to come. It had to come soon, it had to. The commander wouldn't just go down alone after her. He'd be accompanied by a half-dozen executive officers who would know exactly how to bundle her into a stretcher and carry her to the sick bay.

But what if a killer just happened to be crouching in one of the corridors, waiting for the stretcher to pass? A killer with a poisoned barb...

Corriston couldn't stand still. He walked back and forth across the control room while the executive officer continued to talk. He paid no heed at all.

Corriston heard a footfall as he paced. He turned and saw that Commander Clement had returned. He was standing in the doorway with a strange look on his face.

Corriston felt bewildered, unable to quite believe that Clement was really back. It was like a dream that had suddenly turned real, a looking glass reversal with a strange quality of distortion about it.

It was real enough. Clement entered and shut the door behind him, very firmly and carefully, as if he wanted to make sure that Corriston would not attempt to escape.

He walked slowly forward, looking at the executive officer as if Corriston had no place at all in his thoughts.

"Everything he told me was a lie," Clement said. "Everything. There was no girl. The compartment was locked; so was the emergency door leading down to the Selector. The ladder was standing against the wall in the Selector compartment. Miss Ramsey could not have been in the compartment—not at any time. There was nothing to indicate it. She just wasn't there."

Corriston moved toward him, his face white. "That's a lie and you know it. What have you done with her? You'd better tell me. You can have me court-martialed, but you can't stop me from talking. I can prove she was there. The grate—"

"The grate? What are you talking about? There was no ripped-out grate. The grate was in place. I feel very sorry for you, Lieutenant. But I can't let sympathy stand in the way of my duty. In some respects you're very rational. You can think logically and clearly . . . up to a point. But the shock weakness is there. It's very serious when you start having actual hallucinations."

The executive officer had drawn his gun. He was holding it rather loosely in his hand now, triggered and ready for any dangerous or suspicious move on Corriston's part.

There was nothing in Clement's gaze as he swung about to refute the dark mistrust that had come into the executive officer's eyes. He seemed intent only on bolstering that mistrust by driving even deeper nails into Corriston's coffin.

"I'm afraid we'll have to continue to regard Lieutenant Corriston as dangerously unstable," he said "Keep your gun on him when you take him back to the Ward. Don't relax your vigilance for an instant."

"I won't," the executive officer promised.

"Good. You're not going to make any further trouble for us, are you, Lieutenant?"

The question seemed to call for no answer and Corriston made none. He turned slowly and walked toward the door, despairingly aware that a man he had rather liked had fallen into step behind him and would shoot him dead if he so much as wavered.

Just as he reached the door Clement spoke again, giving the executive officer final instructions. "He must not be permitted to leave his cell. Make sure of that, Simms. Post a permanent guard at the door. He must be kept under constant surveillance. If he's the self-destructive type, and I'm by no means sure he isn't, he may attempt to kill himself."

CHAPTER NINE

May attempt to kill himself. May attempt...May attempt...May attempt to kill himself. Corriston sat up on his cot, his mouth dry, his temples pounding.

Had Clement implanted the suggestion in his mind deliberately, with infinite cruelty and cunning? Was Clement really hoping that he would commit suicide? If he took his own life Clement would stand to gain a great deal.

But could Clement be that much of a scoundrel? Was he, in fact, a scoundrel at all? Corriston knew that he could not afford to succumb to panic. Only by staying calm, by trying to reason it out logically, could he hope to get anywhere. Not at the truth, perhaps, but anywhere at all.

Start off with a supposition: The commander was everything that he pretended to be, an honest man with immense responsibilities that he could not delegate to anyone else. A forthright, hot-tempered, but completely sincere man. A little secretive, yes, but only because he took his responsibilities so seriously.

Start off by assuming that Clement was that kind of a man. What would he stand to gain if Corriston killed himself? The removal of one responsibility, at the very least. It was bad for morale if an officer had hallucinations that vitally concerned the Station itself. But a hallucination about the wealthiest girl on Earth wasn't just run-of-the-mill. It could not only disturb every officer and enlisted man on the Station; it could have political repercussions on Earth.

Clement was already in trouble because of the freighter. The chances were a Congressional Investigating Committee would be coming out. They'd be sure to hear about Corriston. His story would be all over the Station, on everyone's lips.

If Corriston took his own life the commander would be spared all that. He'd have nothing to answer for. The entire affair could be hushed up. Or could it?

Wait a minute, better give the whole problem another twirl. Even if the Commander was a completely honest man, he wouldn't stand to gain too much. He might even find himself in more serious trouble. And look at it in another way: It was hard to believe that a hallucination concerning Helen Ramsey could be much more than a gadfly irritation. If the full truth came out, Clement could clear himself of all blame. Would a man of integrity suggest that a fellow-officer take his own life solely to remove a gadfly irritation? Or any irritation, for that matter?

It was inconceivable on the face of it. The first supposition was a contradiction in terms. It did not remain valid under close scrutiny and therefore it had to be rejected.

Supposition number two: Clement was in all respects the exact opposite of an honest man. Clement had something dark and damaging to conceal and was in more serious trouble than he'd allowed anyone to suspect. Clement had some reason for not wanting the truth about Ramsey's daughter to come out.

What would he stand to gain if Corriston took himself out of the world? Unfortunately there were wide areas where any kind of speculation had to penetrate an almost absolute vacuum to get anywhere at all.

The situation on Mars? Was there some as yet undemonstratable link between Ramsey's uranium holdings and the Station itself? Was Clement involved with Ramsey in some way? And was Ramsey's daughter a vital link in the chain?

Had the accident to the freighter put an additional strain on the chain, a strain so great that Clement had been forced to take immediate, drastic action to protect himself?

Corriston tried to remember exactly what the Commander had said over the speaking tube. He had tried to listen intently, but he had been too agitated to make much sense out of the few brief sentences that he had overheard. Clement had been speaking in anger and not too coherently, and it had been a one-way conversation, with the replying voice completely silent, or, at the very least, inaudible. But one thing about the conversation had made a strong impression on him. Clement had not sounded like an honest man with nothing to conceal. On the contrary, he had sounded like a worried and guilty man.

Corriston shut his eyes and relaxed for a moment on his cot. It was an uneasy, tormenting kind of relaxation, because another thought had occurred to him.

What if Clement had not deliberately tried to plant a suicide suggestion in his mind at all? What if he had simply spoken with the malice of a not too kindly man appalled and enraged by a space-shock victim who had not only lied to him, but had given every evidence of being dangerously difficult to control.

It certainly made sense. There was nothing in the cell that might have enabled Corriston to take his own life, even had he been so inclined. Would not Clement have taken care to introduce into the cell some convenient, readily available weapon—a steel file, perhaps or even a small spool of wire?

A cold dream had begun to take possession of Corriston. Was it true then, could it possibly be true? Was he hallucinating? He had seen Helen Ramsey go into a ladies' lounge and disappear. He had seen her a second time, and she had worn a mask. The mask was so strange that it would have made four men out of five question their own sanity. But he had knelt beside her and lifted her into his arms. He had felt the pulse at her wrist. Well? If after that she had disappeared again, was it not more of a black mark against him than if he had failed to touch her at all?

All hallucinations seem real to the insane. The realer they seem the more likely they are to be inescapably damning.

Could a warped mind hope to escape from such a dilemma? Was there any possible way of making sure? No, not if he had actually cracked up. But supposing he hadn't. Suppose he had just passed for an instant over the borderline, as a result of strain, of abnormal circumstances, and was now completely rational again. In that case, proof would help. Proof could convince him that at least a part of what had happened had been real, that he had not been hallucinating continuously for days.

If he could prove conclusively that he had not been hallucinating when he had climbed through the grate, Helen Ramsey's presence beyond the grate would be pretty well established. Even an insane man does not abandon all logic when he performs a complicated act. He is not likely to ascend a ten-foot wall and climb through a grate in pursuit of a complete illusion.

Oh, it *could* happen...possibly it had happened many times in hospitals for the incurably insane. But somehow he could not believe that it had happened in his case. Right at this moment he was certainly not in an abnormal state of mind. How could he be when he was able to think so logically and consistently?

Being sane now, or at least having the firm conviction that he was sane, would enable him to retrace what had happened step by step. What if he were to retrace it in reality...until he came to the grate? If the grate had been ripped out, the torment and uncertainty in his mind would vanish. He would be free then to move against Clement, to unmask and expose him for the scoundrel he was.

Free? The very thought was a mockery. He was free for twenty feet in either direction, free to shout and summon the guard. But beyond that . . .

Corriston sat up straight. Free to summon the guard. Free to summon a man he had dropped to the floor with two quick, decisive and totally unexpected blows. But if he did summon the guard, what then? Could he be doubled up with cramps—the old prisoners' dodge? "Get me to a doctor. I think I'm dying."

Hell no, not that. It was mildewed even on the face of it. The guard wouldn't be that much of a fool. He'd whip out a gun, and slash downward with it at the first suspicious move on the part of a man he hated.

Was there any other way? Perhaps there was...a quite simple way. Why couldn't he simply ask the guard to step into the cell and request permission to talk to him? He would plead urgency, but do it very casually, arouse the man's curiosity without antagonizing him too much. No need to be crafty, await some unlikely opportunity, or anything of the sort.

Simply overpower the man—straight off, without any fuss.

It had happened before, but that very fact would make the guard contemptuous, more than ever convinced that the first time he hadn't really been taken by surprise at all. His pride would make him want to believe that. He was the kind of man who could rationalize a humiliating defeat and blot it completely from his memory.

It not only worked, it worked better than he could have dared hope. When he spoke a few words through the door, the guard became instantly curious. He unlocked the cell and came in, his eyes narrowed in anger...anger, but not suspicion. His gun remained on his hip as he walked up to Corriston and stood directly facing him, well within grappling range.

"Well, what do you want to talk to me about?" he demanded. "Better make it brief. I'm not supposed to talk to you at all."

"I'm sorry to hear that," Corriston said. "You've got no idea how depressing it is to be locked up in a narrow cell with absolutely no one to talk to."

"You don't like it, eh? Well, you brought it on yourself."

Corriston caught the man about the waist and brought his right fist down three times on his curving back. Each blow was a powerful one, slanting downward toward the kidney.

Then Corriston hit the guard directly in the small of the back with an even more punishing blow. The cumulative effect was instantaneous. The guard collapsed and sank down like a suddenly deflated balloon, the breath whistling from between his teeth.

Corriston watched him sink to the floor and straighten out. Forewarned as he was, he was still appalled by the almost instant, shocking change in the man's expression. For the second time the guard's features began to come apart. The entire upper portion of his face seemed to sink inward and broaden out, and the flowing began, the incredible refusal of his forehead and nose to remain in close proximity to his mouth.

One eye closed completely; the other remained open in a wide and almost pupil-less stare. The chin receded and the lips became a puckered gray orifice that looked like some monstrous fungus growth sprouting from the middle of a gargoyle face. The individual features became, paler and paler as they spread, and suddenly there seemed to be no color left in the face at all. It had turned completely waxen.

It was a horrifying thing to watch.

Corriston knelt, opened the man's shirt and stared intently at the exposed throat, something he had not done the first time in the cafeteria. The first time he had simply knelt and searched under the shirt with his hand for a heartbeat which had surprised him by its steadiness. He was quite sure now that the heart was beating firmly and steadily.

Even the peculiar appearance of the throat did not alarm him. But it most certainly did interest him. Far down on the Security Guard's throat, just above his breastbone, were a row of small hooks partly embedded in his flesh. The hooks were very tiny indeed, and their brightness was obscured by a thin film of sweat. Corriston removed the moisture with a quick flick of his thumb and continued, to stare, as if he could not quite believe his eyes.

Finally he wedged his fingers under the base of the mask, and ripped it from the guard's face.

Under the mask, the face had a perfectly natural look. The features were relaxed and vacuous, but there was no flowing, no unnatural distortion at all. And it was quite a different face—the face of a man who had worn a disguise and was now so completely a stranger to Corriston that he might just as well have been anyone of the Station's thirty-seven Security Guards.

Corriston could see where the hook attachments had gone into the flesh in at least thirty places on the man's face: on his brow, his cheekbones, on both sides of his face clear down to the base of his neck. The tiny punctures made by the hooks were faintly rimmed with blood, perhaps because Corriston had torn the mask away too abruptly. Undoubtedly the skin had been anaesthetized, the hooks inserted skillfully by someone familiar with just what should be done to prevent scarring.

He hoped that the guard would not carry tiny scars on his face for the rest of his natural life. He arose and examined the mask. He had a complete false face.

The thing was ingenious beyond belief. It was no mere Halloween assemblage of papier-mâché flimflammery, but an elaborate and flexible mask of very thin plastic, or possibly metal. A prosthetic mask—if one could use that term in connection with a mask. It was certainly more complex in structure than any prosthetic leg or arm he had ever seen on a handicapped man, or would ever be likely to see.

He had a pretty good idea as to how it worked. A general idea. Apparently when the hooks were attached to the muscular structure of the human face underneath, every aspect of the wearer's face would be instantly controlled and altered to conform to the configuration of the false face. In that sense the mask could be said to actually mold itself to the wearer's face and transform it into a completely new and different face.

And yet, in some subtle way, the emotions felt by the owner of the real face would be conveyed to the mask, so that it would express with different features very much the same kinds of emotion.

Ingenious was scarcely the word for it. It was a miracle of technological science, almost beyond belief. But he could not doubt the reality of what he saw, for he held the evidence in his hand. No hallucination could possibly be *that* real.

The way the mask's surface coloration could change when the wearer's emotions changed was perhaps the most amazing miracle of all. He had seen the guard's color come and go, had watched him redden with anger and then grow pale.

It could only mean that there was some mechanically symbiotic, emotion-sensitive electronic coating or skin surface, or series of tubes on the inner surface of the mask, which could simulate actual blood flow much like a network of tiny heat regulators. This network would be so responsive to the slightest change in body temperature that the mask would alter its color the instant the wearer experienced fright or grew uncontrollably angry. What made it seem logical and even likely was the fact that caloric changes do occur in just such a fashion in the human body with every shift from anger to grief or from pain to shock.

There was nothing simple about the inner surface of the mask. It was a maze of complicated gadgetry concentrated in less than eight inches of space, perhaps thirty or forty separate mechanisms in all, some as tiny as the head of a pin, and others about one inch in width.

When the wearer became unconscious, the mask seemingly lost its integrity. The gadgets either stopped functioning or ceased to function properly and the false face became a dissolving, hideous caricature; that bore little or no resemblance to the human countenance in repose, or even to the human countenance convulsed with sudden shock.

How incredibly blind he had been in failing to suspect the existence of a mask when the guard's face had grown unnatural and ghastly in the cafeteria. He had taken it for granted that it was the man himself who had changed.

Fortunately he was spared now from making the same mistake twice, and he took full advantage of the fact. He knelt again and began the by no means easy task of removing the uniform. He had to lift him up and turn him over twice and each time the man groaned and stirred a little. He seemed on the verge of coming to, but Corriston shut his mind to the possibility until the last of the man's garments had been tossed in a pile on the floor.

He quickly took off his own uniform then, and carefully and methodically arrayed himself as a guard, taking care to leave the coat unbuttoned at the throat and even going so far as to draw on the heavy woolen socks and attach to his wrist the guard's metal identification disk.

An audacious thought occurred to him, but he dismissed it at once. He could not attach the mask to his own face. It would have required the administrations of an expert, or, at the very least, someone familiar with the thing and who knew exactly how it was supposed to be hooked into place. He had no way of knowing and he recoiled instinctively from the thought of hooks, however tiny, marring the skin on his face.

No, he'd have to get along without the mask. No one on the lower levels knew him by sight, with the one ugly exception of a killer he'd never seen clearly enough to recognize in return. And in the guard's uniform he might even succeed in deceiving the killer if he moved quickly enough to give the man only a brief glimpse of him as he crossed the wide-view promenade.

CHAPTER TEN

CORRISTON stared down at the still unconscious guard, lying stretched out unclothed on the floor of the cell, then he turned, patting the guard's gun which now nestled in its transferred holster on his angular, bony hip.

Well, there were perhaps even worse ways of ending up, and it was certainly a destiny almost universally shared.

He walked out through the open door of the cell without a backward glance. He had changed his plans completely now. The complicated structure of the mask between his hands had so completely reassured him as to his complete sanity, that he was no longer under a compulsion to return to the Selector Compartment for additional proof.

All of the pieces were coming together and melting into a pattern that remained obscure only because there was still so much about it that he did not understand. He knew there was a killer loose on the Station, the same one who had been loose on the ship that had taken him to the Station. He knew about a poisoned barb that had killed one man and had barely missed killing Corriston himself.

Dismiss the killer for the moment. There was Helen Ramsey, the wealthiest girl on Earth. Think about Ramsey himself and what his wealth had done to Mars. Think about the colonists on Mars, men who had endured unimaginable hardships and privation to stake out uranium claims that Ramsey did not want them to have. Think about the freighter that had gone out of control.

Think about Clement. Think very hard about Clement.

The tragedy had shaken him, had given him the look of a very guilty man. He had not wanted it to happen. He had been alarmed, appalled. Yes, think about Clement—that very secretive man.

The killer? You can't get rid of him, can you? He keeps coming back into your mind. The killer had not tried to spare

Helen Ramsey. He had killed her bodyguard and ripped a mask from her face. No attempt at protection there. But Clement could not have known about that. He had evidently been searching for Helen Ramsey himself. The news that she had been found had startled him, had given him a visible jolt.

Corriston did not think that the pattern would dissolve. A few of its features were becoming too clear now, the implications too inescapable. There was something going on that was ugly at the core of it, and the coming of the killer had simply brought it out into the open. Not too much into the open as yet perhaps, but the handwriting on the wall had at least become almost readable. Perhaps the accident to the freighter had also helped to bring it into the open. In some obscure way everything seemed to dovetail: Ramsey; the situation on Mars; Clement and the freighter; a twice disappearing Helen Ramsey; and an accusation of space-shock which was completely false and unjustified. Each seemed to hover just above the center of a very definite pattern.

And so did the masks! The masks in particular. Think, think hard about the masks and what the very existence of such masks on the Station implied.

The masks could only have been designed to cover the darkest deceit, to cover the most terrifying treachery.

How many officers and enlisted men on the Station were wearing masks? How many? And why? Was every officer on the Station wearing one? If the masks were thought necessary, if their employment had been made mandatory, there could be only one explanation.

Every officer and every enlisted man was masquerading. The Station was officered and manned by—a word he'd never liked from a dictionary of obsolete American slang came unbidden into his mind—phonies!

The thought staggered him. For a moment he rejected it as inconceivable, outside the bounds of reason. But it remained on the perimeter of his consciousness and would not be dislodged. It came back and set itself down where its dominance over his mind could not be contested.

What else could it mean? Masks have only one purpose: to enable the wearer to avoid being recognized.

Quite obviously the phony officers could be wearing masks for only one reason: to conceal their real identities while they manned the Stations, carrying on the tasks of the men they had displaced.

Carrying on the tasks of the rightful officers, but with a difference. And that difference would almost certainly be criminal activity on a wide and daring scale. The only question remaining to be answered was how high did that activity ascend? Did it ascend to the very top, to Commander Clement himself?

Fortunately, the violence of space is a controlled violence, and determined men can slip through it with tools and building materials. They can base themselves on zero-gravity construction rafts and take refuge in pressurized crevices, go Boating along steel girders five hundred feet in length until there has been assembled the greatest of all miracles—a manned Space Station a thousand feet in diameter encircling Earth at a distance of fifteen hundred miles.

The Station had not been built in space, it had been built on Earth section by section. However, the final task of putting it together had been left to the Boating men in their fishbowl helmets, the suicide brigade with their incredible vacuum equipment and remote control welding arms.

Fifty-seven sections had been built on Earth over a period of five years, thirty-four in the Eastern United States, the rest in scattered localities from Chicago to the Gold Coast. They had all been sent up by step rockets into the same narrow orbit around Earth. They were fifty-seven sections "crash landing" in a total vacuum, weightless and yet with sufficient mass and inertia to keep them in close proximity until the great task could get under way.

The assembled Station was cone-shaped, and it had been a colossal undertaking to keep it from developing stress defects over a third of its bulk during the early constructional stages. Under the guidance of experts, the problem had, been solved, but at a tragic price.

Assembling the Station had cost the lives of fifty-three men, for there is no easy way to bring together, join, seal and make safe tons of metal and plastic, intricate machinery and equipment, plus a thousand-and-one small, incidental contrivances fifteen hundred miles above the emergency-alert systems and hospital facilities of

Earth.

Some of the men who had lost their lives had been blown out of transport rocket tubes by mistake. Some had missed their footing too close to a welding operation that had been halted too late. Some had floated into capsules full of nitric oxygen gas under high pressure and had failed to veer away in time. Still others had tugged too strenuously at heavy girders and the slow, but crushing inertia of an enormous, backward-swinging beam in free fall had ripped their space suits asunder and fractured their spines.

There were five thousand ways of dying in space. But the sacrifice, the terror, the tragic toll seemed immeasurably remote now, for the roar of the incoming and outgoing ships made the Station a gigantic reality so completely in the present that it seemed to have no past.

Spinning always on its axis, substituting centrifugal force for the gravity tug of Earth, the Station was a complete world, a self-contained macrocosm so immense that the magnetic-shod mechanics who inspected it in relays, the passenger-carrying shuttle rockets from Earth that came and went, and even the thousand-foot ships that berthed for re-fueling and clearance seemed hardly to encroach at all on its vast central bulk.

And yet, it was something quite apart from the Station's bigness which came under worldwide scrutiny when the freighter crashed and was splintered into fragments, channeling a fiery crater in the earth and causing the most disastrous accidental death toll in United States history.

The news was flashed to the four corners of the earth, and almost simultaneously a flight of United States military jets took off from the Lake Superior airport to explore the wreckage.

The first message from the flight commander, Lieutenant Colonel Hackett, came five hours later. It was tense, grim and it minced no words. "Wreckage radioactive. Main cargo uranium in a rough ore state. Explosion and subsequent intense radioactivity apparently caused by an auxiliary cargo of highly unstable uranium isotopes. If the freighter had berthed at the Station the dangerous character of its cargo could not have escaped detection. We have every reason to believe that it intended to berth at the Station. Its signals to the Station, before some undeterminable shipboard accident sent it out of control, confirm this. We must therefore assume complicity of a double nature: by the freighter's commanding officer, Captain James Summerfield, and by someone in a position of high command on the Station."

After that, there was no silencing the slow, relentless events on Earth.

A week after the tragedy, a U. S. Marine corporal stationed at Port Forrestal, Wisconsin, put through a late afternoon phono-view call to his wife. His face on the screen was haggard with strain, and he seemed not to want to meet his wife's gaze.

"We've been ordered out into space," he said.

"You mean they're sending you out to take over the Station?"

"They're sending out five thousand United States Marines," the corporal said. "We all knew it was coming. We expected it when that Governmental Investigating Committee was turned back."

"But it doesn't make sense. I can't understand it. Why should the Commander of the Station refuse to permit a Governmental Investigating Committee to land?"

"We don't know. He must have something to conceal, and you can be pretty sure it's an ugly something. When that freighter disaster got into every daily press conference of the high brass I knew this was coming. I felt it in my bones."

"But what will happen if the Commander refuses to let even the Marines land? What will happen then?"

"We may have to open fire on the Station," the corporal said. "If the Station is in criminal hands we'll have no alternative."

"You talk as if you were in command."

"I guess every soldier talks like that when his life is in jeopardy. But I'm glad I'm not a five-star general. If I had to make a decision like that—"

But it wasn't a general who made the crucial decision. It was Admiral John Hayes, Commander of the Eighth Spatial Naval Division, acting on behalf of fifty-seven nations.

He stood in the bridge room of a United States naval cruiser of massive tonnage, staring out through a wide-view observation port at the Station's glimmering immensity. The cruiser and the Station were moving at almost the same speed, fifteen thousand miles an hour. But now the cruiser was moving just a little faster than the Station, and Admiral Hayes was growing impatient.

Maneuvering into an orbital position almost directly abreast of the Station had been difficult. Commander Hayes' nerves were badly frayed; and he was not a man who could endure too much frustration. He had signaled the Station twice and received no reply. During that time, both the Station and the Cruiser had completely encircled the Earth at an interval of just a little under two hours.

He turned suddenly from the viewport, his lips set in tight lines. He stared for an instant in silence at the young officer at his side, his mind groping for an argument that would completely justify what he had already decided he must do.

But Lieutenant Commander Kenneth Archer spoke first, saying quietly: "You have no choice, sir."

Hayes' features relaxed a little. It was good to know that he had support from a man whose judgment he respected. For an instant the awful aloneness that went with supreme command weighed less heavily upon him.

"It's absolute defiance, open rebellion," Hayes said. "I'm forced to assume that the Station is in criminal hands. We'll never know, probably, just what happened on board that freighter. But we do know that accidents occur. For every thirty ships that berth securely, one meets with some kind of navigational mishap. The damage isn't always irreparable. More often than not, in fact, it's quite minor. Usually it means only a delay in berthing, a navigational shift, a circling back for another try. But apparently that freighter really had it. So it gave the show away. Commander Clement must be in league, hand in glove, with whoever is interested in smuggling unauthorized uranium shipments through to Earth for his own personal profit. And to hasten his immediate profit that someone apparently found it to his advantage to trigger a little of the shipment into highly fissionable material on Mars."

"You know as well as I do who the someone is, sir." Archer said.

"I guess we both know. But right now my only concern is with the Station. If they ignore my third order to stand by for boarding I'll have to open fire. The Station's stolen property just as long as it remains in criminal hands. You can't get a desperate criminal to surrender your property unless you convince him his own life is in danger. I've got to try my best to convince Commander Clement I mean business without destroying the Station."

"You'll damage it to some extent, sir. How bad do you think it will be?"

"I don't know. I don't intend to launch an atomic warhead. But I can't stop short of that if he stays stubborn. I've no way of knowing what his breaking point will be. But I do know that if he keeps control of the Station he'll be in a position to wipe out New York or London."

"But you'll make your intentions unmistakably clear before you open fire, sir?"

"Yes," Hayes said, wearily. "Yes…of course I will."

CHAPTER ELEVEN

CORRISTON took a deep breath and let it out slowly. So far luck had favored him. Now he felt as though he were walking through a deadly jungle where all the animals had suddenly turned friendly. The teeth they bared at him were smiling. The grins were their masks. But the commander didn't pretend at all . . . whoever the commander really was!

And then that single question began to gnaw at Corriston like some rat feeding on his flesh: Where was the real Clement now? Was he alive? Was he accessible? Or was he dead?

Corriston's mental processes were now governed by the most evanescent of impressions: the depth of the shadows on both sides of the corridor; his own shadow lengthening before him; the drone of machinery deep within the Station; the muffled beating of his own heart. Suddenly he was at the end of the corridor and approaching the main control room, his face as grim as death.

Violence he had determined upon, but it would be a very brief, a very effective kind of violence. It takes only a second to rip a mask from a man's face.

Something was happening just outside the main control room door. The three executive officers guarding the door had moved eight or ten paces down the corridor, and the door itself was standing ajar. The executive officers had their backs turned to Corriston and were making no attempt to conceal their agitation. They were very pale, at least, one of them was. Two had their backs completely turned, but Corriston caught a brief glimpse of the third man's profile, and it seemed completely drained of color, as if the mask had stopped mirroring emotion artificially and had allowed the wearer's actual pallor to seep through.

Corriston glided quickly to the door, passed through it and shut it very quietly behind him.

The commander had his back turned too. He was standing before the viewport, staring out into space.

But the commander did seem dazed, did seem stunned. Corriston could tell by his posture, by the way he held his shoulders, by the utter rigidity of his neck.

Then he saw it, the long cylindrical hull touched by a pale glimmer of starlight, the circular, glowing ports, the massive, atomic-projectile launching turrets at its base. He saw it through the viewport, saw it past the commander's stiffening shoulders—an American war cruiser of formidable tonnage and armed with sufficient firepower to shatter a small moon.

All right, let the Big Dark contain it for a moment, poised out there, ready for any contingency. Right at the moment a scoundrel must be unmasked in a very stark way. Whatever trouble he had brought upon himself, he must be made to face it now without the mask.

Corriston unholstered his gun and walked toward the commander across the deck. He came up behind him and thrust the gun into the small of his back.

"Turn around," he ordered. "Don't make any other move. Just turn slowly and face me. I want to take a good look at your face."

If the commander was startled, he didn't show it. Perhaps the war cruiser had dealt him such a crushing blow that he was no longer capable of experiencing shock. Or his control may have been extraordinary. Corriston had no way of knowing and it didn't concern him too much.

He was chiefly interested in the commander's eyes. He had never before seen eyes quite so piercing in their stare or narrowed in quite such an ugly way.

The commander spoke almost instantly and his voice had a steel-cold rasp. "Well?" he said.

Just a few words—just the shortest possible question he could have asked.

Corriston said: "You're wearing a mask, aren't you, commander?"

The impostor's expression did not change, but his hand went instinctively to his throat.

"Remove your tie and unbutton your collar," Corriston said.

The man made another quick gesture with his hand in the direction of his throat. But it seemed involuntary, protective, for he did not touch his collar.

Corriston shifted his weapon a little, moving the barrel upward until it pressed very firmly against the commander's breastbone. He reached out and unbuttoned the commander's collar with his free hand, very quickly and expertly.

He was staring at the tiny hooks at the base of the mask when something happened which made him regret that he had not followed his original intention of instantly ripping the mask from the man's face.

The door opened and the three executive officers came into the control room. For an instant they seemed neither to see nor understand the situation. They must have seen Corriston, but the fact that he was wearing a guard's uniform may have given them the idea that he had every right to be there. The gun was concealed from view and the commander was standing very quietly by the viewport and quite obviously incapable of making any move, simply because the slightest move would have endangered his life.

So the executive officers went right on talking for an instant, half to themselves and half to the commander, just as if Corriston had not been present at all.

"If that cruiser lands, Ramsey's goose is cooked and ours is too," a tall officer said. "The instant that freighter crashed I knew they'd find out quickly enough how the ships had been carrying smuggled uranium. I knew that under pressure, half of our captains would talk . . . and the crews, too. All the government would have to do is check and they'd find out that we're Ramsey's men, all of us. They might even now know about the masks."

"Why not about the masks?" another officer joined in. "Ramsey paid for the research that went into them, didn't he? Big tycoon . . . fingers in a dozen pies. When the secret's out, and he puts them on the market, he'll make important money out of it. But we'll be in prison with just our own faces staring back at us from a steel wall."

"Don't worry about that. Ramsey won't profit from the manufacture of masks. He won't even profit from the false uranium clearance we gave him. If that cruiser is allowed to land he'll be in prison with us."

"Better think that over, Commander. You refused to let the

Governmental Investigating Committee land. If a single soldier sets foot on the Station we're done for. It's not too late to do something about it. That cruiser can only berth by overtaking us. If we change our orbit fast and start blasting at them with our rear adjusting rockets they'll have to keep their distance…"

"Aren't you forgetting something? A single atomic warhead could blow the Station apart."

"We've got to risk that. They'll think a long time before they'll go that far. The Station's not expendable. If we change our orbit we can still make contact with the Mars ship that's due to berth in an hour. We've got to get back to Mars and whatever protection Ramsey can give us. We'll have his daughter with us. He'll be so glad to see her he'll go out on a limb to protect us."

"He'd go out on a limb anyway. He'd have to in order to save himself. But sure, we'll take the girl. No harm in that. He knows she's here and will be expecting her. He'll thank us for taking things so quickly in hand. If that crazy lieutenant had made his story public that cruiser would have been out there anyway—perhaps even sooner. They'd have wanted to know on Earth why anyone would want to harm Ramsey's daughter, something we don't know ourselves.

Corriston decided then that he'd kept silent long enough.

He returned his gun to its holster, and walked up to the three executive officers, completely ignoring the commander. He heard the commander threaten him in a low tone, heard him say words which would have caused some men to pause in fear. But Corriston did not turn.

There was stunned disbelief in the eyes of the three men facing him. He spoke quickly, knowing that he had only a moment before the commander would see that he was seized and restrained. He had to make sure that the three would hear him out, that the commander would not be instantly obeyed. Perhaps he couldn't make sure, but at least he could try.

"I'll make a bargain with you," he said. "I've done reckless things but I'm not a complete fool. You're going to prevent that cruiser from berthing and I won't be able to interfere. I'm just one man against several hundred. All three of you are armed. If I started shooting I'd get perhaps two of you—no more. Then you'd

143

kill me. I haven't even the advantage of surprise. I gave that up because I can't believe you're complete fools either.

"First, I want to see Helen Ramsey. I want you to let me talk to her. And when the Mars ship berths, I want to go to Mars with her. I've something to offer in return."

One of the officers stared at him, tightened his lips and stared harder. "Good God!" he muttered. "Good God! A bargain. You must be out of your mind. What could you possibly offer? If you had a gun trained on us—"

"A witness in your defense," Corriston said. "A witness who will stand up in court and swear that you did try to protect Helen Ramsey, that you saved her from a very great danger. You may think that you do not need a witness now, but before the year is out Ramsey will be on trial for his life. His wealth won't save him. They know too much about him now. That freighter explosion killed too many people. The public outcry will be too great.

"If you stay on Mars you'll be hunted down like wild animals. They'll get you in the end and you know it. You'll be brought back to Earth; you'll stand trial."

Corriston paused for the barest instant, knowing that the commander too was listening, knowing from the absence of sound and movement behind him that his words were being weighed. "I think you know that I would not break my word. I'll stand up in court and defend you under oath. I'll be speaking the simple truth. You did save Helen Ramsey from a very great danger; you probably saved her life. That is sure to weigh in your favor with any impartial judge and jury. You won't get the death penalty; I can promise you that."

It was the commander who spoke first. He said, very quietly. "He's right, of course. Completely right."

One of the officers nodded. "There's no reason why we shouldn't let him talk to the girl. We can decide later whether we like his offer."

"We're going to like it," the commander said, coming around in front of Corriston. "He has more sense than I would have given him credit for."

"So have you, commander," Corriston said, and meant it.

The commander's eyes were still hostile, unfriendly, but the cold rage had gone out of them.

"All right," he said. "Let him see the girl now. Make sure a guard is stationed at the door. Keeping that cruiser from berthing won't be easy. They'll keep the Station under fire with small projectiles, even if they don't attack us with atomic warheads. They'll risk some damage just to throw a scare into us."

The officer next to Corriston nudged his arm. "All right," he said. "But remember this when you talk to her. She doesn't know the truth about us. She doesn't even know we're wearing masks. We'd like it better if you didn't say anything about it."

"Whether she knows it or not isn't too important," Corriston said. "I suppose you wouldn't care to tell me what you've done with Commander Clement and the other officers."

"No, we wouldn't care to tell you. Anything more?"

"I guess not," Corriston said. "Take me to her."

CHAPTER TWELVE

HE WAS STARING at her across a shadowed room, with the pale glimmer of a cabin viewport above her right shoulder, a very small port that looked like a full moon glimmering high in the sky through a sea of mist.

Her face was very white and she was staring back at him as if he had come suddenly out of nowhere.

She hesitated only an instant and then walked straight toward him, walked right up to him and touched him gently on the face.

"I'm so glad," she said.

She drew back then and looked at him and smiled. "I was afraid you were in trouble because of me," she said, "some terrible kind of trouble, and I couldn't help you at all. I kept blaming myself for everything foolish that I had ever done, going way back to the day when I broke my first doll, deliberately and spitefully, because I was a very headstrong little girl."

"I'm afraid I've always been pretty headstrong myself," Corriston said. "But being a boy, I naturally couldn't break dolls. I just wrecked the family's peace of mind."

"We all go through life with a great deal of foolish luggage," she said. "And sometimes you have an impulse to just drop everything—and run away."

"I can understand that," Corriston said. "But did you have to run away quite so fast? It's hard to believe it was for anybody's good, including your own."

"It might have been," she said. "It might have been for my good and then later, partly for your good. Please don't judge me too harshly before I've had a chance to tell you exactly what happened."

He reached out for her and kissed her even as she came into his arms. He had expected her to be angry, to withdraw, but instead she encircled his strong back with a surprising fierceness. When he released her, her eyes were shining.

"I'm glad you did that...darling! Very glad. But we're still in trouble."

"I know that. But we're in love, too. And you just promised to tell me what happened."

"Well, I guess I just...just regressed."

"You what?"

"Regressed. You know, like when I was a headstrong little brat of a child. We all do that at times. You'll have to admit there was some excuse for me. You weren't born in a house with a hundred rooms, with servants always coming and going, and outside gardens with big red and yellow flowers where you couldn't even run and hide without being smothered, without being searched for and brought screaming and kicking back inside.

"You don't know what it means to know you haven't a father, only a stern, cold, black-coated man standing away of in the darkness somewhere and watching people bow down before him.

"You don't know what it means to be told: 'You're Stephen Ramsey's daughter. *Behave. Behave. Behave!*'"

"I scarcely ever saw my father. And when I did see him he was as cold as one of the slabs in the big mausoleum he took so much pride in, the big family mausoleum which only a Ramsey was permitted to visit. And yet I think he loved me in his own cold way. I think he still does."

She fell silent for a moment and then an overpowering need to tell Corriston more seemed to come upon her.

"I was never allowed to see young men, not even to go for a ride in the park. Anyone of them might be a fortune seeker, because no young man, even if he is madly in love with a girl, can quite shut his eyes to wealth as one additional reason for loving her.

"So I never saw any young men. I wasn't permitted to even go to a dance, or walk in the moonlight on a balcony. I wanted to go to dances, wanted at least one young man to kiss me damned hard."

"Sure you did," Corriston said. I understand."

"I'm going to stop right there, darling. I could tell you what it means to be free to travel, anywhere, anywhere in the world and to see all of the white and shining cities, and to be intoxicated by beauty, and to know at the same time that you are not free, can never hope to be free as other people are free."

"And that's why you ran away."

"Yes, darling, yes, and because that bodyguard was a complete fool. He was just one of thirty bodyguards my father had hired to protect me, year after year. But he was the biggest fool of all. He drank too much and he talked too much. Finally I made up my mind that I would be better off if I went on to Mars alone. My father had told me I could come, the trip had been carefully planned down to the smallest detail. I was to travel incognito. I was to keep to myself until I arrived at the Station and no one was supposed to know I was even on the ship, not even the captain. I'm quite sure he didn't know. I think the invitation to his cabin was a complete fabrication. In fact, I'm sure it was. I think Clakey—his real name was Ewers—was just drunk enough to make up a crazy story like that to get me away from you.

"But I didn't want to get away from you, darling. I wanted to get away from him. I wanted to have a few days of complete freedom before I arrived on Mars, and perhaps after that for a day in the colony before I joined my father. I didn't care how angry he'd be when he saw me without a bodyguard, alone, wonderfully, gloriously alone and free for the first time in my life. I didn't want to be Helen Ramsey at all. I wanted to be somebody else and be completely free.

"So I went into the ladies room, darling, and I put on the strangest kind of mask."

"Yes," Corriston said. "I know."

"You know about the mask?"

"Please go on," Corriston said. "I'd rather you didn't ask me how I know that your father can take pride in at least constructive achievement. The masks are extraordinary. I've seen one."

"But how? Where? I can't believe it. I—"

"Please," Corriston said. "It isn't too important. I made a necessary promise that I wouldn't tell you, not immediately. I'm asking you to trust me and go on."

"Well, I secured one of those very unusual masks. From the Gresham-Ramsey Laboratories, before we left Earth. I could go there anytime I wanted to. All of the research technicians there are quite old. One of them, Thomas Webb, is really quite handsome. I might have fallen in love with him if he had been forty years younger. He showed me just how to adjust the mask. But when I went into the ladies' lounge I had more than just a mask. I had a complete thin plastic change of clothing concealed under my dress. I didn't remove my dress, only reversed my clothing so that the plastic dress covered the one I'd been wearing."

Corriston said. "It was a very courageous thing for you to do."

"I'm glad you think so, darling. Because when I came out of the lounge and saw Ewers killed, I wasn't courageous at all. I became panic-stricken, terrified, beside myself with fear. I knew that my father had many dangerous enemies. I knew that I was in immediate, deadly danger. I had to go on with the disguise then. I had to go right on being somebody else. I couldn't tell anyone. I couldn't even tell you. I had to let you think that in some strange, bewildering way I had gone into the lounge and disappeared.

"I knew you wouldn't really believe that, not for a moment. But I didn't know what you'd think. I could have told you, I suppose, but I was afraid it would only make the danger greater, might transfer some of the danger to you. And I didn't know you'd go straight to the captain and get yourself into trouble. There were rumors on the Station that you'd been confined, put under guard. But they were only rumors. I felt I had to see you, talk to you. I was half out of my mind with anxiety. I bribed one of the guards to let me out of the quarantine cage and went in search of you.

"I searched everywhere, followed passageways at random, got lost in a maze of machinery."

"And someone followed you," Corriston said. "He followed you and tore the mask from your face."

She looked at him with wide, startled eyes. "How did you know?"

"I was there," Corriston said. "You fainted and I took you into my arms—for the very first time. You didn't know that, did you?"

"How could I have known? If what you say is true, I—"

Helen Ramsey did not complete what she had started to say. Had she done so she might not have been thrown so abruptly off-balance by the suddenly lurching deck; she would have moved closer to Corriston and could have seized hold of his shoulders for

149

support.

She did not fall, but she nearly did, and the lurch sent her tottering all the way to the opposite wall. Corriston saw her collide with the wall and sink to her knees. At the same instant his own knees collapsed.

He was lying sprawled out on the deck, too startled and shaken to go immediately to her aid, when the second lurch came. It spun him about, and then he was sliding. He couldn't seem to stop the sliding. He went all the way to the opposite wall too.

For a brief instant they were together again, locked in a desperate embrace, their legs higher than their heads. Then the deck righted itself and the bombardment began.

It was a terrifying thing to have to listen to, and Corriston preferred to listen to it on his feet. Slowly he arose and helped his companion up, holding her in so tight a grip that it seemed to them that they had been welded together and could never part.

He was glad that he could be completely sure of one thing. It wasn't a nuclear bombardment—not yet. The cruiser was merely shelling the Station. When the cruiser launched an atomic warhead he'd know about it—rather, he wouldn't know. The fact that he was still alive and aware of what was going on told him a great deal about the nature of the bombardment.

"What is it?" Helen Ramsey whispered. "Do you know?"

"We're the catspaw in a naval attack," Corriston said. The commander took a very great risk."

It was incredible, but right at the moment he felt himself to be in the scoundrel's corner. He didn't want the Station to be blown apart in the great empty spaces between the planets any more than the commander did.

When Corriston reached the viewport and stared out, the cruiser was following the Station far off to the side, in an obvious effort to outmaneuver it by maintaining a parallel rather than a directly pursuing course. But it was not escaping the swiftly turning Station's stem rocket jets. Blinding bursts of incandescence spiraled toward it through the void, and once or twice scored direct hits.

He saw the cruiser shudder throughout its length, and then draw back, almost as if it were endowed with life and had nerves and arteries that could be ripped apart.

There were mechanical arteries that could easily enough be ripped. For an instant Corriston stared with a strange kind of detachment, freed from the terrible tension and uncertainty by his absolute absorption in the battle itself, freed from the almost mind-numbing sense of participating in a struggle that could end in utter disaster for Station and cruiser alike. He knew that if the cruiser maneuvered in too close, the puffs of flame from the Station's jets could turn into superheated gases roaring through space, destroying everything in their path.

The Station, too, was only a pulse beat from fiery annihilation. And a pulse beat could be terrifyingly brief. But the decision had been made and there could be no turning back.

Aboard the cruiser the decision had certainly come from very high up. Corriston turned the thought slowly over in his mind, still in the grip of his strange detachment. Just what did "very high up" mean?

It meant—it had to mean—a conflict of personalities, the hot-headedness or stubbornness or glory seeking that went with every decision made by strong-willed men.

Aboard the cruiser, someone had acted. After consultation? On just an impulse? In blind rage because the Station had ignored a warning that had been repeated twice?

There was no way of knowing. But on the cruiser men were dying. That was important too. Just how reckless had the decision been?

In space, military science has never been an exact science. Sonic echoes alone can kill, and in a pressurized compartment blowups happen. Jet-supports can be placed at the best of all possible angles and still fly off into space. Compressed air shot out of pressure vents can turn bone and flesh into soft oozing jelly.

The cruiser was changing its course again. It had failed, in a maneuver, twice repeated, to draw close at almost right angles to the Station, and had taken terrible punishment from below, above and straight ahead.

But the cruiser was still firing. And Corriston not only saw the bursts of flame, he felt the blasts in his eardrums, his brain, and the soles of his feet. And suddenly he saw flames darting out directly beneath him, and knew that the Station was on fire.

Corriston knew that at any moment he could be smashed back against a bone-crushing wall of metal; he could be pulverized, asphyxiated, driven mad. And the fear in him—the fear that he wouldn't be able to control—would be a two-edged sword.

There was no pain more ghastly than the final burst of agony that came with a burst open nervous system. It was the most horrible way to die. But even dying that way wouldn't be half as bad as watching the woman he loved die.

Almost as if aware of his thoughts, Helen spoke to him for the first time since he had crossed to the viewport.

"It's very strange, darling. I'm calmer now than I have ever been. I guess it can happen if you love a man so very much that you know your life would have no meaning if anything should happen to him. It's like facing up squarely to the fact that you no longer have any existence apart from him. I've done that, darling, and I'm not afraid."

There was silence in the cabin for an instant. Then another shell exploded, and another, and another. Corriston felt light and dangerously dizzy. It was amazing that he had not been hurled to the floor, still more amazing that he could have remained for so long motionless in just one spot.

Then, abruptly, the bombardment ceased. There was no sound at all in the cabin, just a silence so absolute that the roaring in Corriston's ears was like the sound made by an angry sea beating against vast stone cliffs in a world that had ceased to exist.

There were no longer any exploding white stars coming from the cruiser. It was dwindling into the blackness of space, giving up the battle, conceding defeat. It became thinner and thinner. Suddenly only the reef remained. Where the cruiser had been there stretched only empty space.

Corriston turned from the viewport. He crossed the cabin to the cot, swaying a little, but only from dizziness, and sat down and drew the girl on the cot close to him. He held her tightly, saying nothing.

CHAPTER THIRTEEN

CORRISTON was still sitting on the cot when the door opened and the commander and two officers came into the cabin.

He was not too surprised, for it had been somehow almost impossible for him to believe that the commander could have been killed. A scoundrel's luck and a drunkard's luck were often very much the same thing.

If the commander had succeeded in quickly putting out the fire he rated a medal, he was a man for all of that.

And apparently the commander had succeeded in putting out the fire, or he would not now be facing Corriston with a grimly urgent look on his mask.

Helen Ramsey was staring at him almost as if she were seeing him as he really was for the first time. Did she know that he was wearing a mask? There was no possible way she could know, he told himself, except by intuition. The masks were good. Having worn one herself she ought to know how good they were. She ought not even to suspect the commander unless—

Corriston had no time to finish the thought.

"Get up, both of you," the commander said, gesturing with his braided right arm. "The Mars ship has just berthed. We've got to go aboard before there's any question as to the obedience of the crew. The captain has been taken off, but we're keeping some of the crew."

"You—you put out the fire, Commander?"

"Naturally. I'm not quite the incompetent you think me, Lieutenant."

"I'm quite sure of that, Commander," Corriston said. "Do we take anything with us?"

"You'll get all the extras you need on Mars," the commander said. "Stephen Ramsey isn't likely to want to see his daughter go about in rags."

Corriston decided that the wisest thing he could do was to take the commander at his word in every important respect; for the moment, at any rate. There was the little matter of a killer still at large somewhere on the Station, and the quicker they were in space the safer Ramsey's daughter would be. Not just in space as the Station was in space, but much further out in the Big Dark.

"All right, Commander," he said. "Let's get started."

Getting started took very little time. A great thankfulness came upon Corriston when he saw the smooth dark hull of the Mars ship looming high above him, a thousand-foot long cylinder of inky blackness against a glimmering wilderness of stars.

The ship was berthed securely beneath a towering network of telemetric aerials, on a completely circular launching platform that was like a saucer in reverse, with a contractible metal ramp leading up to the wide-open, brightly lighted boarding port at its base.

There were steps on the ramp, but Corriston knew that when the structure was drawn back into the ship it would collapse like a house of cards, folded back upon itself.

Helen Ramsey ascended first. Corriston made certain that she would by getting in the commander's way with a convincing show of accidental clumsiness. He pretended to stumble as he began the ascent, to be all hands and feet.

The commander swore softly and Corriston was quite sure that he had not been deceived. But there was very little that he could do about it under the circumstances. He had to let Ramsey's daughter climb the ramp first and she was almost at the top before Corriston started up.

Corriston was halfway to the top, and the commander and the impatient, tight-lipped executive officers were just starting up, when three tall figures emerged from the darkness at the base of the ramp.

The attack took place so quickly that it was over almost before it started. The commander and the executive officers didn't have a chance. One of the emerging men had a gun, and he shot the commander in the stomach with it at almost point-blank range.

The commander sank down, clutching at his stomach, bent nearly double. Even from where Corriston was standing, he could see the blood trickling down his right leg. The terrible dark wetness directly over the wound was of course invisible, completely concealed by the commander's tightly laced arms.

The startled, frightened officers turned and tried to get away. But they didn't get far. The man who had shot the commander picked them off like clay pigeons, one by one, as they fled.

His two companions did not even seem to be armed. They just stood quietly watching the executive officers die. They died on the launching platform and on the smooth deck beyond, two of them simply dropping in their tracks, a third sprawling grotesquely, and the last staggering on for a few paces. There were four executive officers, and not one escaped. It was butchery, pure and simple, cruel, savage beyond belief.

Helen Ramsey was already on the ship, and there was no possible way for him to get her off.

The thought that he was himself in the deadliest kind of danger never even crossed his mind.

The killer returned his gun to its holster slowly and deliberately, and then he took it out again. It was a very strange gesture, when every passing second must have been of vital importance to him, but it revealed something very unusual about the man. He evidently liked to feel that he had completed one job and packaged it to his entire satisfaction, before going on to another.

It was that more than anything else that jolted Corriston into complete awareness, and made it impossible for him to doubt the reality, the utter horror, of what had taken place. The killer had gestured to his companions, and he was coming up the ramp.

He came slowly up the ramp, and for the first time Corriston saw his face. It was not a face that he would ever forget or ever want to forget. It was the face of the man he had grappled with in the dark and seen once in the light. But now his features were turned away. It was exactly the kind of face that Corriston had pictured him as having, except that it was just a little uglier looking. The slant of the cheekbones even crueler, harsher, the eyes more venomously narrowed, the mouth an uglier gash.

"All right, Lieutenant," he said, gesturing with the gun. "Go on ahead. Go on board. We're going to need you to help pilot this ship to Mars."

CHAPTER FOURTEEN

THE SILENCE in the chart room was like the hush that comes over a desert when hurricane winds have died down, or like the stillness of a rocky coast when waves have ceased to pound, and dangerous rocks stand out with all of their saw-edged teeth exposed.

It was extraordinary how, at the point of a gun, a man could think and act almost automatically, and postpone making any decision at all. It wasn't cowardice; Corriston was quite sure of that. He felt only anger—deep, relentless, all-consuming. Sweat oozed in droplets from his brow, but it was the heat and the tension that made his skin stream with moisture. There was no immediate fear in him at all.

He'd kept fear at bay by refusing to let his mind leap ahead. Only the gun at his back mattered, and just why it should have mattered so much was the only thing that puzzled him.

It did not occur to him that what some men dread most is the fear of dying too abruptly, without foreknowledge and with just a second's glimpse of something cold and deadly before the final blackout. A gun had that kind of power.

The man with the gun had asked Corriston a great many questions, urgently practical questions that dealt with cold statistics concerning zero-gravity, solar radiation, space drift and the length of time it would take to reach Mars if a single pilot took full advantage of the automatic controls and never allowed himself to become reckless.

Corriston had replied to the best of his ability and knowledge, and the other had accepted his answers with a quiet grunt of satisfaction. It was only after that, when the silence had lengthened almost unendurably between them, that the more personal questions came.

The killer jabbed the gun more firmly against Corriston's spine and asked in a cold, flat voice: "Do you know who I am, Corriston?

Have you any idea?"

Corriston stared out the viewport for a moment without replying, his face deathly pale. "I don't know your name," he said. "Probably that's not too important. I do know that you're a cold-blooded murderer, and that killing gives you pleasure. I am very tired. I wish you wouldn't question me any more."

"Do you think you can pilot this ship to Mars, tired as you are?"

Corriston nodded.

The pressure of the gun barrel diminished. "I am very glad—for your sake. I suppose I might as well tell you my name. It's Henley, Richard Henley. We'll be seeing a lot of each other before this trip is ended, but you'll find that I'm not a particularly talkative man. When I have something important to say, though, I won't leave you in any doubt as to what I want done. Right now I must warn you that I would just as soon kill you as not."

"You're lying," Corriston said. "If you killed me now you'd never get to Mars. You need me and you know it."

"Corriston."

"Yes."

"Don't assume too much. There are practical advantages in keeping you alive but a wrong move on your part could outweigh them. I'd have a fair chance of getting to Mars without your help. I know more than you think about spatial navigation. And the automatic controls are far from unreliable. Without them it would take at least five men to pilot a ship this size to Mars. With their aid a single experienced pilot should be able to accomplish it. I'm pretty sure you've had enough officer training school to qualify as a pilot. A ship's inspection officer has to be able to navigate a ship; I've checked on that. But you're certainly no expert, and if you force my hand I'll take my chance with the auto-controls and my own limited knowledge."

"You'll be taking a chance, all right," Corriston said.

"What would you do if the observation glass started showing small pits in the hull from a very large shower of micrometeorites? Can the auto-controls stop those pits from spreading? I've seen a ship stippled all over in less than ten minutes. The meteor guards won't deflect micro-meteorites, and you've got to alter your velocity and angle of drive and a lot of other things fast. And what happens when your instruments start showing light spectra peculiarities that can't be measured in angstroms? Just a little oddity like that can force you to change your course, but the autopilot won't know a thing about it.

"And when you hit the Martian atmosphere and start firing against the direction of motion, how much good do you think limited knowledge will do you? Remember, nearly all of the journey will have been made in free fall, and in free fall the auto-controls are fairly efficient. But the instant you hit the atmosphere the slightest miscalculation in the utilization of your fuel reserves can lead to absolute disaster. I don't know what makes you tick, of course. You may get a distorted kind of pleasure from thinking of yourself as a man marked for death, the same kind of pleasure you get from killing people."

There was silence for a moment. Then Henley drew in his breath sharply and said: "Are you threatening me, Corriston?"

"Just warning you," Corriston said.

"I don't take kindly to warnings, Corriston. If you're not careful I'll put a bullet right through you."

"Do the men who hired you know how you operate, Henley?"

It was a stab in the dark, but it brought a quick, enraged reply. "How I operate is my own business. And I don't like the word 'hire.' I'd advise you not to use it again. Ramsey's uranium steal made every miner on Mars decide straight off that I was the right man to lead them. They're all in back of me, but they don't control me. I take orders from no one."

"Maybe they wouldn't be in back of you if they knew what a scoundrel you are," Corriston said.

"You may think whatever you please. I don't mind your calling me a scoundrel if it will ease your mind. Just don't use the word 'hire.' "

"I don't see why you should object to it," Corriston went on recklessly. "It protects you, in a way. It's a good word to hide behind. If the colonists knew the truth about you, I don't think you'd last very long."

"I'll last long enough to help you dig your own grave, Corriston, if you keep on with that line of talk. You're the real lucky one. I missed killing you on the Station because my aim was bad. You were an unexpected complication and you were keeping me upset. I didn't like it at all."

"Go ahead. I knew too much. Was that it?"

"Partly. I didn't know how much you knew or how much you'd guessed. But you were in a position to start a lot of high-powered stuff that could have interfered with my plans in a dozen ways. Now I happen to need you—to a limited extent. But I'm warning you again. Don't trade on your luck. Don't force me to kill you, Corriston."

"Perhaps I won't. Perhaps we can strike a compromise. As I see it, there's no need for immediate violence. Suppose you take me just a little more fully into your confidence. It can do you no harm now; and there are a few things I'm still curious about."

"All right, Corriston. What is it you'd like to know?"

"How did you manage to stay concealed on the Station when Ramsey's officers were in full command? You had considerable freedom of movement, apparently, even if you had to move with caution."

"We had everything planned in advance," Henley said. "We got to one of Ramsey's men with bribe money the miners raised, an executive officer named Stockton. We made it worth his while. We had a carefully worked out plan for smuggling Helen Ramsey off the shuttle ship and keeping her hidden until the Mars ship arrived. Stockton had everything prepared: a concealed compartment, food, made our problem more complicated. Stockton helped us get out of the quarantine cage and kept right on protecting us until we no longer needed him."

"Then you must have known about the masks. You must have known before you arrived that Ramsey's men were in complete control of the Station."

"Sure we knew, long before Earth found out. We know exactly what had taken place. You'd be surprised what a few carefully placed bribes can do. We knew that Ramsey had laid himself wide open by substituting his own men for the Station's commanding officers. We knew exactly how vulnerable he was."

"I see," Corriston said. "Ramsey was so vulnerable that any determined attack made upon him would have had a fair chance of succeeding. But you worked out a plan for striking at him in a wholly criminal way, through his daughter. Did the miners know that, Henley? Or did they just give you their backing in a general way? You probably seemed to them the kind of man who would go after Ramsey hammer and tongs."

"Suppose we just say they knew I'd find a way to make Ramsey meet all of our demands." Henley smiled thinly. "The details they left to me." He paused an instant, then went on: "Right after Helen Ramsey disappeared, I did some hard thinking. It occurred to me that she might be wearing a mask too. So I watched all of the women in the quarantine cage and when one of them slipped out I followed her."

"As simple as that!"

"It wasn't simple. The girl's disappearance on the shuttle ship had me completely baffled at first. It wasn't until we reached the Station that the mask possibility occurred to me."

"We talked about that once before, remember?"

"You were lucky then, Corriston. I tried very hard to kill you, simply because I thought you knew more about Helen Ramsey's disappearance than you actually did. In that dark cargo compartment, with time running out on me, I couldn't think very clearly. Anything more you'd like to know?"

"Yes. How many men did Ramsey succeed in substituting for the rightful officers? How many, beside the commander?"

"Eight, including the commander. His real name was Henry Hervet. Five were executive officers, two were security guards. They're all dead now."

Corriston's mouth went dry. "Including the one who sold out and helped you?"

"Yes, Stockton was the first to die. He was dead before the others tried to board this ship. I made sure of that. He was too greedy for his own good."

"You got back the money you gave him, I suppose."

"Naturally. Money is of very little value to a dead man."

Corriston had gone very pale. There was dread in his eyes when he asked: "And the real Commander Clement? What happened to him? Where is he now?"

"Stockton told me that after a mask was made of his face he was imprisoned somewhere on the Station," Henley said.

"Clement and seven others. Ramsey gave Hervet strict orders not to kill them. I don't know where Clement is now; but I can make a pretty good guess. He has probably been released and is in full command of the Station again."

Henley stood very still for a moment, very straight and still, and Corriston could feel the gun nudging the small, of his back again.

"I may as well tell you now that I'm going to have to lock you in, Corriston," Henley said. "When I turn the key on this room your sole responsibility will be right here with the controls. You'll have to sleep and eat here and I don't intend to bring you any fancy meals. You'll hear a knock on the door three times a day. You'll get a tray with some food on it.

"You'll have to decide for yourself how much sleep you can afford to take. And remember this: I'll be keeping a careful check on every navigational move you make. Not a too accurate check, perhaps, but I'll know enough. If you throw the ship off course I'll find out about it, and I'll want to know why. Be ready with your answers and make sure they carry weight. Any more questions, Corriston?"

Corriston shook his head. "No. The quicker you get out of here the better I'll feel."

"All right, I'll leave you now. It's naturally to my benefit to try to see things from your point of view. And just in case you're worrying about Helen Ramsey—don't. Nothing is going to happen to her, provided you stay in line. If you want me don't hesitate to buzz. That's what the intercom is for."

Corriston looked around once when Henley was on his way to the door. The man hadn't turned away from him. He was backing toward the door, his lips tight, his eyes mocking, coldly derisive.

"Did you think I'd give you a chance to catch me with my guard down, Corriston? If you did, you're a bigger fool than I thought you. This gun stays with me, and it's going to be centered on you every time I open this door. Remember that, Lieutenant."

The journey to Mars was a long wait. It was a standing and a waiting, with a hundred corrective power maneuvers to be checked at every hour of the day and night. It was sleep without rest and rest without sleep, and it was a battle against dizziness and the despair which can come to a pilot when a panel starts flickering a red danger signal in the utter loneliness of interplanetary space.

The ship was never too hot, never too cold, for the temperature was kept stable by thermostat-controlled radiation shutters and the air was kept pure with the aid of carbon filters. But to Corriston the air conditioning system with all of its elaborate controls seemed only to point up and emphasize the lack of stability elsewhere, both inside and outside the ship.

There were so many things that could go wrong—tragically, dangerously, fatally wrong. For no reason at all, for instance, a recently inspected filter or gasket could go completely bad, and a "no juice" blow up threaten. Or a magnetic guidance tape could jam and stop recording, and the ship could deviate a hair's breadth from its prescribed path and forget to swing completely back again.

Eventually a correction might be made, but if you failed to correct it in time, that one tiny deviation could spell disaster. With every day out there were more details to check, while obstacles mounted and it was impossible ever to quite catch up with what you had to do, and go on with complete confidence to the next task.

Worst of all, Corriston was denied all opportunity to see or speak to the woman he loved.

The trip to Mars took fourteen days. And in all that time Corriston did not once see Helen Ramsey. He saw only Henley, heard only the deep drone of the engines, and at times, when he was close to despair, the dull, steady beating of his own heart.

The door to his prison would open and a tray of food would be pushed forward into the compartment. Then the door would close quietly again, and he would be alone.

In some respects he was imprisoned in a way that was almost too unbelievable for the human mind to grasp. The walls of his cell were the constellations, the barriers to his freedom space itself.

The chartroom was a cell too, but it had no real confining power over him. He could walk out of the chart room simply by unlocking the viewport and swinging it wide open. He could walk out into the larger prison of space—and die in five seconds with his lungs on fire.

On the thirteenth day Mars loomed out of the inscrutable

darkness ahead like some great accusing eye that had fastened itself on the ship with a malignance all its own. It filled one-fifth of the viewport, rust-red over most of its surface, but also pale blue in patches, a blue which shaded off into a kaleidoscope of colors that seemed to hover chiefly like the shifting, almost hueless cloudiness of a hot summer haze.

On the morning of the fifteenth day, the ship, decelerating under side-thrusts from its powerful retardation rockets, cut off its engines and, free-coasting through a landing ellipse of seventy degrees, landed safely on Mars.

It landed in the open desert, twenty miles from Ramsey's citadel, and eighty-seven miles from the first Martian colony. But Corriston received no praise at all for his navagational skill.

Five minutes after the engines ceased to throb, a blow on the head felled him, a brutal blow from behind.

"Tie him up," Henley said. "We're not killing him, not just yet."

"But I don't see why—" a cold voice started to protest.

"Damn you, Stone, I know what I'm doing. Keep your thoughts to yourself."

CHAPTER FIFTEEN

CORRISTON sat very straight and still in the darkness, his back against cold metal, his eyes on the distant glow of the heating lamp. He could see the lamp through a wide panel opening in the bulkhead directly opposite him. Wherever his eyes fell there was the glimmer of light on metal. But the warmth of the lamp would have left him close to freezing had it not been supplemented by the heating units inside his heavy clothing.

He didn't know how he was going to free himself. His hands were securely handcuffed and the sharp metal was biting into his flesh. Turning and twisting about did him no good at all.

He didn't know how he was going to free himself, but he refused to give up hope. There had to be a way.

You could begin on one of your captors, on a human being with a great deal to lose or gain. You could try to penetrate his armor, sound out his human weaknesses. Or you could set to work on the handcuffs at your wrists, struggling in an almost hopeless attempt to draw your hands through them in some way or get them unlocked without a key.

He decided to try the first way. He raised his voice. "Stone?" he called out. "Can you hear me?"

There ensued a silence. Then Stone's voice came back loud and clear. "Sure, I can hear you. What do you want?"

"I'd like to talk to you," Corriston said.

"About what?"

"About you. What are you getting out of this? You've nothing to lose by being frank with me. Henley would never believe anything I might say."

"You're right about that," Stone said. "But why should I talk to you? I'll tell you something that may surprise you. Keeping you alive was Henley's idea. He figured we might need you. He figured that if Ramsey wouldn't listen to us he might listen to you—a Space Station officer. He figured we might need you to convince

Ramsey we're not bluffing. Someone who knows we're not bluffing. Someone who knows we'd kill his daughter before we gave him a third chance to make up his mind and hand over the dough."

"A *third* chance? I thought—"

"You think too much, Corriston. I'll spell it out for you. Henley is on his way now to give Ramsey his first chance. He may succeed or he may not. If he doesn't succeed he'll come back and take you to the fortress with him. That will be Ramsey's second chance. He won't get a third."

"I see," Corriston said. "But I asked you a question you didn't answer. How much do you stand to get out of this? What is your split, your percentage? Don't tell me; I'll guess. Henley is promising you fifteen or twenty thousand dollars. But how much ransom do you think he'll get from Ramsey? Two million, at least. Possibly twenty million. Does that kind of split satisfy you, Stone? Remember, when that ransom is paid, every law enforcement agency on Earth goes into operation. It starts off in a quiet suite of offices, with just one owl-faced little guy shuffling some papers.

"It starts off that way, but in the space of one hour you're a man marked for destruction. The military goes into action. From Earth to Mars your photograph is televised. Ten thousand trained experts are thrown into the operation. You've suddenly become important, an accessory to the kidnapping of the wealthiest girl on Earth.

"How does that set with you, Stone? They'll get you in the end. No, I'll qualify that. They'll get you unless Ramsey gives you a split of at least a million dollars. With a million dollars you'd have a one in five chance of covering your tracks, of hiding out indefinitely. But Ramsey won't give you anything like that kind of a split. You know that as well as I do. He'll have to cover his own tracks and he'll need all of the two million—or twenty million—for himself. Or most of it.

"I'm not telling you anything you don't know. Your real interest lies in preventing that kidnapping before it's too late. He's getting ready to double-cross you, Stone. It was in the back of his mind all the time. He's looking out only for himself."

"I don't think so," Stone said. "My split, since you brought the matter up, is half a million. He's demanding six million in ransom. That's twelve times what I'm getting and what Jim Saddler is getting. But I've no complaints. He organized and planned everything.

"I'll be honest with you. That doesn't mean a damn thing to me. I'm no good when it comes to taking a risk like that, but does that mean he's better than I am? Do you think I'd string along with him if I believed that for a moment?

"Hell, no. I'm using him, don't you see? I'm letting him take the big gamble, and I stay in the background...doing practically nothing. So if I clear a half million, what have I to complain about?"

"Nothing, I suppose," Corriston said.

"You're damned right. But I don't think I like the way you said that. There's something in your voice that I don't like."

"That's too bad," Corriston said.

"Maybe you think I don't mean what I said. Is that it?"

Corriston tightened his lips. He could hear Stone's footsteps coming toward him through the darkness. They were heavy steps, advancing slowly, with a slight shuffling sound. They paused twice and then came on again, and the silence between pauses seemed almost crushingly thick.

Corriston suddenly realized that he knew almost nothing about Stone. He had taken the man pretty much for granted, a killer's accomplice without much personality, a sullen-faced scoundrel who was good at obeying orders and standing ready to silence anyone Henley disliked with a well-placed kick in the head.

But what if he did have personality after all? Suppose there were hidden depths in him, a hidden reservoir of malice that he kept concealed until he felt a mad impulse to start laughing or bragging or proving to someone he disliked that he was as potentially dangerous as Henley—perhaps even more dangerous. And suppose he decided to back up his boasting with a quick knife thrust or a gun blast at almost point-blank range?

It wasn't a pleasant thought, and the flicker of a match between Stone's cupped hands did nothing to dispel Corriston's uneasiness. The small, bright flame brought Stone's features into sharp relief for an instant. The lips had an ugly set to them, and the eyes were slitted, gleaming. He was making no effort to keep his hate from showing, and the instant the match went out he lit another.

He seemed to be advancing slowly on purpose, as if aware that his stealth and deliberation had begun to unnerve Corriston. Corriston felt himself stiffening, moving more closely back against the wall. Breathing quickly, he told himself that he hadn't much time, that he must be careful not to overreach himself.

There was another moment of silence, of stillness, while the shuffling ceased. Then Stone was very close in the darkness, his hands cupped about a third match, a mocking smile on his lips.

It was a blunder on his part. Before he could move again Corriston was upon him.

There are times when a handcuffed man is at a disadvantage in a furiously waged and uncertain struggle, but Corriston suffered no disadvantage. For ten minutes he had been reminding himself that a blow along the side of the neck, just under the jaw, could paralyze and even kill if it were delivered with sufficient force.

A sharp, flat-of-the-hand blow could do it. But handcuffs were better, and Corriston lashed out now with his manacled wrists upraised, so that the handcuffs grazed Stone's neck twice lightly and then almost splintered his jawbone with a rotor-blade violence.

The blow not only stunned Stone, it lifted him clear of the deck. He staggered forward and fell heavily, his breath leaving his lungs in an agonizing sob.

Corriston leaned back against the wall again for an instant, breathing heavily. Then he knelt beside Stone and went through his pockets until he found the handcuff key. It was difficult. He had to do a lot of awkward fumbling with his fingers, and even with the key in his possession, getting the cuffs off was far from easy. But somehow he managed it, perhaps because he had unusually flexible fingers and knew that if he failed, Stone would see to it that he got no second chance this side of eternity.

He stood very straight and still in the darkness, his eyes focused on Stone's white face. There was no need for him to strike a match. He had taken from Stone not only the key, but a small pocket flashlight that Stone had apparently preferred not to use.

There was something else he had taken from Stone—his gun. He held the weapon now, very firmly centered on Stone, while he waited for him to come to.

Ordinarily he wouldn't have cared if Stone had never opened his eyes again; but now he had to wait and see. The ship was so large that to explore it compartment by compartment until he found the one in which Helen Ramsey was being held prisoner would be dangerously time-consuming. So, if Stone recovered consciousness within fifteen or twenty minutes and could tell him, so much the better.

If not, better wait and see. He waited, shifting his gun only a little from weariness as the minutes dragged on, wondering if he had not made a mistake in waiting at all.

Finally Stone stirred and groaned. Corriston bent and shook him by the shoulders. He took firm hold of his shoulders and shook him vigorously, feeling no pity for him at all.

He got the truth out of him by threatening him with violence, by threatening to kill him if he kept anything back. Stone kept nothing back. Just remembering the blow that had felled him loosened his tongue. But the gun helped too, the gun wedged so closely against his ribs under his heart that he feared that if he breathed too heavily he would breathe his last.

"I won't lie to you," he said desperately, pleadingly. "You haven't a chance. There's a photoelectric alarm system outside the compartment, and Jim Saddler is sitting just inside the door. He has a gun trained on her. His orders are to shoot her dead if anyone so much as attempts to get inside that door."

"Meaning me?"

"It means you, Lieutenant. I'm not lying; I swear it. You won't stand a chance. Henley will be coming back in a few hours now. You'd better get out while you're still in one piece."

Corriston was tempted to hurl Stone back against the wall and shout at him: "It doesn't matter whether I go out of here in one piece or dead on a stretcher. She's the only thing I care about."

But he caught himself just in time. Stone thought in the most primitive imaginable terms. You couldn't go to a Stone Age man and say: "My own skin doesn't mean a gawd dam thing to me. I'm in love. If she dies I die. Can't you understand that? If she dies, my life will be over."

He said instead: "All right. I guess it means I've got to get help."

"You'll never get help." Stone said, summoning from some defiant depths within himself a little courage. "The colony is eighty-seven miles from here. You couldn't cross the desert on foot. No one could cross it on foot, not when the temperature drops at night to fifty below. But you'd better not stay. You'd better head for Ramsey's citadel. That's your only chance. It's only twenty miles from here."

Let him think that, a voice within Corriston warned. Let him think that I'll head for the citadel. Otherwise he may attempt to get word to Ramsey somehow. I can tie him up and leave him in a state of shock, but if he thinks I'm heading for the colony, even a state of shock may not stop him. Saddler may come down here looking for him. Once he's freed, if he thinks I'm heading for the Colony...

Corriston said: "Damn you, Stone, I ought to kill you. I ought to put a bullet through your heart right now. I don't know why I can't. It's a weakness in me."

"I'd kill you, Corriston, if I had the chance. But I'm glad you have that kind of a weakness."

Corriston stared at him incredulously. "You're certainly outspoken. You were pleading for your life a moment ago—going soft, as you'd put it. Now you're talking realistically, analyzing your own motivations and mine."

"I'm not quite as dumb as you think me, Corriston."

"All right. Let's say you're not dumb. Few people are, when it comes to a matter of life or death. That's beside the point right now. I've got to tie you up. Where can I find some rope?"

"It would be much simpler to lock me in a vacant compartment."

"All right. Then I'll lock you in one of the compartments. You can pick your own compartment. I'd advise you not to waste my time. Pick your own compartment and I'll slide the bolt fast on the outside."

Stone showed no disposition to put up an argument. Corriston kept the gun pressed into the small of his back and he seemed to realize that his life hung by a thread.

They found a compartment that was small and dark, and into it

Stone walked at gunpoint, offering no protest, and answering the questions Corriston put to him readily enough.

"You'll find all the equipment you need at the end of this passageway," Stone said. "Activate the third door on your left. Anything else you'd like to know?"

Corriston shook his head. He walked out of the compartment backwards, keeping his gun trained on Stone until he was in the corridor. Then he swung the door shut and shot the bolt home.

He had no trouble at all in finding the equipment he knew he'd need, thanks to Stone's generosity. Stone could afford to be generous, he reflected bitterly. The Henley combine still held all of the trump cards.

He cursed the time it took him to equip himself for a near-suicidal crossing of eighty-seven miles of Martian desert. He would travel on foot, after nightfall, and in freezing cold. The compartment in which he labored was a basal compartment, and set in the massive bulkhead, against which he leaned with his bootstraps still unlaced, was an airlock opening directly on the Martian plain.

He collected the smaller articles first, setting them down in a row on a long metal bench directly opposite the airlock: three compasses, each weighing perhaps twenty ounces; a cathode ray compass; a non-magnetic compass and a sun compass. The sun compass would perhaps prove the most valuable until darkness fell. The sun, shining down with brilliance from the clear Martian sky, could throw a directional kind of shadow, enabling a man on foot to take fairly accurate bearings without the use of sighting and viewing instruments. To the compasses on the bench he added five map coordinates and a Lambert conformal projection chart.

Food concentrates came next: four shining aluminum cubes, four inches by four inches, which would go into the knapsack on his back. Then a canteen, already filled with sterilized water from the ship's central water supply system.

Next, he took from the locker the right kind of clothing: a tubeflex inner suit with a warm lining and a heavy outer suit equipped with heat lamps.

Oxygen masks next—oxy-respirators, to be exact. One to attach to the face and one to hold in reserve as a spare. They covered only a third of the face, but that third had everything to do with a man's staying alive and vigorous in the thin air of Mars. When night fell, and the cold descended, oxy-respirators were not enough. Then you had to pull down the entire front of your helmet and stagger on with your sight impaired, for in a cold that was almost beyond endurance, helmets had a way of clouding over from time to time.

The clouding over of the vision plate was not too important. It could be constantly wiped clean. But if his brain started "clouding over" too...

He dismissed the possibility from his mind. He was clothed now, fully clothed, and ready to depart.

He started moving toward the airlock, feeling and looking like a giant beetle of the tropics, feeling awkward, cumbersome and insecure. His boots were weighted, and the bulge of the oxygen tank on his shoulder made him look almost hunchbacked in the cold light glimmer that turned the bulkhead into a mirroring surface as he advanced.

He manipulated the airlock and it opened with a slow, steady droning and then he was passing through it, still moving awkwardly...

At last! He was out on the Martian desert in bright sunlight, staring up at the clear blue sky.

The first few miles were not difficult at all. He walked away from the ship with his shoulders held straight, the cumbersome feeling dissipated by the lightness of his stride in the incredibly light gravity.

The air pressure about him was less than seventy millimeters of mercury. The thought sprouted in his mind that he was the god Mercury striding along with winged shoes, and for the first five miles his weighted boots did seem to develop wings.

Then the temperature began slowly to drop. The sun sank lower. Its brightness diminished, and his cheeks began to tingle with the cold.

There was a slight wind blowing over the desert, raising dust flurries on the summits of the tallest dunes, causing the gray patches of crust lichen, which were scattered widely over the plain, to change color as their threadlike surfaces were ruffled by the breeze.

Far in the distance he could see a "canal," one of those strange blue-green declivities in the terrain that looked from the air like an actual waterway, and had deceived—or bewildered—three generations of men.

Despite the increasing cold, Corriston did not moderate his stride. He let his thoughts dwell on the most imaginative of the canal speculations. It had been proven completely false, but its originality fascinated him. Long ago, the theory held, there had been volcanic activity on Mars. Great faults or fissures had opened up in the planet's crust, and when the coming of spring thawed the polar ice caps, curtains of fog swirled equatorward, filling those natural crevices with swirling rivers of mist.

Corriston stopped walking for a moment, shifting the weight of his equipment slightly, easing a too heavy drag on his right shoulder. He made sure that the thin flexible tube that connected his oxygen mask with the small tank on his back was securely clipped into place at both ends, tested the harness buckle that supported supplies that were as necessary to him as breathing, and took a turn up and down the sand, stamping, shaking himself, to make absolutely certain that nothing vital had been jarred loose.

Then he was under way again, moving along at a steady pace over the rust-red desert, the ship now lost to view far behind him, his mind leaping ahead to the very great dangers that he was determined to face and overcome so long as one slender thread of hope remained.

CHAPTER SIXTEEN

IT MIGHT have been almost any sleepy little town on Earth, picked at random from a train window—a dust bowl town with a prairie name: Hawk's Valley, Buzzard's Gulch, and the like. It might have been, but it wasn't.

The buildings were thinner, of more precarious construction, and each had been built to house three or more families. They were at unusual angles on sloping ledges where the soil was firm enough to resist overnight erosion from winds of hurricane force, and in many places their prefabricated metal foundations were pierced and supported by shafts of solid rock.

Without modern technology at its most advanced, the town could never have been built. Yet in the streets of the town there was a village rudeness of construction that no pioneering effort could quite efface: a wide main street that gleamed red in the sunlight on which three caterpillar tractors stood stalled, their guard rails caked with yellow mud; a pool of stagnant black water with a wooden plank thrown haphazardly across it; a discarded fuel container upended against a half-rusted away metal cable, and the remnants of an hydraulic actuator overgrown with hardy lichens that had colored it yellow and ash gray. And here and there, projecting from the tumbled sand, were spiny cactus-like growths.

Yet it was not too small a town. Its inhabitants numbered eight thousand, two-thirds of them men. There were ninety-seven children. It was not too small a town, and now, in each of the houses, a new day was beginning.

At least thirty men and a few women had collected about the haggard-eyed desert straggler. Every one of them hung on his words. Every one of these people had been ruined by Ramsey's rapacious greed. Their past accomplishments were destroyed; their futures were non-existent. They lived in a terrorized state, from hand-to-mouth, indifferent now to any more wrongdoing that could be visited upon them. The fires of their hatred for Ramsey gave them the basic energy to go on existing.

Out of grinding desperation they had turned to Henley, had given him a free hand, even when most, in their heart-of-hearts, knew he was a scoundrel. The fact was that he was the only man among them not so cowed as to be actively enraged against Ramsey. He promised that the mines would be given back to the people. And, having nothing, they believed everything.

They came from everywhere in the colony, every trade and profession. Who was this man? And was he friend or foe?

The crowd grew slowly. Despite the shouts and the sudden stir of excitement that had greeted the speaker on his arrival, there was no headlong rush to surround him. The colonists emerged from their lodgings and converged calmly upon the square, some having the look of tradesfolk concerned with a possible interruption of business, and others seemingly intent only on what the stranger might have to say.

It was unusually warm for so early an hour, the temperature well up in the mid-forties, and there was no need for the heat-generating inner garments, only for oxygen masks and heavy outdoor clothing and the careful avoidance of too much muscular exertion in the absence of weighted shoes.

This is madness, Corriston told himself. I am in no condition to convince these people, to make them understand. I should have rested first. Three hours sleep would have helped. I should have asked for food.

Corriston felt suddenly tongue-tied. Words were failing him when he needed them most. His speech became halting and confused. He had been talking for twenty minutes—twenty minutes at least—but suddenly he was quite sure that he hadn't succeeded in convincing anyone that he was speaking only the simple truth.

He looked at the faces before him a little more intently and saw what he had not noticed before: everyone was waiting for him to go on; everyone seemed to be hanging on his words.

Had he misjudged them after all? Or had he misjudged his own capacity to be persuasive, to talk with conviction when his very life hung in the balance?

There could be no doubt on that score. His life did hang in the balance. They'd make short shift of him if they thought he was on Ramsey's side.

"It isn't Ramsey I'm concerned about," he heard himself saying. "I'm pleading with you to face up to the truth about yourselves. You trusted Henley because you were desperate. You couldn't put your trust in a weak or indecisive man. You needed a tool with a cutting edge. That I can understand. But you picked the wrong man. Henley doesn't want to see justice done. He doesn't want to help you at all. He wants to help himself at your expense, to help himself in a vicious, brutal way."

"That's a lie," someone in the crowd said. "Henley's a good man."

Corriston freed himself from his dust-caked coat. He shrugged it off and let it drop to the sand. Then he straightened his oxygen mask and went on: "It's not a lie. It's the simple truth."

He wondered why he had shrugged off his warmest garment. It was cold, he was shivering, and it had been a ridiculous thing to do. Had he intended it as a challenge? In a crazy, confused, subconscious way, was he offering to fight anyone who disagreed with him.

He suddenly realized that he was a little drunk. Not on alcohol, but on a slight excess of oxygen. He fingered the gauge on his mask, cutting down the tank inflow, cursing himself for his delay in doing so.

Had he convinced anyone? He looked at the faces about him and was astonished by their impassivity. Few of the men or women before him seemed either angry or disturbed. They just seemed to be quietly listening.

Suddenly he realized that he was completely in error. They were convinced, persuaded, almost completely on his side. Their silence was in itself revealing, just as the hush that precedes an avalanche can be convincing, or the stillness that precedes a storm at sea.

They were waiting for him to go on.

He talked for thirty more minutes and then there was a long silence, punctuated only by the harsh breathing of a few men who seemed to disagree.

CHAPTER SEVENTEEN

CORRISTON knew that the few who disagreed were prepared to make trouble, but he was not prepared for the violence that ensued.

Fights broke out in the crowd, singly and in groups. The colonists with strong convictions took issue with the few who disagreed. And the few who disagreed had strong convictions, too.

Two men about the same in height were suddenly down on the ground raining fisticuffs at each other.

"Damn you, Reeves, I'll break your jaw. From the first minute I saw Henley I knew he was a scoundrel."

"Yeah, and who else but a scoundrel could hold his own with a rat like Ramsey. We can call the turn on him if he goes too far."

There was an explosion of cursing and Corriston could see five more men fighting, moving backwards as they exchanged blows toward the periphery of the crowd.

There was nothing he could do to stop the fighting. He was close to exhaustion, hardly able to stand. He desperately needed food and rest—a long rest flat on his back.

Suddenly he realized that he had victory within his grasp. Most things worthwhile in life called for a decisive effort of will. He decided suddenly that he couldn't just let the fighting go on. He had to take a firm stand himself, had to convince everyone that he was prepared to fight for his convictions.

He moved forward into the crowd. He grabbed one doubter by the shoulder, held fast to him for an instant, and then sent his fist crashing into the astonished man's jaw.

The doubter folded in complete silence. Corriston stepped back from him and said in a voice loud enough to carry to the rim of the crowd: "I don't care how many of you I have to take on. Every word I've said is the truth. If you can only settle it by killing me, you may as well start trying."

There was a silence then. Even the sound of the breeze rustling

176

the garments of the colonists, stirring little flurries of sand along the main street, seemed to become muted. Far off between the houses a clock struck the time. It seemed very loud in the stillness.

It amazed Corriston a little, even in his exhausted state, how determinedly a challenge like that could be accepted at face value. He was quite sure that he had won a victory; that nine-tenths of the colonists were on his side. But everyone remained silent, everyone drew back in tight-lipped silence while the issue was put to the test.

A tall man with a lean, lantern-jawed face approached Corriston and said: "I'm going to tell you exactly what I think. Henley isn't an easy man to understand. He keeps his thoughts to himself and he may have had his own special reasons for pulling the wool over your eyes. He's looking out for our best interests; I'm sure of that. But what good would it do me to knock you down to prove it?"

"No good at all," Corriston said. "But try knocking me down if you want to."

"I'm not going to try," the lantern-jawed man said. "I think you're lying. That's all I have to say."

Corriston watched him disappear in the crowd and shook his head. He felt like a man with a fly swatter in his hand. He had won a victory and yet if he failed to swat a few flies no one would believe that he was telling the truth.

Finally he got his chance. A thickset, dark-browed man with a trouble-seeking aspect came up and hurled insults at him in a markedly offensive way.

Corriston hit him three times. The first blow doubled him up, the second dropped him to his knees; the third flattened him out on the sand.

Corriston stepped back and surveyed the crowd. Their response now was overwhelmingly favorable.

It wasn't a complete victory. There were still doubters, still arguments going on, still a hatred for Ramsey that overflowed and made a mockery of the few voices raised in his defense.

And Corriston was glad that not too many voices were raised in Ramsey's defense. He had not come to plead Ramsey's cause, and he wanted all of the colonists to know that. He only asked that a truce be declared, an end to the fierce, immediate hatreds, while a scoundrel was attacked by men who had been lied to, cheated and betrayed. He moved still further forward into the crowd, prepared to fight again if he had to, prepared to back up his arguments with the simple, primitive and direct use of his fists.

He swayed suddenly and realized that he was at the end of his endurance, and now would in all probability make a complete fool of himself. He would commit the unforgivable folly of issuing a challenge that he couldn't back up.

He shook his head violently, trying to clear it, but his dizziness increased. The landscape about him began to pinwheel and he saw the streets of the colony through a wavering yellow mist. The storefronts danced, the rusting and discarded machinery on a side street began to move and come to life, to clatter and waltz about.

A woman moving toward him seemed to grow in height, her oxygen mask widening out, overspreading her face. For a moment she seemed like an impossible ballet figure in a danse macabre, pivoting about on her toes as a caterpillar tractor came rushing toward her through the thin air of Mars.

Then two colonists were supporting him, holding him tightly by the elbows, refusing to let him collapse. It was outrageous, because he wanted to collapse. He wanted to sink down, to let sleep wash over him, to forget all of his troubles in merciful oblivion.

But the two colonists were very stubborn. They refused to let him collapse. He only wanted to go to sleep, to forget all of his troubles, but the two colonists were like doctors in a hospital, very stern, very patient, and seemingly determined to keep him on his feet.

Somehow they must have failed. They must have failed because when he became fully conscious again he was lying between cool white sheets, and a woman in a white nurse's uniform was bending over him. By straining his eyes he could see two men who looked like doctors standing just beyond her.

The two men appeared to be discussing him, but when he struggled to a sitting position and stared hard at them they came toward him with reassuring smiles, and one of them said: "Take it easy, now. You're going to be all right."

"I...I must have passed out," he stammered. "I was ready to pass out before I started talking. Is this a hospital? I guess it is. I should have come here immediately. Forty hours in the desert and I arrive half-delirious and make a fool of myself."

"Take it easy," one of the doctors said. "You didn't make a fool of yourself. Quite the contrary."

Oh, brother, he thought. They're lying to me to spare me, or something. "I have a vague recollection of not being able to stand, of talking my head off and then collapsing and making a complete fool of myself, of accomplishing nothing at all. I swung hard at two or three people. I knocked one man down, flat on his back. But that was a crazy thing to do. It's no way to win the confidence or respect of anyone."

"Look," one of the doctors said, taking firm hold of his shoulder and shaking him gently. "Don't go reproaching yourself. You've got nine-tenths of the colony behind you."

"You mean—"

"Sure, you convinced almost everyone. And that was a miracle in itself, considering how close to collapse you were. You were running a high fever. You were dehydrated. Your skin was as dry as a parched lichen. Yet you stood there and convinced them. That's the gospel truth."

"They've chosen you as their leader," the second doctor said. "They're going after Henley before it's too late. They feel exactly as you do about Ramsey's daughter. Not about Ramsey perhaps— but about the kidnapping of a helpless girl. None of them have any liking for Henley now."

CHAPTER EIGHTEEN

CORRISTON walked out into the central square and stood there. For a moment no one said a word. One of the doctors was there with him. He'd had a sandwich and coffee before leaving the hospital and his nerves felt steady and his voice was pitched low.

"I don't know a single one of these men, Dr. Tomlinson," he said. "I spent a week in the colony four years ago, but I just don't see anyone I recognize. I'm afraid you'll have to introduce me around."

It took a full hour to really get acquainted, to plan what had to be done, to check over the tractors, the ammunition supplies, the equipment of each and every man.

They had to cross eighty-seven miles of desert to a heavily guarded cave and then move on perhaps to Ramsey's fortress. They had to be prepared for any eventuality.

The morale was good. Corriston could sense the grim determination in every man, the faith in their mission, the anger. It cheered him.

He walked around between the tractors, listening to stray bits of talk, getting better acquainted with everyone as the minutes sped by.

He took out his watch and looked at it and decided that time was running short.

Give each and every man twenty minutes, he thought. Then we get rolling. Thirty caterpillar tractors and two hundred and ten men. And in the ship are two men holed up—possibly three now—with all the portable fighting equipment of a two thousand-ton spaceship at their disposal. And if Henley has returned—"

Suddenly Corriston found himself sweating in the silence, despite the cold, despite the hoarfrost that was beginning to collect on the rim of his oxygen mask. There was a split second of shouting from one of the tractors and then it started up, with a coughing and spitting that drowned out the human voices.

All along the wide, rust-red street other tractors came to life. In the thin air of Mars, in the pale sky, a single blue cloud hung suspended.

It was wispy thin, incredibly thin, a hollow mockery of a cloud. But the scene below would have been less remarkable had the sky remained cloudless, for then Mars would have seemed completely unlike Earth and the human drama less compelling.

There was something tremendous in the forward march of the tractors, in the clatter and the rising dust, the shouts of the men at the controls and the women who ran swift-footed along the sand to urge them to greater fortitude. The women knew that endurance would be needed, for twenty-first century weapons of warfare could destroy a hundred tractors and spatter the desert with blood before retaliation could become complete and justice be fully satisfied.

So the women did not weep or lament. They ran parallel, with the tractors, urging their men onward, stilling their own inner fears in the greatness of the moment.

Corriston waited for the last tractor to come abreast of him before he leapt aboard it. There was the smell of acrid grease in the air, a smell of burning. The mechanical parts set up a dull rumbling, and as Corriston swung himself aboard, a voice said: "I'm Stanley Gregor. If I had any sense I wouldn't take part in this. I came to Mars with the second expedition. I'm sixty-two years old but somehow today I feel young. There's no longer any doubt in my mind that Henley is a scoundrel. Why we trusted him I don't know. I'm here to do my part in rectifying an error."

"Sure," Corriston said, settling down at the side of a big, awkward-looking man with red hair. "Sure, I understand. Take it easy. We're all in this together."

"We've got eighty-seven miles of desert to cross. It's going to be tough. Have you seen the fortress Ramsey built to protect himself?"

"No," Corriston said.

"There are twenty-five square miles of fortified defenses—photoelectric eye installations. They spot you when you're a half-mile away. Try to storm those installations even with a dozen armed tractors, and you'll be pulverized into dust. Try to storm them on foot with the most formidable of energy weapons, and you'll be electrocuted. You'll hang suspended on barbed wire. Think that over, Lieutenant."

"I've thought it over," Corriston said. "We won't have to storm the fortress unless they've taken Ramsey's daughter there, or if Ramsey himself is in danger. And if he is in danger, he'll welcome our help. We're going to the ship first and there are only two men on the ship."

"But they've got plenty of ammunition, haven't they? They've got the ship's military installations. Anyway you slice it, it's a dangerous gamble."

"I never thought it was anything else," Corriston said.

CHAPTER NINETEEN

CORRISTON woke up to the hum of human voices, the soft whisper of the wind, the gentle stirring of sand. He awoke to coldness and brightness, to sunlight that dazzled him with its brightness.

Corriston remembered then. Not everything at once, but just the first thing. There were no guideposts. That was always the first thing to remember when you woke up from a brief, twenty-minute sleep on Mars.

In islands scoured by trade winds and bright with blown sea spray a man does not talk of traveling east or west, and even familiar streets are no longer given names or marked by intersections. A man talks instead of walking into the wind, of setting his course by the north star, of moving straight into the teeth of the gale or huddling for shelter beneath a high chalk cliff where all directions converge in a hollow drumming that has neither beginning nor end. It was that way on Mars. It would always be that way, it could never change.

Just lie very still and listen, listen to the voices of men who are risking their lives to help you. Listen and be grateful; listen and be proud.

All at once Corriston realized that an amazing discussion was going on. They were discussing an eleven-year old boy who had done an absolutely crazy thing. He had followed his father into the desert by concealing himself in one of the tractors, behind a liquid-fuel cylinder, and was now a member of the 210-man rescue team.

"Mars is no place for a kid. Dr. Drever ought to be ashamed of himself. If a man has children—well, Mars is simply no place for children."

"That's right. A boy of eleven needs companions his own age to help him over the growing-pain hurdles. He needs a backyard to play in. When I was a kid I had a bike of my own, a bull terrier pup, a collection of butterflies, a stamp collection and a simply amazing talent for roughing up my clothes.

"Mars is the worst of all possible worlds for a kid like Freddy. We're buoyed up by the bigness and the newness and the strangeness of everything. The mile-high granite cliffs don't really belong to a planet smaller than Earth. But they're here and we accept them. We pit our technical brilliance—or lack of it—against the rugged grandeur of the mountains and the plains and we can take even the sandstorms in our stride. But to bring a kid here—"

"Drever is a widower. He quite naturally didn't want to put his son in an orphanage. Besides, there are thirteen other young kids in the Colony."

"That doesn't excuse it. There are plenty of childless, single men."

"How many of them could step into Drever's shoes and grow to his stature as the first really great medical specialist on Mars? You're forgetting the hell he had to go through just to pass the preliminary screening. It's rugged for a man of his attainments. They not only insist that he be good; they want him to be the best."

"That's true enough, I suppose. And now that he's here he probably couldn't be replaced. Experience of a very special sort does things for a man. And *to* a man, if you like."

"I'm simply stressing that Mars is not a place for a kid of Freddy's age. When he goes roaming he gets his lungs choked with dust. He couldn't ride a bike on Mars—even if he had a bike. Worst of all, he has no kids of his own age to play with. And now he comes on a trip like this. Does he hope to rescue the Ramsey girl all by himself?"

Corriston got up then. The three men who had been discussing Dr. Drever's son stood by the smoldering embers of a burnt out campfire. They were kindly looking men but a certain narrow-mindedness was stamped on the faces of at least two of them.

Corriston shrugged off his weariness and walked up to them. "Nonsense!" he said.

A startled look came into the eyes of the oldest, a grizzled scarecrow of a man whose beard descended almost to his waist. He was a Martian geologist, and a good one.

"Eh, Lieutenant. I was just going to ask you. Shouldn't we get started?"

"We should and we will," Corriston said. "But a good many men collapsed from the cold this morning. If we don't arrive at that ship in force, we may live to regret it. Where's Freddy? Have you seen him?"

The grizzled man raised his arm and pointed: "Over there," he said. "His coming along was just about the craziest thing I ever heard of."

Corriston walked across the churned up sand to where Freddy sat perched like a disconsolate gnome on a metal-rimmed food container shaped like an old-fashioned water barrel.

Dr. Drever's son was almost twelve, but he was small for his age and Corriston had seen boys of nine who were much huskier looking.

Corriston had no way of knowing that on Earth, shoulder to shoulder with other schoolboys, Freddy had never thought of himself as particularly small. It was only on Mars, all alone with his father and other grownups, that he had felt even smaller than he actually was. He had felt like a dwarf child.

"Why did you do it, Freddy?" Corriston asked. "Your father is very upset and worried."

Freddy looked up quickly and just as quickly lowered his eyes again.

"I had to come," he said. "I had to."

"But why?"

"I don't know."

"I see."

Corriston stared at him for a long moment in silence. Then he said: "I think perhaps I understand, Freddy. Just suppose we say you succumbed to an impulse to roam. The exploring urge can be overwhelming in a boy of your age. It usually is. If you were on Earth right now you'd be dreaming about exploring the headwaters of the Amazon. You'd be dreaming about birds with bright, tropical plumage and butterflies as big as dinner plates."

Freddy looked up again, not quite so quickly this time. There was wonder and admiration in his stare. "How did you know?" he gasped.

"I guess I was pretty much like you, Freddy—once," Corriston said.

"Gee, thanks," Freddy said.

"Thanks for what?"

"Thanks for understanding me, Lieutenant Corriston."

Corriston walked out between the tractors and raised his voice so that everyone within earshot could hear him.

"We're starting again in ten minutes," he said. "Better have another cup of coffee all around."

CHAPTER TWENTY

THE SAND had been blowing for forty minutes. It was a flying avalanche, a flailing mace. Even inside the tractors it set up an almost intolerable roaring in the eardrums, and when it struck the wind-guards head on, the battered vehicles shook. For five or six seconds they would rumble on and then come to a jolting halt. Often they would start up again almost immediately but equally often they would remain stalled for several minutes, and at times there were more stalled tractors than moving ones across the entire line of advance.

The pelting never ceased, never let up even for a moment. Minute after minute the sand came sweeping down in red fury, tons upon tons of it, in great circular waves from high overhead and in jet velocity flurries close to the ground. In that assault of billions upon billions of spinning particles the brightly colored lichens which covered the Martian plains were uprooted, lifted high in the air, and carried for dozens of miles, flying carpets so small they scarcely could have supported the tiniest of elves.

For three hours the sandstorm continued to rage in fury, and then, abruptly, the wind died down, the last flurry subsided, and the colonists got under way again. And just for a change a few of them descended from the tractors and advanced on foot, keeping a little ahead of the swaying vehicles.

Dr. Drever, a tall, stooped man with graying temples but surprisingly youthful eyes accelerated his stride a little and fell in with the scarecrow geologist who was walking at Corriston's side.

"We can't be far from the ship now," he said. "I wish there was some way I could send Freddy back. If I thought you could spare a tractor and one man to accompany him…"

"Freddy will be all right." Corriston said. "You don't know what it means to a kid like Freddy to ride through a sandstorm in the company of grownups. He had to prove something to himself, and I think he's done it."

The stillness was almost unnatural now, and Corriston could see that most of the men were becoming uneasy about it. The desert seemed too bright and far too quiet. It was one of those mysterious, brooding silences that are a menace to start with. You think of unsuspected pitfalls, hidden traps. Imagination leaps ahead of reality and leaves an insidious kind of demoralization in its wake.

"I'm not surprised that all the animal life on Mars went underground," the scarecrow geologist said, and it seemed a strange thing for him to have mentioned at that moment, when the stillness was so absolute and the thoughts of everyone should have been on the ship, which had to be very near now.

"Yes, and what a vicious, horrible kind of animal life it is," Drever said, as if he too welcomed the opportunity to talk irrelevantly, perhaps to relieve his inner tension.

"They're a very primitive form of life, really," the geologist said. "They look like large gray snakes, but they're actually more like worms. Worms with sucker disks instead of mouths. When once they've attached themselves it's almost impossible to dislodge them. You've seen marine worms on Earth often enough, I'm sure. They come in all shapes, sizes and colors, but there are one or two species that look quite a bit like lamprenes in miniature. Lamprenes are usually about three feet in length. But some of the very old ones grow to eight feet or longer. Their natural prey is a small running lizard—the galaka—as you know."

"All right," Corriston said, a little of his raw-nerve exasperation returning. "Now I suppose you're going to tell us exactly how they kill their prey."

"I don't have to tell you how they kill men," Macklin said. "You know as much about that as I do. You've been on Mars before. You've seen at least a few of the victims. You know exactly how they come up under a man when he's asleep, puncture his clothes and attach themselves. He doesn't just get nipped; the lamprene can seldom be pulled off that quickly. And when two or three of them attack you, it can be pretty horrible. They're more than just vampires; they sting. The poison is as deadly as aconite. It works a little slower, but almost immediately the victim starts to degenerate, his nerves first, and then—"

"All right, now I've heard an expert confirm it. I'd be grateful if you'll just shut up."

"Lieutenant, I told you—"

"Never mind, Doctor. I'm asking him to shut up."

In silence they continued on, the tension between them increasing almost intolerably, their nerves becoming more and more frayed. And then, finally, it seemed to them that they could see the ship, and the great cliff wall surrounding it through the slight haziness left by the sandstorm and the vaguer haziness that distance imposes, could see the tumbled, flat slabs of rock that radiated out from it in all directions across the desert.

But it was hard to be sure it was really the ship. It was perhaps only one of the many desert mirages, which were far more common on Mars than they were on Earth. A man who has once looked at the bright, scarred face of a cliff wall in the Martian sunlight will remember it even in his dreams and no mirages are really necessary. He is certain to see it a second and a third time, like an after-image so indelibly imprinted on the retina of the human eye that its recurrence becomes inevitable. And yet, the running man could not have been a mirage. He was much nearer than the ship appeared to be, and he was falling and getting up and falling again in so frenzied a way that his movements bore the unmistakable stamp of reality.

Corriston came to an abrupt halt. For an instant he simply stared, watching the distant figure fall to the sand for the fourth time and drag himself forward over the sand, his shoulders heaving convulsively.

For an instant Corriston could not have moved if he had wanted to. The scarecrow and Drever were standing too close to him, so that the shoulders of the three men formed a compact unit, and their arms were in each other's way to such an extent that no real freedom of movement was possible.

Corriston almost had to disentangle himself by sheer physical effort. Disentangle himself he finally did, turning completely about and shouting to the colonists behind him.

"Get to that man as quickly as possible!" he ordered. "There's no time to be lost. Try to tear the lamprenes off him, but watch out for your hands. Don't let them coil around you, watch out for the disks. Get them off if you can. If you can't, bring him here. Carry him slung between you."

Two men left the line of march and started off across the desert, walking very rapidly but not breaking into a run. Corriston had forgotten to warn them that running with their weighted shoes would be difficult, and would only delay them, and he was glad that they had thought of it themselves.

He turned back to the scarecrow, who was staring in white-lipped horror at what must have seemed to him an unbelievable occurrence—a man attacked by lamprenes when he had been talking about lamprenes only an instant before.

But Corriston knew that it was a common enough occurrence, not to be in any way coincidental. No one who slept in the desert for any length of time could hope to avoid an attack if he failed to take the necessary precautions. And even with precautions the death toll was high; almost as high, perhaps, as cobra fatalities in India.

Corriston turned abruptly, his lips white. "If a man is attacked by just one lamprene, and it's pulled off quickly, how much chance has he?"

It was Drever who answered him. "Not much, I'm afraid. The poison gets into the blood stream and acts quickly. You can't get it out with a suction disk the way you sometimes can with a snake bite. It's a nerve poison and it spreads very fast. And there's no way of neutralizing it, no serum injection that does any good. Of course, there have been a few recoveries."

Corriston swung about and stared out across the desert again. The two colonists had reached the stricken man now and were attempting to tear the lamprene—or lamprenes—from his flesh. They were bending over him, and it was hard to tell for a moment whether they were succeeding or not. Then, abruptly, one of them rose and made a despairing gesture, unmistakable even from a distance of five hundred feet.

The next few minutes were like a nightmare that has no clear beginning or end. They brought the man back and laid him down on the sand. The man was Stone.

It was Drever who got the lamprene off. He did it with an electric torch, taking care to manipulate the jet of fire in such a way that it scorched only the head of the creature and not Stone's exposed flesh.

Corriston bent then, and gripped Stone firmly by the shoulders and shook him until a look of desperate pleading came into his eyes. He forced himself not to feel pity, seeing in Stone's closeness to death a threat that could have but one outcome if the man refused to speak at all.

"Where's Helen Ramsey?" he demanded. "Where is she, Stone? We're not likely to do anything more for you if you don't tell us."

"I—I don't know," Stone muttered. "Saddler…double-crossed Henley. I guess…he wanted her for himself. I don't know where he's taken her. I'm telling you the truth. You've got to believe me."

"All right," Corriston said, easing Stone back on the sand. "I believe you. Take it easy now. They've got the lamprene off."

He stood very still, waiting for his heart to beat normally again, telling himself that Saddler had taken an almost suicidal risk in leaving the ship on foot with no certain refuge in mind. By taking along a helpless girl he was making himself a target for the rage and relentless enmity of men who would never rest until they had tracked him down.

There could be no sanctuary for him anywhere. If he escaped Henley's vengeance, the colonists would capture him in a matter of days. But Corriston wasn't thinking in terms of days. He was thinking in terms of minutes, hours. He stared at the empty stretch of desert ahead, trying desperately to control the despair that was welling up inside him. How long a head start did Saddler have? Had he left the ship only a few minutes, or hours before?

He'd have to ask Stone one more question. Like a fool he'd put off asking it, dreading the thought of what Stone's answer might be. But now he had no choice. He must ask, and risk knowing that pursuit could not be immediately undertaken by one man, that Saddler was miles away across the desert, hiding out in some remote and inaccessible cave and that tracking him down and putting a bullet through his heart would have to be a joint undertaking.

It was a cruelly frustrating possibility. It increased Corriston's rage, his bitterness. The hate within him seemed suddenly violent enough to destroy anyone or anything. He preferred to go on alone, in relentless pursuit of Saddler and if it took days to track him down…

It was Freddy's voice that brought him back to reality, startling and sobering him. Freddy was coming toward him between the tractors, shouting at the top of his lungs.

CHAPTER TWENTY-ONE

CORRISTON couldn't quite catch what the lad was shouting at first. Something about the dunes and the ship and footprints. Then he caught the name of Helen Ramsey and his mouth went dry and for an instant he couldn't seem to breathe. Freddy was shouting that he had found Helen Ramsey.

Dr. Drever started and leapt quickly to his feet, his eyes darting with an understandable solicitude toward the small figure coming toward them across the sand. He moved quickly to place himself directly in front of Stone, as if fearing it would be bad for Freddy to see a man so close to death. Then the full significance of Freddy's words seemed to dawn on him, and his solicitude for his son was replaced by a larger concern, a wider sympathy.

"You talk to him, Corriston," he said. "You've been living through a short stretch of hell. If he's really found her—"

Corriston needed no urging. He swayed a little forward, steadied himself and broke into a run, meeting Freddy almost midway between the nearest tractor and the hollow where Drever was crouching.

Freddy's eyes seemed almost too large for so young a face, large and immensely serious. But along with the seriousness Corriston could sense something else, a taper glow of excitement burning bright.

Freddy had gone exploring. As he told Corriston about it, the words seemed to flow from him as if they had a mysterious life of their own, and were somehow reshaping Freddy, making him over into a grown man with a heavy stubble of beard and eyes that had looked on far places and a thousand brilliant suns.

Freddy had found Helen Ramsey by following her footprints in the sand. Corriston let Freddy tell it in his own words, shaken by doubts for a moment, but finally convinced that the lad couldn't possibly be making any of it up.

"There wasn't a footprint anywhere near the ship, Lieutenant

Corriston. The sandstorm covered them over. I looked everywhere just to be sure. I mean there wasn't any prints that could have been made by a woman leaving the ship with a man. The sand was trampled in a few places, because about ten minutes ago Mr. Macklin and two other men started looking too. But that was all.

"I remembered then that the sand sometimes stays nearly smooth close to very high dunes, even in a storm. There's a—a wind-breaking buffer zone where the dunes keep the sand from piling up. I asked Mr. Macklin about that once and he told me. I got to thinking that if I just wandered off I could be back again before anyone missed me."

Freddy turned and gestured toward the ship. "You can see the dunes from here. Not the ones right behind the ship. Those two bigger ones over there...that sort of look like the humps on a camel. I guess nobody would have been crazy enough to go looking for prints that far away from the ship. But if I hadn't done it I wouldn't have found her. That's for sure."

Corriston said: "You're so much the opposite of crazy, Freddy, that I'm afraid you're trying to spare me. It's hard to hurt someone you like, but I've got to have the truth."

His hand tightened on Freddy's shoulder. "Do you understand, Freddy? I must know. Don't lie to spare me. Is she all right?"

Freddy looked up at him, troubled, uncertain. "I think she is. She's lying down near the bottom of the dune, right where it slopes up again toward another dune. It's like one, big, hollow dune. I didn't see her move. I guess she must have fainted. He's there, too, lying face down in the sand halfway up the dune, like he was hurt..."

"All right," Corriston said. "Now you'd better stay here with your father."

"Can't I go back with you? I was afraid to climb down to her alone. I was afraid he'd catch me and kill me, and then no one would ever know I'd found her. He'd be warned and try to get away—"

"It was the right thing to do, the level-headed thing," Corriston said. "You couldn't have used better judgment."

"Then it's all right if I go back with you?"

Corriston shook his head. "No, Freddy. I'd rather you didn't. Don't you understand? You've done more than your share. Now it's my turn."

Freddy tightened his lips and stared for a moment at the glitter of sunlight on the caterpillar tread of the nearest tractor. Finally he said, "All right, Lieutenant Corriston. If it's an order—"

"It's an order, Freddy."

Corriston gave Freddy's shoulder a pat. Then, after the briefest pause, he said: "There's no substitute for the kind of fast-thinking resourcefulness you've just displayed, Freddy. In a dozen years you'll be heading an expedition—and it won't be the kind that gets bogged down after the first thousand miles. You can take my word for that."

He turned then and walked toward the ship. In a moment he had passed the ship and was moving out into the desert beyond, and Freddy wondered how a man could remain so calm in an affair of life and death such as this. It was just as well, perhaps, that he could not see Corriston's face as he moved still further away from the ship into a loneliness of desert and sky.

She was lying in a wind-scoured hollow beneath a seventy-foot dune, her head resting on one sharply bent elbow, a look of utter exhaustion on her face. Her eyes were closed, and even from where he stood Corriston could see that she was breathing heavily. He could see the slight rise and fall of her bosom, the trembling vibration of her oxygen mask. She was completely alone.

He stood for an instant absolutely motionless on the summit of the dune, staring down at her, noticing in alarm the hollow contour of her cheeks on both sides of the oxygen mask, and the slight tinge of gray that had crept into her countenance. Then he started downward. Almost instantly the sand rose like an unsteady sea on all sides of him, and a warning signal sounded in his brain.

He could connect it with no cause. Beneath him stretched only the wind-scoured inner surface of the dune, dazzling his eyes with its brightness, mirroring the sunlight like a burning glass. For a moment the brightness deceived him, and he did not realize that there were shadowed hollows directly beneath him, dark fissures in the tumbled sand wide enough to conceal a crouching man. He did not even see the shadow creeping toward him over the sand. Only the dazzle for an instant and the gleam of sunlight on Helen Ramsey's tousled hair.

Then, suddenly, he was aware of the danger, fully awake and aware. But realization came too late. Abruptly, without warning, a knife blade flashed in the sunlight and he felt an agonizing stab of pain just below his left kneecap.

A dark shape rose before him, and then dissolved into the shadows again, darting downward and sideways as it disappeared. Corriston threw himself backwards and froze into immobility, thrusting his elbows deep into the sand behind him, using that moment of surprise forced upon him by his assailant to lower his eyes and seek him out.

He saw Saddler's face clearly for an instant, saw the gleaming knife and the hand holding it, and the wavering outline of the man's crouching body three-fourths in shadow. He heard Saddler mutter: "I'm done for, Corriston. But I'll get you first."

It all seemed to happen in slow motion. Corriston's hand went to his hip, but with a nightmare feeling of retardation and his fingers seemed to move without any assistance from the motor centers of his brain. Then even more slowly he was facing the hollow with the gun in his clasp, and the weapon was exploding into the shadows, filling the hollows and windy places with reverberating echoes of sound.

There was complete silence after that. No groans, no outcry— nothing but silence. It went on for so long that Corriston could not shake off a numbing sense of unreality. Surely only a dream could have had so violently unreal a beginning, so terrible an outcome. Then he looked down, and saw the blood on his leg where the knife had grazed it, and knew that it could not have been a dream.

He was still facing the hollow, with two bullets left in his gun. But he knew that he would not have to fire again. Saddler was lying on his back on the sand, his eyes wide open, his jaw hanging slack. There was a spreading red stain on his chest and a rim of blood around his lips. The wind that was blowing across the crest of the dune seemed suddenly to turn malevolent, striking out at the dead man with a sudden, down-sweeping gust, ruffling his hair and making him seem to be still enveloped in violence.

Corriston felt his throat muscles contract. He forced himself to bend over and search for a heart beat he knew he wouldn't find, remembering the other times when the outcome had been less fatal, when only a man's face had changed.

As his palm rested for an instant above the dead man's heart, the stirring of the sand immediately beneath him seemed to increase, to become a loud and continuous rustling sound that filled him with a vague sense of disquiet. He could not quite dismiss from his mind a feeling that he was still in danger, that in some strange, almost terrifying way Saddler was still a menace, and that the terrible reality of his death had not destroyed all of the hatred and savage violence that had forced Corriston to kill him in self-defense.

Suddenly Corriston realized that what he heard was not the wind stirring the sand at all, but something quite different. It was closer to him than the sloping rim of the dunes, and it was accompanied by movements directly under his hand, a sudden tightening of the dead man's skin, a contraction more pronounced than could have been produced by the abrupt onset of rigor mortis, however freakishly violent or premature.

The rustling continued for perhaps ten more seconds. Then, abruptly, it stopped and the heads of two lamprenes came into view, moving slowly across Saddler's unstirring flesh until their writhing mouth parts were less than two inches from Corriston's outspread hand.

The sight of them brought an instant of terror, an awareness of peril so acute that Corriston's breath caught in his throat. His hand whipped back and he leapt to his feet with a convulsive shudder.

It was suddenly very still on the dune again. Corriston stood for a moment with his body rigid, fearing to look downward, his mind filled with a growing sense of panic.

Had Helen Ramsey been attacked by lamprenes too? No, no, she was all right; she had to be. Everything confirmed it, her quietness, her steady breathing, the simple fact that her eyes had been closed and not opened wide in torment.

He descended the dune like a man ploughing in frantic haste through a snowdrift, sinking to his knees and floundering free again, lurching backward and sideways, sliding a third of the way.

She was all right when he got to her. He dropped down beside her and lifted her into his arms, and for an instant there was complete silence between them. She just looked at him, looked up into his face steadily and calmly, as if she could read his mind and had the good sense to realize there could be no more certain way of reassuring him. Then her arms tightened about him. "Darling," she whispered. "Darling, darling…"

Corriston started fumbling with his oxygen mask and suddenly he had it off. He held his breath and more slowly helped her free her lips so that he could kiss her. Their lips met and the kiss was longer and more intense than any they had ever before shared.

A half-hour later the tractors were in rumbling motion again, their destination Ramsey's Citadel. And Corriston had a plan. He knew that it was riddled with risks and that he was perhaps quite mad to think that it might succeed. But the fact that Helen Ramsey was now completely safe and had dropped off into a brief, outwardly untroubled sleep at his side made him feel reckless to the point where a cautious, level-headed man like Drever could only stare at him and shake his head.

There was a swaying and a creaking all about them, the slow, steady rumble of caterpillar treads, and Drever had almost to shout to make himself heard. He stood directly opposite Corriston, supporting himself by a guard rail, and watching the desert through the weather-shield change color in the wake of the heavy vehicle's heaving, churning, torpedo-shaped rear-end.

"Stone's been unconscious now for an hour," Drever said, dividing his gaze between Corriston, and the loosely strapped-in, sleeping girl at his side, both swaying with the swaying tractor. "We can't count on getting any more information out of him. I can't wake him up. Drugs would be dangerous. I don't think he'll live, but we can't deliberately kill him to get him to talk."

"I know that," Corriston said.

"But he's the only one who knows why Henley is staying so long at the Citadel. He should have been back hours ago. He left before you escaped from the ship. For all we know, he may be dead. Ramsey may have lost his head and had him shot, although that seems unlikely. Ramsey would go to any length to save his daughter. But we've no way of knowing whether he believed Henley's story or not. Anything could have happened. Henley may have attacked Ramsey."

"I've a feeling that he's still at the Citadel," Corriston said. "I'll have to gamble on that—the one-in-five chance that for some reason the negotiations have been prolonged. He may be lying dead in the desert somewhere. He may have been attacked by lamprenes. As you say, anything could have happened. But when I make up my mind to do something I usually go through with it. It's just a matter of plain common sense. You don't toss aside a decision you've given a great deal of thought to just because the arguments against it are weighty, too."

"I see. So you're still determined to walk right up to the gate and tell them you're Stone."

"Why not? They've never laid eyes on Stone and they don't know me from Adam. I won't be wearing this uniform. I'll tell them that Henley's expecting me, that he left orders for me to join him if he failed to come back at a specified time. I'll watch the guard's face and change my story a little—if I have to—as I go along."

"It's a very long gamble. I hope you realize that."

"It's either that or no gamble at all. And we've got to gamble. We're holding at least two high cards and a joker. Henley has had the ground shot right out from under him. He's completely alone, and the only thing he has left to gamble with is his nearness to Ramsey, his ability to terrify Ramsey by making him believe that his daughter's life is still in danger. Ramsey has to be told that Helen has been freed, has to be warned in time, before he does anything foolish.

"Don't you see? With that threat hanging over him, Ramsey would never let us get within fifty yards of the Citadel, let alone walk through the gates. And if Henley finds out that we've got Helen, he'll know that he has nothing left to gamble with except that desperate bluff. And he may doubt his ability to win with a bluff. That would be the worst tragedy of all. He may turn on Ramsey in blind rage, and kill him. He gets a horrible, pathological pleasure out of killing. I've told you how he went berserk on the

Station."

Drever nodded, and, quite suddenly and unexpectedly, the look of stubborn opposition was gone from his eyes.

"I guess you're right, Lieutenant. You can't always tell how the cards will fall."

"You can never tell," Corriston said. "And there are some games where the important moves can only be made by just one player, and he usually has to be something of a reckless fool."

CHAPTER TWENTY-TWO

CORRISTON left the tractor a hundred and seventy yards from the gate, well hidden behind a hundred-foot dune. The other tractors had come to a halt a much greater distance from the Citadel, and were spread out across the desert in a slightly uneven, double line.

He walked slowly forward across the rust-red sand, with a feeling in his bones that he was going to be lucky. Yet he knew that he'd have to be convincing, or he wouldn't stand a chance. If there was more than one guard at the gate he might never get inside. With luck he might be able to convince two guards—even three—but never four or five, for you couldn't forge words into persuasive enough weapons to disarm the suspicion of that many observant men. Not the kind of men who would be guarding Ramsey, at any rate.

The massiveness of the fortified gate shook his confidence a little as he drew near to it. It was at least fifty feet in height, a solid oblong of inches-thick steel with a desert-mirroring surface. He could see his own reflection as he advanced, but it did nothing to reassure him.

He knew what he'd have to do, of course. Walk right up to the gate and trust to luck that he could find some way of announcing his presence without getting himself killed. How did you gain entrance to an impregnable fortress? Surely there had to be some way by which a man could gain admittance without being instantly shot down as a hostile intruder.

He was surprised by the simplicity of the answer. There was no need for him to press a bell or a buzzer, to manipulate a mechanism of any sort. There was not even any need for him to proclaim his arrival by shouting.

The gate swung inward without a sound, and in the shadows cast by its moving bulk two figures silently materialized. They were guards, heavily armed, one tall with shaggy brows and piercing dark eyes, the other a wiry little man with reddish hair, his expression peculiarly bland and noncommittal.

It was the little man who said: "All right, come inside. We've been expecting you."

It was impossible, but true. There was nothing threatening in the way the words were uttered, just calm acceptance, just the matter-of-fact indifference of a man who has a duty to perform and doesn't care what happens afterwards.

But it would have perhaps been better if Corriston had not moved so quickly forward, for almost instantly the second guard barred his passage and laid a firm hand on his arm.

"Hold on. Just a minute," the tall guard said. "You're Peter Stone, aren't you?"

With a quick pretense of anger Corriston jerked his arm free and looked the guard up and down. "Naturally I'm Stone. Who in hell did you think I was?"

"Sorry," the guard said, shrugging. "Don't take it out on me. I just had to be sure."

"Well, you're sure now. I guess you know why I'm here."

The guard nodded. "Ramsey just phoned down about you. Your friend is with him now. See that big gray building, the one on the left with the shuttered windows? There's a guard stationed at the door, but he won't stop you. He has his orders. Climb two flights of stairs and go down the long corridor on the third floor. Ramsey and your friend are in the last room on the left."

Corriston drew a deep breath, wondering if the guard had noticed the tightening of his facial muscles. He turned away from the gate slowly, staring out over the interior of the fortress, letting his emotions of the moment take complete possession of him.

He had entered as if by magic a world apart, a small, shut-in world of massive magnificence, of undreamed of material power and wealth. There were five buildings within the encircling wall of the fortress, each monumental in architectural sweep. Each was a citadel alone and apart, monuments to man's creative genius erected by one man with a determination to make himself unique.

It was a folly almost beyond belief, a terrifying distortion of human creativeness that could lead only to ultimate disaster and defeat.

But greedy and cruel and ruthless as Ramsey undoubtedly was, there still burned in him a little of the spark that had created Athens in white marble. Had it not been so, he could not have even commissioned men of creative genius to transport to Mars the materials for such a project and have taken pleasure in its completion.

"Your friend got here two hours ago," the tall guard said. "They've been talking ever since. He came down to the gate once and said we should let you in, you and another man. Saddler, I think his name was. I see he's not with you."

"No, Saddler is not with me," Corriston said.

"What happened to him?"

Corriston ignored him. "The big gray building with shuttered windows, you said. If the guard tries to stop me, what do I say?"

"I told you he had his orders."

Corriston looked up at the massive gate swinging shut behind him. For good or bad, he was completely trapped, completely at the mercy of the armed guards inside the citadel.

They hadn't taken his gun away from him, but nevertheless, he was trapped. What chance would one armed man have against seventy-five or a hundred guards? They were keeping out of sight, all but the two at the gate. But at any moment they could converge upon him and shoot him down. They could choose their own moment, precisely as a research medical man could choose his own moment to experiment upon a laboratory animal, knowing that the creature was safe in its cage and couldn't possibly get away.

Corriston's lips tightened and from a shadowed corner of his mind came a determination to brush all that aside, to ignore it completely. The guards at the gate might very well be telling the truth. It stood to reason that Ramsey would have remained secretive about his daughter. Kidnappers do not like to have their ransom demands discussed too openly. If Ramsey had been a complete fool he would have gone down to the gate and taken the guards completely into his confidence, but Corriston could not believe that Ramsey was that much of a fool.

In all probability Henley had threatened Ramsey and provoked him almost beyond endurance. There had arisen the questions of how the ransom was to be paid, the girl set free.

Damn it, Corriston thought, the thing to do now is to go straight toward that building and straight up the stairs to the third floor and straight down the corridor until I'm confronting Ramsey face to face. I'm Peter Stone. I'm one of the two men who helped Henley kidnap the girl and I've come to help Henley convince Ramsey. I've come to help him really put the screws on Ramsey. I can improvise from that point on.

He moved away from the guards without looking back. Within the citadel there was silence, stillness, the five massive buildings cutting a rampart of pure, fragile design across the sky. There was a strange kind of perfection about the interior of the citadel. It was akin, somehow, to the perfection of solitude and even the sky seemed hushed, expectant, remote from reality, as if awaiting the unfolding of some impossible event, some terrifying drama of violence and retribution that could take place nowhere else.

But Corriston's reason told him that to believe any such thing would have been the height of folly. The sky inside the citadel was just as real, just as cloud-flecked and palely blue as the sky outside, and the notion that architecture or scenery of any kind could influence events was absolute nonsense. Things would happen exactly as he willed them to happen, provided nothing stood in the way of immediate drastic action and the kind of luck which had saved him at the gate continued to smile upon him.

The big gray building with the shuttered windows continued to occupy most of his attention, and he walked very resolutely toward it, his eyes on the glimmer of pale light that marked its wide doorway. He was still fifty feet away when he saw the guard, standing very quietly just inside the door with his hand on his gun holster.

Corriston's lips tightened, but he did not moderate his stride. He had a reply ready if the guard challenged him. He preferred to believe that he would not be challenged, but he had no intention of taking anything for granted.

He continued on until he reached the doorway and then he stopped abruptly. He waited for the guard to say something, but the man did not speak at all. He simply stared quietly at Corriston for an instant, and then stepped quickly back into the shadows. Corriston went on past him, and advanced along the wide corridor that stretched before him.

The wide central staircase that circled up did not seem appropriate to a building that was not a residence and Corriston found himself wondering if Ramsey had turned the other four buildings into similarly unusual expressions of his own strong-willed orientation to reality.

The buildings had undoubtedly been designed as administrative units of an industrial empire—a beginning empire in a new world. An empire predatory, avaricious, merciless. Yet Ramsey had seemingly allowed his desire for a home to gain dominance here, had allowed the emotions common to all men to influence his taste in interior architecture in at least one of the buildings.

Chalk up that much to Ramsey's credit. In that respect at least, he was superior to Henley. In that respect at least a man of good will could take sides, all apart from the personal issues involved. Henley was a predatory vulture on all counts, his talons constantly spread, constantly crimson-tipped. Ramsey was a vulture too, but in the depths of his mind he knew it. Part of the agony was shared by him, and in one desperate, despairing part of his personality he had tried to be creative.

Corriston ascended the staircase swiftly, casting one brief glance at some murals and then ignoring them. The second floor landing stretched away into shadows, bisected by a wide corridor dimly lighted by overhead lamps. The second floor had an administrative building aspect and so did the third floor, which seemed in all respects its exact duplicate.

Corriston's excitement grew as he mounted the stairway. He felt like a man poised on the brink of a precipice with no assurance that he would not be hurled to his death; a man aware that tragedy would not strike him like a thunderbolt at any moment; and yet also like a man who thought and felt differently from the trapped and the desperately despairing. He felt very confident, very sure of himself, and it seemed to him that there was no danger that he could not surmount, and deep within him there was something that exulted in the thought and kept him moving steadily upward.

The third floor was like the second, its long central corridor dwindling away into shadows. Down it he moved cautiously, remembering what the guard at the gate had said. The third floor, the last door on your left.

Ramsey was in conference. But it wasn't a conference of industrial associates planning a division of spoils. Ramsey was talking to a killer under duress.

Corriston was half way down the corridor when he heard the shot. It rang out in the stillness with a terrible clarity, sending echoes reverberating throughout the building, stopping Corriston in his tracks.

For an instant the silence remained absolute, as if the shot had somehow silenced all life within the building. Even Corriston's breathing was affected by it, so that for an instant he remained like a man horror-blasted into immobility, frozen, a statue with waxen features and widely dilated eyes.

Then, abruptly, he ceased to be a statue. He broke into a run, heading for the door from which the shot had come.

He came to the door and saw that it did not slide open on a panel. It was massive, with a knob jutting out from it, and when he grasped the knob it swung inward instantly and soundlessly and he found himself in a large, blank-walled room brightly illumed by three circular overhead lamps.

Ramsey was sitting stiff and straight before a desk that was cluttered with reference files, manuscripts in folders, pens, pencils and other writing materials. His face was drained of all color, and his eyes were wide and staring. He was looking directly at Corriston, and yet he did not seem to see Corriston.

He did not appear to be staring at anything in particular, that small, shrunken, unimpressive-looking little man with graying temples and a look of blank incomprehension in his eyes that chilled Corriston to the core of his being.

Shaking, wishing that the eyes would close or brighten with relief, or do anything but remain so stonily indifferent, Corriston moved closer to the desk.

He saw at once that Ramsey was close to death. He had been shot in the chest. There was a dull red stain on his chest, and even as Corriston stared it widened, a butterfly pattern of red, like a Rorschach seen through the eyes of a homicidally inclined psychotic.

Suddenly Ramsey moved. He caught hold of the desk edge,

and swayed a little, but his eyes remained filmed, blankly staring.

Corriston was bending above him when a familiar voice said: "He's done for. Nothing you can do for him. We had an argument and he lost his head. He just couldn't see it my way. So I made a mistake and shot him. It was a mistake, all right. I lost my head. Now I've got nothing to lose by killing you."

Corriston raised his eyes slowly. He had one chance in a hundred perhaps. He knew it; he sensed it. Henley had somehow managed to stay out of sight for an instant. The room was very large. There were shadows in it, and Henley had apparently flattened himself against the wall behind the desk, in deep shadow.

But now he was standing very straight and still behind the desk, ignoring the shuddering form of the man he had shot, little dark deathheads dancing in his eyes.

Henley's nearness did not bother Corriston. Death at ten feet could be no more final than death at a hundred yards.

Only one thing bothered him. Events could move fast when you were close to a killer.

He didn't intend to let them move fast. Not for him, at any rate. He let his eyes rest for an instant on the gun in Henley's hand, his thoughts racing. He knew that he'd be as good as dead if he made a single concession.

Don't let him know that the gun worries you. Pretend that the odds are even, even though he's got the drop on you.

Corriston said: "How do you know he's fatally wounded? The wound's three inches below his heart. You're taking a hell of a lot for granted. You just said you made a mistake in shooting him. If he's rushed to a hospital that mistake may not be your last. You'll have a chance to go to work on him again."

Henley shook his head, his lips tightening. "Don't be a fool. He'll be dead in five minutes."

"I'm not being a fool," Corriston said. "What will you stand to gain by shooting me and letting him die? You've got his daughter, but a dead man won't be able to ransom her."

For a moment, nothing happened. Henley had made no attempt to draw his gun, and he did not draw it now. He stood very quietly staring at Corriston, breathing heavily, a strange, withdrawn look in his eyes.

Perhaps he was thinking over what Corriston had said. Corriston wondered about that for an instant, and then dismissed it from his mind. You did not take anything for granted when you were standing that close to a killer.

It was probably too late to save Ramsey. But for the first time he was standing very near to Henley with a weapon beneath his hand. If he drew his gun instantly and shot Henley through the heart Ramsey might have a chance. Otherwise...

Somehow he couldn't do it; not without giving the other some slight warning, not without whipping his hand to his gun with a vigor that was clear and unmistakable. In matters of crime a fair man is at a disadvantage. He can only deal with a murderer in one way.

He drew a split second ahead of Henley. He shot Henley three times, the gun blazing in his hands, and it did not seem important to him that Henley had also drawn his gun. A tight knot reached into his stomach as Henley's gun blazed, but he kept right on firing.

Henley died missing him, not scoring at all. That was the incredible thing. Henley, an expert shot, a genius at massacre, had missed him clearly with five shots and now he was down on the floor, clutching at his stomach, dragging himself along, while beneath his fingers a dull red stain grew.

His eyes turned glassy suddenly. He tried twice to raise himself but he fell back each time. He did not speak at all. Blood from his punctured lungs flooded up into his mouth, and with a terrible, convulsive trembling of his entire body he rolled over on his side and lay still.

Corriston's hands began to sweat beneath the hard, cold gun. He wanted to drop the weapon, to hurl it from him, but he couldn't somehow. He had killed Saddler in immediate self-defense. This had been a little different—a new experience, a frightening experience and he had been forced to grit his teeth even in firing, and now that it was all over he was tormented inwardly in a way that left him badly shaken.

Henley was gone now. Dead and still and forever removed from a world he had contaminated. Henley had been warped and twisted largely by circumstances outside himself; nevertheless a deadly reptile has to be crushed when it is about to strike.

Corriston looked up from the limp form sprawled out on the floor, and for a moment the tight lines of his face relaxed a little. Henley was no longer a menace; the breath of life that had sustained him had expired so completely that he had become now a kind of hollow mockery of something monstrous and distorted that could never harm anyone again.

It was Ramsey who had to be considered now, Ramsey who was in peril.

The light in the room seemed somehow a little dimmer than it had been. He turned slowly back to Ramsey, and for a moment could not quite believe what he saw.

Ramsey's face was changing. The hollows beneath his cheekbones were deeper than they had been, and his mouth had gone completely slack, and his eyes were uprolled in a quite ghastly way, so that only the whites showed.

Slowly as Corriston stared Ramsey's features began to come apart. The familiar, hideous pattern began to repeat itself on Ramsey's blanched features. The mouth widened until it turned into a shapeless, colorless gash in a face that was hardly recognizable. The nose widened and spread out, the chin receded, and the cheeks became a flattened expanse of wrinkled flesh that stubbornly refused to stop spreading.

Ramsey's face became a pumpkin face, with slits for eyes and a hideous caricature of a mouth that seemed almost to pout as it expanded.

Suddenly Ramsey was no longer sitting upright before the desk. His body swayed and began to slump, tilting at first only a little sideways and then sliding completely from the chair to the floor.

Ramsey did not descend to the floor with violence. It was a slow, barely perceptible gliding motion of his entire body that carried him from an upright position to a prone one in less than thirty seconds. His body seemed to collapse inward upon itself, as if he had suddenly become too skeleton-thin for his clothes, as if so much vitality had been drained from him by the shot which had put an end to his life that he had given up all hope of maintaining his dignity in death.

But perhaps the man on the floor had no dignity to maintain. He wasn't Ramsey. He was a hired substitute, an impostor, and quite obviously no man would undertake to play such a role without calculating all of the risks in advance. Perhaps he expected to die without dignity. Perhaps that was one of the risks which went with the bargain—the assumption that Ramsey might very well be killed in a violent fashion, and that anyone who stepped into Ramsey's shoes and masqueraded as Ramsey might expect a similar fate.

Corriston felt a nerve begin to twitch violently in his cheek. Why had Ramsey kept Henley occupied in so strange a manner, talking to a nonentity, a stand-in, a double who could never bargain and come to terms unless Ramsey ordered him to do so? Had Ramsey been incapable of dealing with Henley directly, and had taken this means of complying with the ransom demands?

It seemed incredible on the face of it. Ramsey was quite obviously the kind of man who could live through any kind of private hell if he had to.

He'd have stood up to Henley no matter how great his inner torment. He'd have met the ransom demands or rejected them—and it was almost inconceivable that he would have rejected them—without for an instant losing his outward composure. And even inwardly he would have kept a tight rein on his emotions. He was not the kind of man who would hire someone else to protect him from anything that vitally concerned him, even with the masks so conveniently at hand.

Why then had he employed a double to bargain with Henley and keep him occupied for so long a time? It didn't matter if Ramsey had made use of doubles in the past. Probably he had, in order to protect himself in dealings with the colonists when the advantages of deception would favor him. But he would never have done so under these present circumstances—when a criminal who would stop at nothing was holding his daughter under threat of death.

He would never have done so unless he had some very special reason that dominated his thinking to the exclusion of all else.

Suddenly Corriston had the answer. It came to him in a lightning-swift flash of intuition, which carried with it complete credibility. It was more than a guess. Somehow he was sure; he knew. A full minute before he heard the dull rumble of the tractors as they came through the gate, and went to the window and stared down, he knew.

He had the answer and yet what he saw eclipsed what he knew. It was a little like watching a rocket take off, hearing the roar and seeing the flames through all of its burning time, and seeing at the same time the men on the proving ground moving swiftly about, and the space-helmeted men at the controls of the rocket itself, each grimly intent on one particular task.

Ramsey was returning into the Citadel with armed guards on both sides of him, and his daughter was walking with her head erect at his side. Five colony tractors had followed him into the Citadel and two more were just coming through the gate, moving ponderously on their caterpillar treads because each tractor weighed two tons even in the light gravity of Mars.

Corriston did an almost unbelievable thing then. Standing quietly by the window he raised his right hand and saluted Ramsey in silent tribute to the man's courage at the most threatening moment of his life.

What Ramsey had done in no way lessened his guilt. But Corriston would have just as readily repeated the salute in public, without caring what anyone might think. What Ramsey had done was as clear to him now as a series of moves on a chessboard laid out in advance, but hidden from the man who was to be outwitted and outplayed.

Ramsey had made use of a double to keep Henley occupied— no doubt with repeated, skillful evasions, a constant insistence that more proof be forthcoming, more details supplied. Perhaps a half-dozen conferences had taken place in all, extending over many hours. And while Henley was being encouraged to believe that Ramsey was being softened up, and would accept all of his demands in the end, Ramsey had gone out into the desert alone, armed, furious, and determined to rescue his daughter if it cost him his life.

Or perhaps he hadn't gone alone. Perhaps he had taken a dozen armed guards with him. Somehow it didn't seem important, couldn't take away Ramsey's moment of victory. It was a moment of victory for Ramsey even though he hadn't played a major role for long, even though he had found his daughter already rescued and safe on his return. And Corriston had been the one to move out into the center of the board and deliver the coup de grace. He had kept a restless killer immobilized while the play was under way, and that was victory enough for any man.

Corriston suddenly realized that neither Ramsey nor the Colonists had any way of knowing that Henley was dead. They had probably joined forces outside the Citadel for the sole purpose of rescuing him from the deadliest kind of danger. And he wasn't helping them at all. In another minute they'd be trying to get to him with tear gas.

It didn't make any kind of sense, but when Corriston went down the wide central staircase he wasn't thinking about the colonists at all. He was wondering only how Helen Ramsey would look standing alone on a strange dark headland at midnight. Then the vision dissolved and another one took its place. She wasn't on a headland any more.

She was standing at the door of a small, white cottage and there were a couple of kids beside her: a boy of about Freddy's age, or maybe a little younger, and a little girl with golden curls, her hair like a crown.

He realized suddenly that it could never be a small, white cottage. There were no small white cottages on the Station, and never could be. But the Station would be all right for a married man with kids. The kids could come and visit him, and his wife could be with him about one-fourth of the time, both on the Station and on Earth.

What more could a happily married man ask, if the Station was so much a part of him that it was never wholly absent from his thoughts? He'd have to ask her, of course—at least a dozen times to make sure—that she really wanted that kind of man for a husband. But he knew what her answer would be even before the vision dissolved; and he was soon out in the central square between the five buildings, holding her tightly in his arms.

From the way she kissed him he knew that she must have endured an eternity of torment just from uncertainty, just from not knowing whether he was dead or alive. For an instant he could think of nothing else but the wonder of it, the absolute reassurance which she had brought to him with her closeness, her gratefulness, the intensity of her concern.

Across the square they could see the tractors, looking in the dazzling light like massive blocks of metal standing almost end to end. There was a great deal of movement and shouting between the buildings, and Corriston knew that in another half-minute they would no longer be alone together, that the closeness couldn't last.

A change was coming over her face, and he was suddenly afraid for her, afraid that when she was told the full truth about her father just the pain of knowing might make her withdraw from him, even though it could never really come between them or separate them for long.

So there it was. He could see it in her eyes, the fear, the shadow, and because he had no way of knowing just how much she already knew he decided that only complete honesty could keep the shadow from lengthening.

His hands moved slowly up over her face, and he drew her chin up and said, very gently: "There's something I'd like to say now, about your father. Without his help Henley would have finished what he started out to do. There are different ways of paying off a debt, and your father—"

She raised her hand as if to put a stop to his words. "Darling, I know he's in serious trouble. Don't try to spare me; there's no need to. There will be a trial and we both know what the outcome will be. He'll never walk out of the courtroom a free man. But he's not afraid...and neither am I. These last few terrible hours have changed him. He's not ashamed now to admit that he loves me. All the hardness, the coldness, is gone."

Something in her voice stilled the questions he wanted to ask. She seemed to sense what was in his mind, for she said quickly. "I don't think father has any enemies now on Mars. He's going to give the colonists back their land. Not because he has to, but because he wants to. They came to his assistance when they could have used the way he cheated and robbed them as an excuse for not helping him at all. There are few men who wouldn't feel grateful, who wouldn't be shaken by remorse. But I think it goes deeper than that. Even now I'm not completely sure, but I think he knows it's the only way he can free himself from the prison he's been building around himself since I was a little girl."

She was silent for an instant, while the pain in her eyes seemed to deepen. Then she said. "I can't leave him now, darling. Not right away. It would be too cruel a blow."

Ahead now Corriston could see three of the colonists coming toward him. They were less than forty feet away. "I think I know how it is," he said. "When you've been through too much, you just go dead inside. You can feel sympathy for someone very close, like your father. But that's about all…"

"Darling, that's not what I mean. We'll be apart, but just for a little while. It will be so short a time we won't even miss it later on…two or three weeks, at most. And this time you won't have to wonder about me at all."

Corriston noticed then for the first time that her hair had been blown in all directions by the wind. He remembered how, on their first meeting, it had been disarranged in much the same way. She'd been wearing a beret then, and just the casual tilt of her hat had done the fluffing. But wind or no wind, he'd always like the way her hair looked, the gold in it, and the way it set off the great beauty of her face.

"I'd be more than unreasonable if I tried to pick flaws in a promise like that," he said.

"You can never go home again," someone had once said.

You can never go home because people change and places change with them, and familiar scenes take on an aspect of strangeness as the old, well-loved landmarks fade.

But in space, the landmarks are as wide and deep as the gulfs between the stars, and it is not too difficult for a man to return to a steel-ribbed Gibraltar in space and experience again the emotions he felt when he first sighted it, and hear again the long thunder-roll of the ships berthing and taking off.

The ship that was bringing Corriston back had begun to loom up behind the telemetric aerials with her bow slanting forward. She had almost berthed, and, standing with his face half in shadow, Commander Clement watched the landing lights flashing on and off and wondered just what he would say to the young lieutenant he'd never met—the very famous lieutenant who would be emerging from the boarding port and descending the ramp any minute now.

He told himself that it ought to be something very simple and direct, accompanied by a friendly handclasp and a nod. "Welcome back, Lieutenant. Welcome back. I guess you know how I feel about the scoundrels who kept us from meeting the first time."

Yes, just a few words and a friendly handclasp would be best. No salutes either given or returned. No stiff-necked salutes, and damn the regulations for once. It was truly a very great occasion.

THE END

If you've enjoyed this book, you will not want to miss these terrific titles...